John Hayden Wells was born in Brighton and lived there for many years before emigrating to Australia, and now lives in the Northern Beaches part of Sydney. John had a long and successful career in IT before deciding to concentrate on his writing and spend more time travelling.

Evolving Perspectives is John's first book but he is already writing an exciting follow-up book.

John Hayden Wells

EVOLVING PERSPECTIVES

AUSTIN MACAULEY PUBLISHERS™

LONDON • CAMBRIDGE • NEW YORK • SHARJAH

A CIP catalogue record for this title is available from the British Library.

ISBN 9781398496460 (Paperback)
ISBN 9781398496477 (ePub e-book)

www.austinmacauley.com

First Published 2023
Austin Macauley Publishers Ltd®
1 Canada Square
Canary Wharf
London
E14 5AA

Thank you to my wife, Mandy and Gareth Denyer, for your input and encouragement during the writing of the book. Thanks to friends and family for all the kind words and encouragement on my first version of the completed book.

Preface

This book has been split into three separate parts. You can read each part as a separate book. They can also be read in any order. These parts share characters and events, so after reading one part, you will find additional insights and perspectives in the other parts. The order you choose to read the parts will produce slightly different results regarding how you will feel about the events that unfold. The three parts are as follows:

Connect—A cyber-thriller based on what happens to a woman who has her Facebook account hijacked and enters the world of hackers and the Dark Web to try and find who did it and get revenge.

One for You—A comedy romance that follows a group of single people who sign up for a speed dating event to find their perfect partner. Some of the dates that result from the event lead to true love, but others provide hilarious results.

Only Hope—A morality tale about a man who pins all his future dreams in life on winning the lottery. Has he wasted his life waiting for something that will never happen or will he win and be happy as he always hoped?

Connect

Chapter 1

It was 11.30 AM and Sally was still in bed. It was Saturday, so she had no intention of getting up until lunchtime. Sally had first woken up at 7.00 AM as she did every day, thanks to her annoyingly reliable body clock. Three hours ago, she had slipped into her kitchen for a coffee and cigarette. Two hours ago, she had turned on her bedside radio and dozed off the sports program on Radio 5. Sally hated football but loved to fall asleep listening to men talking about it.

Suddenly, Sally was awoken with a jolt as the sound of her front doorbell filled the room.

Her first thought was to ignore it and go back to sleep, but then she remembered the parcel she was expecting. She briefly weighed up the pleasure of returning to sleep with the hassle of collecting the package from the post office later. She recalled the two hours she had spent queuing on the last occasion and got straight up and rushed to the front door.

"Morning, darling," said the postman with a disconcertingly lecherous grin on his face.

Sally suddenly realised that apart from a small t-shirt, she was naked. She snatched the parcel from the salivating postman and shut the door.

She had been warned of the parcel's imminent arrival by an email from the Internet bookstore the day before.

Unfortunately, Sally's 'Customer Delight' was soon shattered as she opened the parcel. Rather than the latest novel from her favourite author (which she had just planned to spend the weekend reading), she found the cover of 'How to pick up horny women—100% guaranteed' staring up at her.

"Bollocks," she shouted—she was unsure if she meant this as a somewhat premature critique of the book or simply a rant due to her frustration. Sally threw the book down onto her kitchen table and went back to bed to re-plan her day.

Sally got up again about 30 minutes later, with no plans other than to have another cup of coffee. She sat at her kitchen table and as she waited for the kettle to boil, she picked up her mobile and checked her social media accounts. A message from her friend Caz immediately got her attention, "Is your Facebook posting a wind-up or have you been hacked?"

She immediately went to her Facebook app to check, but all she got was an invalid password message. She also now recalled seeing an email about her account being accessed from a new computer that she had stupidly ignored. She had been hacked and her account hijacked. Sally phoned Caz who answered straight away: "So, what is?"

"Hacked," replied Sally. "I have not posted anything in weeks. So what does the post say?"

"You have two tickets for the Adele Concert at The Brighton Centre that you cannot now use and are happy to sell."

"I hate Adele."

"I know; that's why I thought you had been hacked!"

"Why would they bother to post something like that?"

"Guess they hope a friend will transfer money for tickets, not realising it will be their account, not yours, they are sending money to."

"Scumbags."

"I will post a new message on your page to say it is a scam and you have been hacked. You should contact Facebook and get your account back; though, sure the hacker will delete my message pretty quickly."

"Will do and many thanks, Caz."

"No worries, let's catch up soon."

"Yes, that will be great. I will get back to you once I have this sorted."

"Cool."

Sally hung up and went to Google to search for how to get her Facebook account back. She quickly found the links to the Facebook recovery forms but then had another thought. Why should the scum who hacked her get away with it? She would find them and get revenge. She hardly ever used Facebook and still only had about 20 friends. All could easily be contacted by one of the other apps and warned of the Facebook post. Not that she had Adele fans as friends anyway. She quickly posted the messages to her friends and then returned to Facebook.

She was about to start implementing her cunning revenge plan when her mobile suddenly rang and the theme tune to *Sex in the City* filled her kitchen in all its polyphonic glory. Sally saw from the phone display that 'ZoeMobile' was calling her.

"Hi, Zoe, what's up?"

"Not much, just bored and fancied a chat. What are you up to?"

"Planning a bit of cyber revenge."

"What are you talking about?"

Sally explained about her hacked Facebook account and her cunning revenge plan.

"You need to get out more," quipped Zoe. "Is that the best you can find to do?"

"OK, you win. I am a nerd at heart and what do you suggest instead?"

"How about going down the beach and catching some sun, might even have a small drink as well?"

"Yes, OK, it's too nice to spend all day inside."

"Great, see you at the 'Meeting Place' in 30 minutes."

"See you there."

"Bye then."

"Bye."

The Meeting Place was a café on the promenade at the border between Brighton and Hove. It was about 15 minutes' walk from Sally's flat, so she decided she had better hurry and get ready. She went into her bedroom, stripped off, put on her swimming costume and quickly checked in the mirror that she did not look too hideous. She was pleasantly surprised; she was in better shape than she thought. She slipped on a T-shirt and shorts and grabbed her rucksack. She put in a towel, sun lotion, her phone, purse, keys and a bottle of water, slipped on her beach sandals and left the flat for the beach.

The sun was shining strongly in the clear sky as Sally strolled along the promenade. The sun sparkled on the deep blue sea and for once, Sally considered going for a dip. The seafront was packed with people enjoying one of the few warm sunny days the English summer offered each year. She reached the Meeting Place but could see no sign of Zoe, so she reached into her rucksack and pulled out her phone. Just as she was looking up ZoeMobile in her phonebook, she heard somebody shout her name.

"Hi, Sally."

She turned around and saw Zoe walking towards her from the pelican crossing opposite the café. Zoe was wearing just her bikini and her brown-toned body looked sensational. Sally suddenly felt much more insecure about her own physique despite her little ego boost from the mirror a few minutes before.

"Wow! You look fantastic," exclaimed Sally to her friend.

"I got a personal trainer just after Christmas and you are looking at six months of bloody hard work and a small fortune in fees."

"It was worth it; you could become a model with a body like that."

"Funny you should say that as a bloke down the gym did offer to do a portfolio and get me some work."

"Are you going to do it?"

"I thought about it but was worried he would turn out to be a sleaze bag, so I told him I was already signed up with a London agency. I found out afterwards that he runs the best fashion agency in Brighton so I might still try and persuade him if I see him again. Make up some story about not being happy with the London agency or whatever."

"You should, although you were right to check him out first."

"Where shall we go?"

"Let's go along towards Brighton and find a beach nearer the action."

They walked along the boulevard that ran along the top of the beach. They passed the wreck of the old West Pier and the i360 tower before reaching the large children's pool and playground. Zoe spotted a friend and she stopped to talk. Sally walked onto the pebble beach and lit a cigarette.

As she smoked, a thought popped into her mind. Sally was not thinking about the Facebook revenge plan she had devised earlier, but her mind must have been working away in its subconscious. She suddenly knew how to REALLY screw the hacking scumbag.

Zoe returned from talking to her friend and they walked further along the boulevard and reached the main part of Brighton Beach. This was tourist central and it looked like the whole of London had come south and was in Brighton. You could not see the pebbles on the beach from all the people jammed together taking the sun.

The bars and cafes behind the beach were also packed. Undeterred, Zoe led Sally down onto the beach and they eventually found a couple of square metres of pebbles to lay down their towels. Sally took off her T-shirt and shorts and applied some sun lotion to her pale skin.

"Blimey, you're so white," exclaimed Zoe with her St Tropez tan.

"White is the new brown," joked Sally. "The last time I sunbathed was over a year ago when I spent a week in Spain and even then, we only had two days sun."

"Love your cosie," said Zoe. "Where did you get it?"

"I got it when I was in Spain. Shopping was all we had to do most days. This is the first chance I have had to wear it."

They both lay down on their towels and soaked up the sun. Zoe put her airpods in her ears and gently moved her body to the sound of the music. Sally luxuriated in the warm sun soaking into her body and slowly drifted into a light sleep. She was then woken by a prod to her arm from Zoe.

"Fancy a swim, then lazybones?" said Zoe.

"Yes, OK," replied Sally and they both got to their feet.

Sally walked down to the shore in her beach sandals while Zoe made a far less elegant sight as she hobbled across the pebbles in her bare feet.

"Shit, these stones hurt," cried Zoe. "I wish I had brought my beach sandals."

"Don't worry, it will hurt more on the way back," teased Sally.

They reached the sea and Sally slipped out of her shoes and left them on the shore. Unfortunately, it was high tide, so they would have to plunge straight in. Sally was not expecting the water to be very warm, but the icy cold was a shock and she could not help letting out a loud scream. Zoe joined in almost immediately. They both swam as hard as they could in the hope of warming up. Within a few minutes, it worked and the water temperature seemed bearable.

However, it still did not feel warm enough to prolong their swim and so they were soon back on their towels, drying in the warm sun.

"How is your love life?" asked Zoe.

"Non-existent and you?"

"Same. Unfortunately, the only decent guys I seem to meet are married or gay."

"Have you tried a dating app or website?"

"No, but I was thinking of trying that speed dating."

"How does that work?"

"Well, you turn up at the venue and spend 10 minutes chatting one-to-one with about 5 or 6 different blokes and afterwards, you write down which ones you would like to go on a date with. The guys all do the same and then, the organisers give you the details of the blokes you wanted to see and who also wanted to see you again."

"Have you tried it before?"

"Yes, once, last year. That was when I was out of shape and so the two gorgeous guys I fancied never picked me. I would like to try again although I would much prefer it if I went with somebody. Will you come with me?"

"I am not sure I fancy it."

"Oh, go on, it will be a laugh."

"When is it?"

"There is one next Tuesday at the Old Market. That's just around the corner from you."

"I'm still not sure."

"What have you got to lose? You might even meet Mr Right."

"I would rather meet Mr Randy; I'm gagging for it."

"Sally! You wicked girl."

"Yes, OK, count me in."

"I will phone up and get us enrolled when I get home."

They stayed on the beach until they were both dry and then headed up to one of the beach bars for 'a little drink'. Two hours and two bottles of wine later, Sally staggered back home to her flat. She had broken both her rules about drinking during the day and drinking on an empty stomach. She felt awful and so slumped onto her bed and drifted off to sleep in a drunken stupor.

Chapter 2

Sally woke up at precisely 7.00 AM as always. She was relieved that she did not have a hangover, but then she had been asleep for 13 hours. Sally headed straight to the shower to clean off the salt and suntan lotion from the day before. After she had showered and dressed, she headed to the kitchen and put on the kettle. She had not eaten for over 24 hours, so she opened the fridge to see what she could find to satisfy her aching hunger. Sally found some eggs and set to work on making herself an omelette.

After the coffee and eggs, she turned on her laptop and checked her email but found nothing to interest her and turned off the PC. She decided to go down to the gym; after meeting Zoe, she had started to feel a bit frumpy and decided she needed to get back in shape. Her gym membership was still live and costing her 20 pounds per month, although she had not been for over six months. She changed into her gym kit and slipped a hand towel and her water bottle into her rucksack.

The gym was right on the beachfront, near where she had gone with Zoe the day before. Today's weather was grey and a fine drizzle filled the air. As she walked along a now deserted promenade, it was hard to believe such a vibrant summer scene was in the same place only 24 hours before. She entered the gym, checked in and headed for the exercise bikes. She did a 10-minute warm-up on a bike, followed by some stretches before getting into the actual workout. Her routine was written on a card she had collected from the file at reception when she checked in.

After such a long break, restarting the training would be challenging, but Sally was determined to get through it. An hour later, she was exhausted and dripping with sweat, but she had finished the entire routine. Sally now regretted not bringing a change of clothes and a good towel, as she badly needed a shower. Instead, she hurried home as quickly as she could and ran herself a hot bath.

After a good long soak, Sally made herself a coffee and sat down at the kitchen table and turned on her laptop. She checked her email and was pleased to see, amongst all the usual spam and junk, a genuine email from an old friend.

From: Lucy Cunningham
Sent: 6 June 2020, 13:15
To: Sally Tompkins
Subject: What's Up!

Hey Sal,
    Long-time no see, old friend.
    I'm still working in LA and having a ball. Don't ask me why but you just popped into my head and I thought I'd send you an email and see how things are going at your end.
    Have you met your dream bloke yet?—The only guys I meet are at work and they are all real creeps, but I guess that's what you would expect if you work with geeks. I can't wait to come back next month and catch up with you all.

Luv
Lucy XXX

Lucy was an old friend from university. Sally found the comment about geeks ironic, as Lucy was the biggest geek Sally had ever known. Sally composed her reply and sent it.

From: Sally Tompkins
Sent: 7 June 2020, 14.34
To: Lucy Cunningham
Subject: Re: What's Up!

Hi Lucy,
    Great to hear from you.
    Think all geeks are creeps—look in the mirror, girl!. The guys I work with are all married and every other decent guy in Brighton seems to be gay. It looks like I will have to become a mistress or fanny muncher. One last chance, though,

as I am going to a speed dating event on Tuesday with Zoe. I will let you know how it goes.

It will be great to catch up next month. Please come down and stay for a few days.

Love
Sally xx

Sally deleted all the junk emails she had also received and then shut down the PC. She was feeling hungry so decided to go and make herself a sandwich. After eating, Sally sat down in front of the TV and watched her favourite film for what must have been the 30th time. She never tired of the film and even on her own could not resist singing along.

"A spoonful of honey helps the medicine go down," echoed around her lounge. Just before the film had finished, her mobile rang. It was Zoemobile.

"Hi, Zoe."

"I have booked us both in for the speed dating next Tuesday."

"Great, what time is it?"

"It starts at 8.00 PM but do you fancy meeting in the Farm Tavern at 7.00 PM for some Dutch courage?"

"Sounds a good idea, see you then."

Chapter 3

The alarm on Sally's phone woke her up with a jolt and for a moment, she was utterly disorientated, but the fog slowly cleared from her mind. She remembered she set the alarm to remind her to phone an old friend in New Zealand. It was 6.00 AM in Brighton, which made it 6.00 PM in Auckland.

She had written the number of the University of Auckland where her friend worked on a small scrap of paper. She got up and went in search of it, vaguely recalling she had stuck it on her fridge.

The friend was a guy called Simon; she had worked with him in Brighton when he was doing his obligatory UK working holiday. Many Kiwis of Anglo-Saxon descent take advantage of the two-year working visa they can get to work and live in the UK before settling down back in New Zealand. Simon worked in Cyber Security and she hoped he would help her with the cunning plan she had to exact revenge on the Facebook hacker.

She found the number on the floor in front of the fridge and dialled the number.

"Good afternoon, the University of Auckland. How can I help you?"

"Could you please put me through to Simon Hall in the IT department?"

"Certainly, please hold."

The line went silent, then after a couple of minutes, a male voice said, "Simon Hall, here."

"Hi Simon, this is Sally Tompkins from Brighton. Do you remember me from working together at Anglo Credit?"

"Wow, Sally, of course, I remember you. How are you doing?"

"Not bad, still working at Anglo Credit and still single."

"What's wrong with the guys in Brighton? If you were out here, the guys would be swarming around like bees around a honey pot."

"Would that include you, Simon?"

Sally instantly felt embarrassed by what she just said and regretted how the call had suddenly become so flirtatious.

"You must know I have always fancied you rotten," replied Simon.

Sally did not know this. She remembered Simon as a miserable git who hung around with her and a few other work friends. She could not remember him paying her any attention, let alone making a pass.

"You are kidding, right?" exclaimed Sally.

"No, not at all," replied Simon. "I wanted to ask you out but never had the nerve to do it. To be honest, I think I was a little bit scared of you."

"How could you be scared of me?"

"You were so self-confident and strident. I was just a timid, miserable bloke."

"As a matter of fact, I like miserable guys," responded Sally, feeling sorry for Simon.

"Fat lot of good that is now we are on opposite sides of the planet. Why have you phoned me, by the way?"

Sally explained about the Facebook hacker and her plan for revenge. Simon loved her idea and said he would be able to help her with what she wanted. He would need a few days to sort it out but would get back in touch as soon as he had it ready.

After the call with Simon, Sally had a shower and made herself a simple breakfast of cereal and fresh fruit. It was now 7.30 AM and just about time to head to work. The office where Sally worked was only 15 minutes cycling from her flat. She kept her bike padlocked to a drainpipe on the side of the building. She unlocked it and cycled down her road to the seafront, where the wide cycle path would take her most of the way to work on safe off-road cycle paths.

Once she had passed the Palace Pier, she headed north and rode on the main roads in rush hour. Never much fun. Sally arrived safely and parked her bicycle in the racks provided in the underground car park. She got the lift from the car park up to the second floor where her office was.

The lift opened into the kitchen/lunch area and Sally grabbed a cup of coffee from the machine before heading to her desk. The coffee from the machine was awful, but it provided her with the caffeine hit she needed first thing before dealing with her work colleagues. She would grab a proper coffee later from one of the nearby coffee shops.

The office was operated on a Hot Desking basis, so she could pick any desk she liked. She usually came in earlier than most of her colleagues, so she had a good choice. Her favourites were the motorised desks that you could raise and use as a standing desk. Unfortunately, they had already been taken, so she settled for a regular desk next to a window and placed her coffee on the desk to claim it.

Next, she went over to her locker and took out her laptop, keyboard and mouse. She then returned to the desk and plugged them into the docking device that connected her PC to power, as well as the two large monitors hanging on stands in front of her.

She took a sip of coffee as the PC booted up and her login sequence started loading all her applications. Sally was a software developer on a team that looked after the local websites. She enjoyed her job and loved the team she worked with, so she was pretty content. However, she sometimes thought she was in a bit of a rut and lacked ambition. She had intended to look for a fresh challenge and a new job 'in a few months' for the last four years.

The office was now starting to fill up and a middle-aged man Sally did not know claimed the desk next to her. He caught Sally's eye and introduced himself in a broad American accent.

"Hi, I am Steve from the Dallas office, over here for some workshops for a couple of weeks."

"Hi, I am Sally. Nice to meet you. I am a developer here and if they are the workshops for the new Local Shopping website, then I will see you there."

"Cool, looks like I picked the right desk. Can you show me the way to the conference suite when we need to leave? I have not been to the Brighton office before."

"No problem, it is not far, so we should leave at about 9.50."

"OK, I will make sure I am back here by then."

Another middle-aged guy came over at that point and greeted Steve. They were obviously old friends and both left to grab a coffee together.

At 9.45, Steve returned as promised and Sally and he went together to their meeting.

Chapter 4

Sally arrived home from work at about 6.30 PM. The meeting had gone on from 10.00 AM until 6.00 PM with just a 20 min break for lunch. Sally was mentally exhausted. There were over 30 people in the conference room and they all had strong opinions on what the project should be doing. She had sat through nearly 8 hours of people arguing. Nothing had been agreed. The whole day was a complete disaster and she had nine more to come over the next two weeks.

She desperately needed a glass of wine and poured herself a generous measure of her favourite Australian Chardonnay from the bottle she had in the fridge door. She slumped down on her sofa and sipped some of the cold wine. She immediately started to relax and feel better. She was still too tired to cook but was starving, so she ordered pizza delivery from an app on her phone. While she waited for the Pizza to arrive, she phoned Zoe.

"Hi, Zoe."

"Hi, Sally. What's up?"

"Can you do me a favour and log in to Facebook and look at my page?"

"Sure, got it here now."

"Is the post from Caz warning about the ticket post being a scam still there?"

"No, it has been deleted, but the ticket post is still there."

"Great, can you do me a big favour and let me borrow your Facebook account. I have a plan to get even with my hacker but need to reply to the post with one of my friend's accounts."

"Sure, hardly use it anyway. I will SMS my username and password."

"Thanks, Zoe. I really appreciate it and see you tomorrow night at 7."

"Looking forward to it, going to be so much fun."

As soon as she had hung up the call with Zoe, her phone pinged, announcing the SMS with Zoe's Facebook credentials had arrived. Sally opened her laptop and logged in as Zoe. Sally soon found her profile and the ticket post. She replied as Zoe, "Hi, Sally. I would love the tickets. How much do you want for them?"

An alert popped up on her phone to let her know her pizza delivery man was near her house. She got up and walked down to the front door. The Pizza guy knocked just as she got there, so she opened the door and collected her dinner.

After she had finished the pizza and wine, she went back to her laptop and went to check if she had a reply to the message she had sent as Zoe. She was delighted to see the hacker had responded.

"Hi Zoe, tickets are 300 pounds for the pair. They are five rows back in the middle, so the best seats. Need to sell today, so reply quickly and I will give you details to transfer money."

Sally needed more time to set her trap, so she replied to stall the hacker. She was confident they would not be pulling out. Making a deadline of today was just a pressure-selling trick.

"Really want tickets but need a couple of days to get money. I will message back when I have it and if they are still available, I will take them."

She got an almost instant response.

"Do not wait too long as sure tickets will sell soon."

'Scumbag,' thought Sally and closed her laptop. She would enjoy getting revenge on the scamming bastard. She picked up her computer and went to the kitchen table to start building her hacker trap.

Her plan involved setting up a false website that she would lure the hacker. To do this, she had to take a considerable risk. The false website needed to look 100% authentic. To achieve this, she planned to make it part of the Anglo Credit website. As a developer, she was able to update the site and a couple of extra pages hidden away in an obscure part of the site for a couple of days would hopefully not be noticed. If they were, she would certainly lose her job.

The new pages were for a service called 'Anglo Credit Pay on Demand'. It would be how she would tell the hacker to get his money. Once he went to the site, the booby-trap that her friend Simon was writing for her would download onto the hacker's computer and she would start getting her revenge.

It took Sally over 2 hours to finish producing the new pages for the website. She was determined to make them perfect. She would install them once she had the additional boobytrap code that Simon had promised. Once all that was in place, she would message the hacker to tell him she would buy the tickets. She was feeling tired again, so she decided to call it a day and go to bed. Tomorrow was going to be a big day.

Chapter 5

Sally got up early and arrived at work before 8.00 AM. She was delighted to see a stand-up desk free, so she took it even though she would have to leave it and go to the tedious workshop again in less than an hour. She had emailed the new website pages to her work email account from home. She opened the email and added the web pages to the development branch of the company website, so they were ready to implement when she needed to. Just as she finished, she felt a pat on her shoulder and 'Good morning, Sally' in a now familiar American accent.

"Hi Steve, how are you?"

"Feeling great but not looking forward to this workshop session. Yesterday was a nightmare."

"Could not agree more. We achieved nothing except annoying each other."

"I had a word with Bruce last night and he promised to do something about it. No way am I sitting through 9 more days of that crap."

Bruce oversaw all the European operations based in Brighton. Steve was very senior himself or had friends in high places. Sally was relieved that Steve had shared her feelings and something was to be done.

At 9.50 AM, Sally and Steve left the office and went across to the conference centre for their workshop. They found most of the other attendees already present and sitting in silence, looking at laptops and phones when they arrived. Then, at 9.58, Bruce appeared and took charge.

"Listen all, yesterday's session was totally unacceptable. It costs the company a fortune to have you guys here and the Local Shopping project is critical. You collectively achieved nothing in nearly 8 hours. No way am I paying for nine more days like that. I am putting Steve Johnson from the Dallas office in charge from now on. I have known Steve for 20 years and trust him to sort this. Listen to what he says and do it without argument or you are in big trouble. Goodbye."

By 10.00 AM, Bruce was gone, leaving a stunned and remorseful audience for Steve to address.

"OK, guys, you heard it from Bruce. I am now in charge and this is how it is going to work."

Steve asked everybody present to stand up and explain what they did and why they should be at the workshop. After each person spoke, Steve would either dismiss them and they left the room or let them stay. By the time everybody had spoken, only six remained, including Sally.

The rest of the day went brilliantly. The much smaller team had all the skills and knowledge needed to get the job done and was small enough for a team dynamic to develop. They debated constructively and were happy to compromise when needed to allow things to move forward. Sally left the meeting at 5.00 PM feeling really excited about the project and the next week or so of workshops. She was also feeling excited about her night out with Zoe, so she hurried home to get something to eat and get ready in time.

Sally stopped off at Waitrose supermarket on the way home and picked up one of their pre-prepared meals for her dinner. She tried to avoid too much takeaway and junk food, but these uncooked meals were as far as she would compromise. Sally found cooking from scratch for one person unrewarding and not very efficient. Once home, she put her dinner in the oven to cook and had a shower.

Forty-five minutes later, she was clean and fed. She went to her bedroom and pondered what to wear for the speed dating. She decided something low-key was the best bet and slipped on a pair of old jeans and a plain T-shirt. The pub where she was meeting Zoe was a 20 min walk, so she gathered up her phone and keys, put them in her handbag and left the flat.

Sally arrived at the pub just as Zoe pulled up in a taxi and they entered together. The Farm Tavern pub was not very big, but it was laid out in an open plan with pine tables and chairs, which meant it felt airy and bright. Sally went to the bar and ordered a bottle of Chardonnay with two glasses. Zoe found a free table near the window and Sally joined her with the drinks.

"I suddenly feel so nervous about tonight," exclaimed Zoe as Sally poured her a drink.

"Don't be silly. It's just a laugh. Relax and enjoy it."

"I don't know why but I have this feeling that I am going to meet HIM tonight."

"What do you mean HIM?"

"You know, Mister Right, the man I am going to have children with and live with happily ever after."

"Sounds like you have been reading too many of those romance novels you like so much."

Two guys came over and sat at the table next to them. Both were in their early twenties. One was a fit and tanned, handsome guy with a 'Manly Beach' T-shirt and the other a serious-looking man with small glasses and, despite a pointy nose, still good-looking. The tanned guy caught Zoe looking at him and gave her a big smile in return.

"What's a Manly Beach?" said Zoe to explain what she was looking at.

"It is not a type of beach. It is the name of the place I come from in Australia," replied the tanned guy. "My name is Andy, by the way."

"Hi, I am Zoe and this is my friend Sally. Would you and your friend like to join us?"

Sally could not believe how forward Zoe was being and was dreading what she may have got them into.

"That would be great," replied Andy as he got up and moved towards their table. "This is Colin," he said as he beckoned his friend to join them. Both guys sat down at their table and Colin asked, "Do you come here often?"

Andy laughed out loud and teased his friend, "Is that your best line Colin, no wonder you are single and need to go to speed dating nights."

"No!" explained Zoe. "Are you going to the event at the Old Market tonight?"

"That's the plan," replied Andy. "Surely you two are not going as well!"

they all burst out laughing as Zoe and Sally both replied, "Yes!"

They spent the next 30 minutes chatting about speed dating and Colin shared some anecdotes about some of the things that had happened to him at previous events. Then, when it was time to go, they all agreed to meet back in the pub after the event to share their experiences.

Chapter 6

There was a small queue outside the speed dating venue. Sally waited a few minutes before entering the foyer and going to the table under the sign 'Girls' to register. She was given an instruction sheet, a small card with six numbered boxes and a number 12 written in purple felt tip.

The instructions let her understand that the number 12 was her table number in the main hall and the six boxes related to the 'Boys' that she would meet in order. The boy's name was to be written next to the box and if she wanted to see any of them again, she was to put a tick in his box and, if not, a cross. If they did not show up, then just leave their box blank.

The first date would start at 8.15. Each date lasted 10 minutes with a 5-minute gap in-between. The date began when a whistle was blown and ended when a siren went off. You were free to end the date early if you wish, but in no circumstances could the date go on more than 10 minutes.

After the final date, you should post your card in the box on the registration table as you left. The organisers would collate the results and send an email with the contact details of the dates when both parties wanted to see each other again. The email would be sent to all participants by 10.00 PM. You would get an email even if you had no matches.

This all seemed straightforward enough, so Sally went through into the main hall with Zoe and they found their tables. They were too far apart to talk, so Sally sat and looked around to check out the competition. There were about a dozen other girls waiting for their dates. Most seemed to be about the same age as Sally and all except one seemed pretty ordinary. The exception was a tall blonde girl who looked like she had just come from a Hollywood movie set. She was stunningly beautiful, with amazing makeup and very expensive designer clothes. *'What the hell are you doing here?'* thought Sally.

After about five more minutes, a whistle blew and the boys came in. A tall guy with long greasy hair and a black leather jacket strode purposefully towards Sally's table and sat down. Sally let out a silent inward sigh of disappointment. He did not look her type at all.

"Hi darling, my name is Slash. What is your name then?"

"I am Sally. Is Slash your real name or a nickname?"

"Nickname really, but everybody calls me that."

"What is your real name?"

"Nigel, but nobody calls me that except my mum."

"OK, Slash it is then. How did you get the name?"

"The kids I grew up with called me that 'cos I was always going for a pee, but I kept it as that guitarist bloke made the name really cool."

"Do you play guitar then? You look like a rock musician with the jacket and hair."

"No, but I am in a motorcycle gang and we all dress like this. Do you like bikes?"

"Only bicycles. I ride one to work."

The inane Small-talk went on easily enough until their ten minutes were up, but Sally had decided after the first 30 seconds that she would not see Slash again. She was surprised when, as he left, Slash said, "Thanks Sally, I think you are gorgeous and hope I can see you again."

She was touched and flattered but still put an X in the box next to Slash's name.

A few minutes later, the whistle went again and the boys returned for their next dates. At first, Sally thought she had been stood up as everybody had sat down and she had no date. However, her date did arrive a minute or so later and he apologised for being late.

"Hi, I am Tim. Sorry for being late, but I tried to grab a sneaky ciggy between dates."

"Hi, I am Sally and I wish I had joined you; this is pretty stressful and could have done with one myself."

Sally was pleased to meet a fellow smoker. She was about the only one of her friends who still smoked and often felt a bit of a leper. Tim was a stocky guy with curly blond hair and he was wearing a lumberjack shirt.

"Cool, a fellow smoker," replied Tim. "I like you already. Is this your first time at speed dating?"

"Yes, I came along to keep a friend company, the blonde girl with the deep tan at the end of the next row."

"Does that mean you are already attached?" said Tim with a clear tone of disappointment in his voice.

"No, very much single," replied Sally. "Just that I would not normally have considered coming to such an event."

"Do you use Tinder or any dating apps then?" responded Tim.

"No, nothing, just hoping to meet somebody in the normal course of life. It probably explains why I have been single for so long. What about you then, Tim?"

"Same as you, really. I tried Tinder once and it was a disaster, so I burned off that one. I decided to try this as I was not meeting anybody by just going to the pub with my mates."

Sally resisted the temptation to find out what happened on his Tinder date. She had already decided she wanted to meet Tim again, so she spent the rest of their 10 minutes making herself appear as attractive to him as possible. Apparently, she loved watching rugby, was a fantastic cook and her massage skills were legendary.

Next up was a guy called Pete, who did not ask Sally a single thing about herself. Instead, he spent most of the ten minutes saying how great he thought he was and what absolute 'mingers' his previous two dates were. Definite X.

The fourth date was a really shy and timid guy called Peter. Sally could barely hear what he said as he spoke so softly. He seemed a really lovely, sweet person, but Sally was not really interested in being a mother figure, so it was another X. Only one out of four was not as good as she had hoped.

When the next date sat down and she saw who it was, she was taken aback. There was no reason to be that surprised, but for some reason, she had not really thought about the possibility of one of her dates being Colin, who she had met in the pub earlier.

"Hi, Sally. I was hoping you would be one of my dates. It looks like it is my lucky day!"

"Wow, Colin," responded Sally. "Seems a bit of a wasted date given you already met me in the pub."

"Not at all," replied Colin with a big grin on his face. "It gives me the opportunity to say how fantastic I think you are. You are everything I would want in my dream woman. But, of course, I would never have the nerve to say that in front of Andy and your friend."

"Oh, thanks, Colin," replied Sally. "You are not so bad yourself."

Sally had not made up her mind up about Colin even after the further 10 minutes of chatting. He was pleasant enough, but there was no spark, nothing to excite her and make her want to see him again. She also found the dream woman comment a bit creepy. The problem was that if she rejected Colin, it would be really awkward in the pub afterwards. She could not give the pub a miss, as she knew Zoe was keen to go back and meet Andy again. She reluctantly put a tick in the box next to Colin's name.

Sally's final date was with a short Scottish guy called Ian. He was amusing and made Sally laugh several times. She was thinking of giving him a tick, but he blew it at the last minute. He told her he was a big Adele fan.

Back in the pub after the event, they sat down at the same table they had been at earlier.

"So, how many ticks did we all put down?" asked Sally.

"I put a tick down for the last guy, not because I particularly liked him but seemed a waste of the evening not to give at least one a go," said Zoe.

"I ticked them all," said Andy. "Any port in a storm, as they say."

"Andy is more interested in their sofa than anything more romantic," quipped Colin.

"What does that mean?" said Zoe.

Andy explained that he had been couch surfing but needed to find a new place by the weekend.

"You can stay with me," replied Zoe.

"Wow, that would be fantastic. So much rather be with you than any of the girls at speed dating."

Zoe blushed and Sally gave her a 'what the hell are you doing' look.

At that moment, Sally's phone pinged to say she had a new email. She picked up the phone and saw it was from the speed dating. She only had one match, but to her surprise and delight, it was with Tim and not Colin.

"Hey, Colin, how come you did not tick my box? What about all that stuff about me being your dream woman?"

Colin looked very embarrassed and squirmed in his seat. "Sorry, Sally, but the last date was beyond my wildest dreams, so I changed the tick to a cross."

"Fickle bastard," teased Zoe. "Don't worry. I have found a better date as well."

Andy's phoned then pinged and after reading the email, he proclaimed, "Full house, got six matches!"

"I hope you are not going to meet any of them," said Zoe.

"I told you, I fancy you much more than any of them, so I am all yours," quipped Andy.

Zoe's phone was next to ping. "Well, I have a backup date if you mess me around, Andy."

Colin's phone pinged last and after looking at his phone, he looked devastated.

"She turned me down," said the distraught Colin.

"Which one was she?" asked Andy.

"The curly-haired girl called Rachael," replied Andy.

"I got her contact details as she matched with me," said Andy. "Here they are. Give her a ring and pretend they told you it was a match. Maybe correct, sure they make mistakes."

Colin took the details down from Andy's phone and rang Rachael. He looked much happier after a brief conversation with Rachael. She had ticked him off and was keen to meet up the next night.

After they had finished their bottle of wine, Sally made her excuses and left the others to it. Assuming Simon had finished his booby-trap and would send it in time, she wanted to get in early to work so she could set up her website trap. She also wanted to contact Tim in private.

Chapter 7

Back in the privacy of her flat, she was about to phone Tim when he beat her to it.

"Hi, Sally. It is Tim from the speed dating."

"Hi, Tim. I was about to give you a ring."

"So, how about I buy you dinner tomorrow night?"

"That sounds great. Where do you fancy going?"

"I heard about a great new restaurant in the Lanes. How about I book a table for 7.30 and we meet in the Bath Arms at 7.00 PM?"

"Sounds great, see you then."

Sally was elated to have an actual date again after such a long time. She was so pleased Zoe nagged her into going to the speed dating. Finally, she went to bed and slept with a smile on her face.

Sally's body clock woke her the next morning at precisely 7.00 AM as usual. She got straight up and headed for the shower. Afterwards, over a quick breakfast of cereal and fruit, she checked her email. She was delighted to find a reply from Simon. He had sent across the boobytrap program as promised. He went on to explain how it worked and what it did. Sally was super impressed; it was much better than she ever hoped. She forwarded Simon's email with the attachment to her work email. If it got past her work firewall and virus scanners, it would have passed its first test.

Sally got to her desk by 8.00 AM and was pleased to see the first test had been passed as the forwarded email and the attachment were at the top of her email inbox. Simon promised to ensure the boobytrap did not have any of the signatures virus checkers looked for to identify such things. He had kept his word. Sally copied the attachment into the website code repository. She then attached the code to her new web pages and prepared everything ready to go onto the main company website.

However, she was not authorised to deploy the code to the live website. This was strictly controlled and she had to raise a formal request that needed to be approved by one of the heads of development. She sent a quick message to her local Head of Development.

"Hi, Shane. Can you authorise CR45637 for me? It is an urgent but straightforward fix to the website navigation bar."

She got an almost immediate response. "No problem, Sally, now approved and will be implemented at 10.00 AM."

Sally was relieved it all went so smoothly. This was the riskiest part of her plan. If Shane had bothered to look at what her code actually did, she would have been in big trouble. She would send the hacker a message saying she wanted the tickets when she got home that evening. As soon as he had downloaded the boobytrap, she would remove the code from the company website and nobody would ever know what she did.

At 9.50 AM, Sally left her desk to head down to the conference centre for the next day of her workshop. The large meeting room was far too big for the much-reduced team, so they all huddled in one corner. Steve had been in very early and placed all the work to date and plans on the walls of the room. As soon as everybody arrived, they all got stuck in and the day flew by. Steve was excellent and Sally enjoyed working with him. She felt they were going to create something special on this project.

Sally got home about 5.30 PM and wasted no time getting back in touch with her hacker. She sent a message that said, "Hi Sally, great news. My mum lent me the money as she wants to come with me. She has put it on her Anglo Credit card. Just go to www.AngloCredit.com/payondemand. If you put in the code TRE435DFG*UI and my surname (Tonys), it will transfer the 300 pounds to whatever bank account you nominate or even bitcoins, apparently. Let me know when you have the money and we can sort getting the tickets to me."

Sally hoped the lure of the bitcoins option would be an extra incentive for the hacker to click straight away.

Sally went to get ready for her date with Tim. She still had 10 minutes after she had got ready before she needed to leave, so she phoned Zoe to see how things went after she left.

"Hi, Zoe, Sally here. How are things?"

"Things are moving fast."

"What do you mean?"

"Andy stayed last night and he was not on the couch."

"You naughty girl, how was it?"

"Fantastic, best ever. You know I said I had that feeling about meeting HIM before the speed dating event, well I was right and I have."

"I am so happy for you, Zoe."

"Did you get in touch with Tim?"

"Yes, meeting him in the Bath Arms tonight and he is buying me dinner at this new place in the Lanes."

"No! Andy works at the Bath Arms and is on tonight."

"I will make sure to say Hi."

"Do that and hope you have a great night. I look forward to meeting Tim soon."

"Thanks, Zoe, catch you again soon."

Sally booked an Uber on her phone. As always, it was 2 minutes away and she rushed outside to meet it.

Sally's phone pinged as the driver made his way through the maze of one-way streets in central Brighton. It was a message from the hacker.

"The website does not work. I put in the code and nothing happened. Can you pay me directly in bitcoins?"

Sally smiled and said silently to herself, "Got you—now you will pay for trying to rip off my friends."

The Uber driver dropped her next to the nearest entrance to the Lanes for the Bath Arms. The Lanes themselves are a pedestrianised labyrinth of old fisherman's cottages that now form the beautiful heart of the city. The old cottages have been converted into an eclectic mix of shops, pubs and restaurants. The Bath Arms is the oldest pub in the Lanes, having opened in 1864. Sally entered the pub and was pleased to see Tim waiting for her just inside the door.

"Hi Sally, you look fabulous," said Tim as he leaned forward and gave her a gentle kiss on the lips.

"Thanks, Tim, you look pretty good yourself," replied Sally and she meant it. Tim was a lot more handsome than she remembered from the speed date.

"What can I get you to drink?" asked Tim.

"A glass of Chardonnay, please," replied Sally and she followed Tim up to the bar to get the drinks. As Zoe had mentioned, Andy was working behind the bar and he served Tim.

"Hi Andy," said Sally as she caught his eye.

"Hi Sally," replied Andy. "What are you doing here?"

"With Tim, my date from last night. I heard you and Zoe are now an item."

"Yes, she is a wonderful girl."

"She is; make sure you treat her well. She is my best friend and I am a vindictive bitch to people who mess with my friends."

Tim heard this and felt a little voice inside his head say, "Be careful with this one, Tim."

Andy seemed less worried and replied, "Don't worry, Sally, I am one of the nice guys and will take good care of her."

Sally and Tim took their drinks and sat down at a quiet table near the back of the pub.

"Don't worry, Tim. I am not really a bunny boiler. I just said that vengeance thing to make sure Andy had second thoughts if he ever thought of messing Zoe around."

"That's a relief. You had me worried for a moment. I was thinking about what I may have got myself into here."

They both laughed and Sally said, "So, what is this new restaurant you are taking me to?"

"It is called Zero," replied Tim. "It was started by one of the Master Chef winners from the TV program."

"I love that show," replied Zoe. "I watch them all. Which winner is it behind the restaurant?"

"I think her name is Suzie Ryan," responded Tim.

"I remember her well. She did this fantastic French/Malaysian fusion food."

"Yes, that's right. A friend from my rugby team took his wife last week and he was raving about it."

The food was indeed remarkable and the wine flowed freely. Tim turned out to be the most charming and funny guy Sally had ever been out with on a date. After paying the bill, Tim said, "How do you fancy coming back to my place for a nightcap?"

It was a corny line, but just the one Sally hoped he would say. They caught a taxi from the rank near the restaurant and headed to Tim's flat, which turned out to be just around the corner from where Sally lived.

"We should have shared the cab in, as well," joked Sally.

Inside Tim's flat, he poured them both a glass of brandy but not much got drunk before they were undressing each other and heading for Tim's bed.

Chapter 8

Sally woke up at 7.00 AM in Tim's bed.

"I need to leave to go to work," said Sally.

"Let's have sex one more time before you go," pleaded Tim.

Sally could see that he was ready from the bulge under the sheet, so she pulled back the sheet and rode him cowgirl style.

After the sex, Sally took a shower in Tim's bathroom and then headed back to her flat, where she quickly changed clothes, grabbed her bike and then cycled to work. As usual, she parked her bike at the top level of the underground car park and went to the lift to get to her work floor. The lift arrived and had a middle-aged guy already inside from the floors below. She stepped inside and pushed the button for her floor. The smell inside the lift was disgusting and Sally nearly retched. The horrible looking man had obviously farted in the lift.

As she left, she gave him a killer stare and said, "You are disgusting."

She got into her office at 8.30 AM and was just about to log in to her computer when Shane, the Head of Development, approached her and said, "Don't bother, your login credentials have been suspended. Come with me to Frank's office."

Frank was the CIO and she followed Shane to his office. Once inside the office, she was horrified to see her 'Pay on Demand' web pages displayed on Frank's computer monitor.

"What the hell have you been doing," barked Frank. Sally was about to come clean on the whole booby trap plan for her hacker when Frank said, "The new parts of the site came up on the Web Site Analytics reports that go to the Head of Digital in New York. He wants to know what this Pay On Demand thing is and who approved it."

'Shit,' thought Sally. She had forgotten about the analytics. She should have added a tag for them to ignore the new pages. Sally then realised they probably had no idea about the boobytrap and thought they were just a few web pages.

Thinking quickly on her feet, she said, "It was an idea I had for the innovation competition. I mocked up the concept for my submission. I have no idea how they got on the website—OH NO!—I must of put the wrong code in that emergency fix I got Shane to approve yesterday. I am SO SORRY."

Sally took a deep breath, inside she was very proud of herself and hoped it had fooled them.

Frank turned to Shane. "You approved this without checking it?"

"I must admit, I was swamped yesterday and as it was Sally, I assumed it would be OK," responded Shane.

"Really sloppy work from both of you. I am very disappointed. Be more careful in the future. Take it down immediately and make sure nothing like this happens again," said Frank.

They both turned to leave and as they were doing so, Frank said, "By the way, Sally, Head of Digital loved the Pay on Demand idea—you might do well in the competition."

Sally went back to her desk and prepared a new Change Request to take the code off the website. She took it to Shane and he approved it for immediate implementation.

Sally returned to her desk and could not believe how she had managed to get out of this without being in big trouble. She was so close to confessing and if they knew about the boobytrap, she would have been sacked and possibly reported to the police. Shane had reinstated her credentials, so she logged in and checked her email. There was an email from Steve saying he had to go to an urgent meeting first thing and putting back the start of the workshop to 11.30. This pleased Sally. She would now have time to check how the booby trap went.

The boobytrap that Simon had written for her was a very sophisticated computer virus that installed itself on the computer of any person who visited the Pay On Demand pages of the website. The virus first used the camera on the computer to take a picture of the user. It did this very quickly so they would not notice their camera light coming on. The image was then sent to a secure cloud storage area that Simon had set up and given Sally access to.

The virus also captured other information about the user, such as the geographical coordinates, IP address and User ID/Passwords and sent them to the cloud storage are. The next trick that the virus had was the bit Sally had not expected and delighted her when she found out. The virus read every document on the user's computer, including emails and social media messages.

It had a sophisticated AI algorithm that could decide if the document contained any useful personal information. If it decided it did, then it sent a copy to the cloud storage. This part took time, so it would be several days before the virus would complete an initial scan of everything on the user's computer. It ran slowly to avoid using too much computer power and alerting the user that something was wrong by slowing the computer down.

Her work computer and network blocked access to the cloud storage, so she took her personal computer out of her rucksack and used that with the 4G internet connection on her phone. On the cloud storage site, she was surprised to see four sets of user's data had been captured. She clicked on the latest one and saw a picture of a concerned-looking Frank. She also noticed that the virus had already collected over 500 documents from Frank's computer.

'*Holy shit,*' she thought, '*that will make interesting reading later.*' The next set of files had a picture of a middle-aged man in a suit from New York who she assumed was the Head of Digital. She would check later by reading his emails. The next one had a picture of an attractive goth-looking woman in her early twenties and a location in Adelaide, Australia. She had looked at the website about 10 hours ago. There was no other data collected from her computer.

'*How strange,*' thought Sally. "Who are you?"

The last one had a picture of a guy in his mid-thirties with heavy stubble and bleary red eyes. Exactly what she had imagined her hacker would look like. The time he had accessed the website was 6.30 PM yesterday, so confirmed it was almost certainly him. To her delight, the virus had already harvested nearly a thousand documents from his computer.

Sally was surprised that the hacker's location was like the goth girl, also in Australia but this time in Sydney. She expected the hacker to be in Russia or China or even a third world country. Eager to find out more about him, she started working her way through the various emails and messages the virus had captured. It was soon clear he was indeed the hacker, as many of the messages related to more victims of his 'tickets' scam.

Sally was surprised at how successful the scam was. He seemed to get an almost 50% hit rate on the post where the victim was not quick enough to remove it straight away. Sally was also intrigued by how the scammer got his money. She assumed he would ask for it to be transferred into a bank account, but that was not how it worked. He had a bullshit story he sent as the person he had hacked, telling their friend that they wanted the money to buy an Amazon Gift card for their nephew's 18th birthday.

The bullshit explained that to make things easier, the buyer should buy an online gift voucher for the amount and send it to an email address that was supposed to be the nephews with a message of Happy 18th Birthday from Uncle/Aunty whatever. Looking at the number of emails and doing a quick calculation, Sally deduced he was making over 20 thousand pounds a month out of this simple scam. Time was getting on and Sally left for the postponed meeting in the Conference Centre.

It was nearly 11.45 before Steve eventually arrived. He was really animated and energised from the earlier meeting. "Listen up, big news, everybody. Our little project has been put on the Global Big Ten. Isn't that fantastic? It means we will be a top priority and we will get whatever resources we need."

They all cheered and there were big smiles all around. "Can we start by ordering some coffee and doughnuts for lunch?" quipped one of the team.

"Better than that, let's all go to the Pizza place down the road and have a proper lunch," replied Steve.

With that, they all left and walked down to the local Italian Pizzeria. Over lunch, Steve elaborated on what being on the GBT list would mean. They would be able to scale the team when they needed to and would have priority in getting any IT system changes. In return, they would be closely scrutinised by some of the company's senior executives. Starting tomorrow, the Global Head of Digital will be joining their weekly meeting. Sally's head was spinning. This was the guy she had accidentally hacked and got access to all his personal messages.

Chapter 9

After she arrived home, Sally phoned Tim to see how he was and if he fancied coming round for dinner.

"Hi, Tim, Sally here. How's it going?"

"Hi, Sally, been thinking about you all day. I can't wait to see you again. What are you doing tonight?"

"I was hoping you would come round to my place for dinner," replied Sally.

"I would love to, especially as you are such a fantastic cook."

'Shit,' thought Sally. She had forgotten about her little white lie at the speed dating. "Bit short notice for one of my culinary masterpieces, but sure, it will be good," bluffed Sally. "How about 8.00 PM and you can stay over if you like?"

"You bet I like," replied Tim. "Fantastic meal and sex with a beautiful woman, what's not to like."

"See you at 8.00 then," replied Sally.

As soon as she had hung up, Sally started to panic about what to cook. She had initially planned a SpagBol that would not fit with Tim's view of her as some kind of Nigella Lawson clone.

She rushed out to the supermarket and got some scallops for the starter and some venison for the main. She planned to sear the scallops and serve them with crispy bacon and pea puree. The venison was to be pan-fried and served with a blackcurrant sauce and potatoes dauphinoise.

By the time she had got all the preparation done for the meal and had a shower and changed, it was almost 7.30 PM. She would not have much time to check on the latest data harvested by Simon's virus, but she could not resist a quick scan. She was delighted and amazed to see a file called passwords.docx had been collected from the hacker's computer.

'Surely, he would not be so stupid,' thought Sally, but she was delighted to see he had been on opening the file. The document contained usernames and

passwords for all his website accounts, including his banking one. Based on the usernames, she had a good idea what his real name was.

She was sure he was called Spencer Howard. She knew he had a Facebook account from the password document, so she did a quick search and there he was. Not so bleary-eyed as in the snap the virus took, but the stubble was a permanent feature. Sally could not wait to get stuck into this information and have some fun at Spencer's expense, but Tim was arriving in 10 minutes. She rushed around the flat to tidy up the last bits of mess and had just finished when the doorbell rang.

The meal turned out to be delicious. Sally surprised herself by how good it was and Tim said, "You were not lying when you said you were a fantastic cook. If that was a quick mid-week meal, then I cannot wait to try one of your culinary masterpieces."

However, Sally was concerned about how much work she would have to put in to maintain her Nigella facade. To make matters worse, Tim had also mentioned his hope of one of her legendary massages later and had invited her to a rugby match on Saturday.

After dinner, they snuggled up together on the sofa and finished the rest of the wine. It was not long, however, before they drifted off to the bedroom. Unfortunately, Sally's legendary massage did not go down as well as her dinner. Tim was polite and said it was lovely, but Sally could tell she had not hit the right buttons. The actual sex, however, was even better than the night before they both drifted off to sleep in contented post-coital bliss.

Sally woke at 7.00 AM and Tim was also awake soon after. This time, there was no morning sex as Tim needed to catch the train to London for a work meeting at 10.00 AM. He left straightway to go back to shower and change at his flat. After he had left, Sally had a shower and grabbed some breakfast.

She opened her laptop and went back to look at Spencer's password document. She was keen to get into some of his accounts but wanted to make sure that he was not alerted to something being wrong just yet. Many websites send alerts when your account is accessed on an unfamiliar computer. She knew that the websites used something called a 'Cookie' stored on your computer once you have visited it. If the website cannot find one on your computer, it assumes this is the first time and sends the alert out.

Luckily for Sally, she had noticed yesterday that amongst the files taken from Spencer's computer were his cookies. She found the Facebook, LinkedIn, Twitter and Gmail cookies and copied them to her laptop. She then went to

Facebook and logged in as Spencer. His Facebook pages were pretty unremarkable. He used to post regularly, but recently there were only a couple of posts per month.

He was obviously a keen surfer as most of the posts related to that, but there were also a few family posts and Sally found out that both his parents lived with his only sibling in a farmhouse near a place called Bowral. His sibling was a sister, but she was not the goth that Sally had captured the picture of using the virus. Sally looked his at Twitter feed and found that he never really posted there. The LinkedIn profile was more interesting and Sally found out that he was a graphic designer. His last job was with a small Australian design agency and ended about 12 months ago. Clearly, hacking paid better than graphic design.

Sally felt she could understand and perhaps sympathise with hackers from 3rd world and oppressed countries. They did what they did out of desperation. They had very few other opportunities to make money and improve their lives. This Spencer guy was a different case. He lived in one of the most prosperous and open countries in the world. He had so many ways to improve his life without doing it at the expense of his innocent scam victims. Sally was determined he was to pay the price starting now.

She changed the passwords on his Facebook and Twitter accounts so he could not quickly undo what she was about to post. She also changed the password on his Gmail account so he would be locked out and not receive any notifications. On Facebook, she posted under the title 'A Confession'.

"I am the person who ripped you off by fraudulently getting you to pay me for tickets your friend never had. I did not need to stoop so low to make money. I am a vile and worthless person and need to be punished. If you already reported the scam to the police, then follow up and give them my name. If you have not yet reported it, then do so now."

Sally tagged every victim she had found in the emails from his computer. By tagging them, they would all receive alerts from Facebook to look at the post. To make sure he would be caught, she also sent a direct message via his Twitter account to the Australian Federal police with a similar confession and a link to the emails she had harvested and copied to his Google Drive.

Time was moving on and Sally needed to get to work, so she packed everything up and headed out. She arrived a bit later than usual and no desks were free, so she parked herself in one of the collaboration spaces until the meeting was due to start in the conference centre. While waiting, she checked on

Spencer's Facebook page. The message had undoubtedly got out. It was flooded by vitriolic messages from the victims of his scam, all vowing to get revenge.

At 9.55, she left and went to the conference room, where everybody else had already arrived and was ready to start. Sally had forgotten that the Head of Digital guy would join them for a weekly briefing later that morning. He was to participate by video conference at 11.30 AM, which was 6.30 AM in New York, where he was based.

The next 90 minutes were spent preparing for the briefing to the Head of Digital, who was called Ryan Brown. Steve was keen to make a good impression and had obviously spent many hours preparing what Sally thought was an excellent pack of slides, summarising what they planned to build. Steve was keen to give everybody 'airtime', so he allocated a portion of the presentation to each team member to speak to.

When 11.30 arrived, Ryan popped up on the giant video screen and introduced himself. He was taking the call from home and was sitting at his kitchen table. They all went through their individual parts of the presentation. Ryan nodded and smiled, but he never asked any questions. At the end of the presentation. Steve asked him what he thought. He replied he thought it was good and he was happy. With that, he ended the call.

They all sat in silence. '*What an anti-climax,*' thought Sally. Steve looked confused and worried. He suggested they break for an early lunch and meet back at 1.30 PM.

Sally found a now vacant desk and got out her personal laptop from her rucksack. She had not looked at any of the messages harvested from Ryan Brown or Frank up until now, as she was still a little nervous about breaking the bond of trust she should have with her employer. Ryan's strange, detached behaviour had changed her mind.

He was obviously hiding something and she needed to know what. She connected via her phone and browsed the cloud drive with Ryan's messages. It did not take long to discover what was going on. Ryan's brother-in-law was an out-of-work IT Program Manager and Ryan's wife was putting pressure on Ryan to get him a job. Ryan had identified the Local Shopping project as an ideal candidate, but first, he had to get rid of Steve. Ryan had wasted no time in starting that task.

As soon as the briefing they had given him earlier had finished, Ryan sent an email to his boss saying that he had reviewed the project and was sorry to see it was a complete mess and lacked any half-decent leadership. He went on to say that he felt it urgently needed a 'big hitter' program manager bought in to sort it. He added that he knew of such a person who was luckily soon to be available. They were expensive but would be well worth it. Sally was fuming.

Steve had done a fantastic job and this weasel was not only treating him unfairly but also about to execute a terrible example of nepotism. She was determined to stop it from happening. Unfortunately, at this point, she had no idea how. She could hardly confront him head-on and admit she had hacked Ryan's computer. She needed to find a more subtle way to expose him.

The rest of the afternoon session with the project team was very downbeat. Everybody sensed that something terrible was going to happen. They finished early and Sally was back home by 4.30 PM. She used the time to go to the gym and work out her frustration with some physical exercise. She was jogging back home from the gym to shower when she bumped into Tim, who was coming back home from the station.

"Hi, Sally. Did not know you were a runner?"

"Hi, Tim, not really. I prefer the gym but do run there and back. Finished work early, so just been down there for a workout. How was your day?"

"I have some exciting news. How about coming round to my place for dinner and I will tell you all about it."

"Sounds intriguing. Will 7.00 PM be OK?"

"Perfect, see you then."

Sally jogged back home and had her shower. Afterwards, she phoned Zoe for a quick catch-up.

"Hi, Zoe, Sally here."

"Hi, Sally. What's up?"

"You will be pleased to know I have got even with that scumbag who hacked my Facebook account," Sally explained to Zoe what she had done and Zoe responded.

"Well done, girl. How clever. I told Andy about it and he said he was nearly caught by the same thing the other day. Glad you have put the scammer out of action."

"How are things going with Andy?"

"Wonderful, he is such a kind, funny and sexy guy. I cannot believe my luck. How are things with Tim? Andy said he saw you on Wednesday night in the pub."

"Having a really good time. We have seen each other every night. I went back to his place after dinner in the restaurant and stayed the night. I cooked a meal for him last night and he stayed over at my place. He is cooking for me tonight."

"He still wants to see you after tasting your food?" teased Zoe. Sally explained about the white lie at the speed date and the enormous effort she put in.

"Sounds like we have both done well. How about the four of us meeting up next week for a night out?"

"Yes, sounds good."

"I will check when Andy is not working and get back to you."

"Cool, speak soon."

Sally went and got changed and then headed off to Tim's flat for dinner.

On the way, Sally stopped at an off licence to get some wine. When she arrived at Tim's place, an Uber Eats driver was dropping off some food.

"Caught me red-handed," joked Tim. "It was supposed to be delivered 20 minutes ago so I could put it in the oven and hide the packaging before you arrived."

They both laughed and took the food up to Tim's flat. They were both hungry, so they skipped the pretence of a home-cooked meal and put the containers of food on the table. Tim got a couple of plates, some cutlery and wine glasses. The food was from a small French restaurant around the corner that Sally had eaten at before but did not realise also did take away. It was delicious and they soon demolished the whole lot. After eating and settling down with their wine on the sofa, Sally asked, "So come on then, what is this exciting news you have?"

"I have been offered a promotion and a big pay rise," responded Tim.

"Wow, that is fantastic. Well done. Why did you say *offered*? Have you not accepted it," quizzed Sally, sensing a catch with the job.

"It is in Sydney, Australia," explained Tim. "I would have bitten their hand off if the job was in Brighton or London, but Sydney is so far away."

"How long have you got to decide," asked Sally.

"Now we get to the exciting bit," teased Tim. "They have said they will pay for my partner and me to fly over there for two weeks. All expenses paid to meet the team I will be heading up. I will then need to decide and tell them before coming back."

"Wow, that is generous of them. They must think a lot of you," said Sally.

"So, *Partner,* will you come with me?" said Tim with a big grin on his face. "Flying business class and staying at a 5-star hotel with a view of the opera house." Sally was flabbergasted and lost for words. "I know we have only been dating for a few days, but I would love you to come with me. Just look at it as a free all expenses holiday you have just won."

Sally eventually managed to speak. "That is a wonderful offer and so lovely that you asked me. I am tempted to say yes now, but can you give me until tomorrow to get my head around it all? I don't want to say yes and then get cold feet and let you down."

"Fully understand," said Tim, "but need to confirm by lunchtime tomorrow and we will be leaving next Wednesday."

"OK," said Sally, her head spinning again, "I think I need another drink."

Tim poured her a large glass of wine and they carried on discussing the trip. By the time they had finished talking, Sally was 99% certain she would say yes. Tim insisted he was not asking her to emigrate with him, just come on a free holiday. Sally left Tim's flat at about 11.00 PM. Sally decided that she would be able to think more clearly about what to do with a bit of space. She also wanted to speak to Zoe. She did this by phoning her as soon as she got back to her own flat.

"You OK to talk," said Sally.

"Sure, just waiting for Andy to get back," responded Zoe. Sally explained about Tim's job offer and the offer he made her to go on the trip to Sydney.

"If you like Tim and would be happy to go on a holiday with him, then it is a no brainer. This is the opportunity of a lifetime. You have always wanted to visit Australia and this way, you do it in style for free."

"To be honest, the thing I am scared about is that I fall in love with Tim and then he accepts the job and leaves me," responded Sally. "I am tempted to tell him now that we should not see each other again but if he turns down the job, we could start again."

"That is the worst thing you could do. If you tell him that you will definitely never see him again and miss out on the trip."

"It is all just so scary," responded Sally.

"It is not like you to over analyse things like this," responded Zoe.

"I know," said Sally. "I am going to tell Tim I am going and deal with the rest if and when it happens."

"That's the spirit," responded Zoe. "And by the way, Andy is not working on Sunday night if you and Tim are free."

"Pretty sure that will work, will get back to you," replied Sally.

Sally went to be a bed but did not get much sleep.

Chapter 10

Sally may not have slept much, but she did plenty of thinking. She got up at 6.30 AM refreshed from now, having a clear view of what she would do and a firm conviction it was the right thing. She sent Tim a text saying she now had everything straight in her head would love to go to Sydney with him. He replied immediately, asking for her to send her passport details so the travel agent could sort tickets and visas. She did this and then headed to the gym.

After getting back from the gym, she showered and had a bacon sandwich for breakfast. This was her 'Saturday Treat'. As always, it tasted fantastic and she found she was still licking her lips for several seconds after she finished eating it. Roll on next Saturday. She thought before suddenly realising she would be in Australia then. The realisation sent a brief shiver down her spine. She pulled herself together and decided to get on with the other thing she had decided during her sleepless night. She phoned Steve.

"Hi, Steve, it's Sally from work."

"Hi, Sally. What are you doing, phoning at the weekend?"

"I need to speak to you urgently about something very important and extremely sensitive," replied Sally.

"You have me intrigued and worried, but can this not wait until Monday?" responded Steve.

"You should be worried and no. I think it is best if we meet and I explain as soon as possible."

"OK," said Steve. "Meet me at the Pavilion Gardens Café at 11.00 AM."

"Great, see you there."

The café was set in the grounds of the Royal Pavilion. The royal palace was built by the Prince Regent in the mid-19th century in the centre of Brighton and is one of the most eccentric buildings ever built. The gardens surrounding the palace provided a beautiful botanical oasis and were a major tourist attraction in their own right. Sally arrived early and sat at an empty table under some shade to wait for Steve. When he did arrive, he ordered them both an iced coffee and then sat down.

"So, what is this all about?" asked Steve. Sally came completely clean on the whole thing from the Facebook hacker, bogus web pages and the booby trap. She had printed copies of Ryan's emails and presented them to Steve.

"Fucking Hell!" exclaimed Steve. His bad language caught Sally by surprise and he got some dirty looks from the two old ladies sitting at the table next to them.

"I fully intend to expose Ryan Brown. I always thought of him as a brown-nosed little creep," added Steve. "The problem here is that when I present the evidence and explain how I got it, you are going to be in as much trouble as him."

"I am happy to accept whatever the consequences are," responded Sally. "I could not stand by and watch him get away with it."

"I cannot thank you enough for what you have done. I promise I will do all I can to find a way for you to come out of this with as little damage as possible. Let me go and speak with Bruce and see what he suggests."

"OK and thank you," responded Sally.

"It is me who should be thanking you. Try not to worry and I will get back to you as soon as I can," replied Steve.

Sally walked away from the Royal Pavilion towards her flat. On the way, she passed a Japanese restaurant and picked up some sushi for her lunch. When she got to her flat, she got her phone out of her handbag and noticed she had missed a text from Tim. He said the tickets would be ready on Monday and that he was playing Cricket that afternoon at Hove Rec from 2.00 PM and he hoped she could come along. After finishing the sushi Rolls, she started feeling really tired from her lack of sleep. She set her alarm on her iPhone and had a power nap before leaving to meet Tim.

Sally arrived at Hove Recreation Ground at about 2.45 PM and the game was already underway. She joined a small crowd watching the game from the side-lines. Sally knew very little about Cricket, so she struggled to follow what was going on. She spotted Tim in his whites standing in the middle, near the man with the wooden bat. She knew enough to know that Tim's team was fielding and that the scoreboard showing 23 for 4 was good.

It was a lovely sunny afternoon, so Sally found herself some space in the sun and sat down to enjoy the warmth of its rays. The batting team made a minor comeback, but it did not last long and they were all out for 76. At 'tea', Sally joined Tim and the rest of his team for some sandwiches and soft drinks that had been laid out on a picnic table near to the scoreboard. Tim introduced Sally to his teammates and some of the other players' wives and girlfriends.

When Tim's team came out to bat, Sally joined the other girlfriends to watch. Tim was an opening batsman and made quick progress in getting his team to the target runs with two fours and a six in the opening over. Things slowed down a bit, but it was still under an hour before Tim's team had won by 9 wickets. Tim top scored with 45.

After the match, Tim and Sally declined an offer to join a few of the others for a 'quick pint', they both knew how they usually turned out. They decided instead to head out for an early dinner. They first went back to Tim's flat, where he got changed and then headed for the seafront. It was now a beautiful summer evening and they sat at one of the beach restaurants and enjoyed a jug of Pimm's followed by some locally caught seafood and a local Sussex sparkling white wine. While they were contemplating what desert to select, Sally's phone buzzed. It was Steve.

"Hi, Steve," said Sally.

"Hi Sally, look, I have been talking with Bruce and he would like to talk to us both at his house tomorrow morning. He lives locally, so can you make 10.00 AM?"

"Yes, sure," responded Sally.

"Great, I will text you his address and see you there at 10.00."

"Let's share the chocolate brownie with cherry ice cream," said Tim as he noticed Sally hang up.

"Sounds yummy," responded Sally.

After dinner, they went for a stroll along the beach and then up into the Lanes. As they passed the Bath Arms, Sally suggested they pop in for one last drink. Inside, Sally was happy to see what she had hoped for. Zoe was sitting at the bar while Andy was working.

"Keeping an eye on him then Zoe," teased Sally.

"Hi Sally, what are you doing here?" responded Zoe.

Sally ushered Tim forward and introduced him to Zoe and explained where they had been. Tim bought a round of drinks and the three of them found a table where they could talk.

"So, are you love birds off to Oz next week?" asked Zoe in her typically direct style.

"Yes, I have accepted Tim's offer and we leave on Wednesday," replied Sally.

"I am so jealous. I have always wanted to visit Sydney and even more so since meeting Andy and him telling me more about it," said Zoe.

"Of course, I forgot Andy was from Sydney. We must get some tips on what to do and where to go."

"You will have the chance tomorrow if you are free. Andy is doing an Oz style BBQ at my place and you are both invited."

Sally looked at Tim for confirmation and then said, "That would be great."

Chapter 11

Sally left Tim's flat about 8.30 AM, so she had plenty of time to get ready to meet Steve at Bruce's house. Bruce lived in a very upmarket area of Hove situated high up on downland at the edge of the South Downs National Park. The area was made up of grand detached houses with extensive gardens and sea views. Brighton and Hove were compact cities and Sally would be able to cycle to his house in 20 minutes. She left her flat at 9.30 to make sure she had plenty of time.

Bruce's house was surrounded by a high wall and had a single set of large metal gates protecting the entrance to the grounds. Sally clicked on the video intercom next to the gates. Without anybody bothering to reply, the large gates silently opened and Sally walked through up to the front door of the house.

Before she had reached the front door, Bruce appeared from around the side of the house and said, "Hello Sally, come with me to the garden. Steve is already here."

Sally followed Bruce to the rear garden, where Steve was sitting at a large wooden table on a raised patio area. Sally sat down and joined him. The views from the patio over the city and down to the sparkling blue sea were spectacular.

"Right, let's get down to it," said Bruce. "I have taken this problem to the very top and I think we have a way out that will work well for everybody, except Ryan, of course. We have already arranged for our internal security team to analyse Ryan's emails as part of an investigation into alleged drug dealing on his part. There had been rumours of Ryan being a Coke Head for some time, so we should probably have done it before anyway."

"This investigation gives legitimacy to finding the emails Sally discovered showing his plot to undermine Steve and place his brother-in-law in his job. The internal security team was furious when they found out what Sally had done and pressed hard to prosecute her. I pointed out that the publicity would severely damage our reputation and the CEO has agreed."

"If you agree, Sally, we would like you to resign and sign a non-disclosure agreement regarding what you did. In return, we will provide you with good references and 100,000 pounds as a tax-free lump sum."

Sally was flabbergasted. She had hoped to get away without going to jail. To not be prosecuted at all and be given a hundred grand in cash blew her mind and she was momentarily speechless. She pulled herself together and timidly responded, "Yes, that seems fair."

"Fantastic," said Bruce and took out the non-disclosure agreement for Sally to sign. She glanced over it and signed straight away. "All we need now is a cover story on why you are resigning," said Bruce after she handed him the signed papers.

"That's easy," said Sally. "I am going to Australia with my boyfriend next week. I will say I resigned because you would not give me the time off."

"That works for me," said Bruce.

"And me," said Steve and then added, "when were you planning to ask for this time off, anyway?"

"I only found out about the trip on Friday and we need to leave on Wednesday, so probably Monday," responded Sally.

"You would have needed to resign if you wanted to go anyway then. I could not let you leave at such an important time for the project," replied Steve.

"Never mind all that now," said Bruce. "Things have all worked out well, so let's move on. I am playing golf in 20 minutes, so I need to leave. I will speak to you on Monday, Steve. Sally, have a great trip."

Bruce opened the gates using a remote attached to his key ring and Sally and Steve left. Outside, Steve said, "I am getting an Uber if you want a lift."

"I am fine," said Sally as she pointed to her bike that she had left leaning against the wall by the gates.

"Guess this goodbye then," said Steve. "Just want to say thanks again for sticking your neck out and exposing what Ryan planned. Enjoy your trip to Australia and if you need help getting a new gig when you come back, then let me know. I have some good contacts who I am sure would be able to help."

"Thanks, Steve. I would not have stuck my neck out if I did not admire you as much as I do. You were a great manager during the short time we worked together," replied Sally. She got on her bike and headed back to the city centre.

She headed down to the seafront to get back to her flat along the promenade cycle lane. Once back home, she started to organise her packing for the trip to

54

Sydney. She put on a load of washing as she discovered most of her better clothes were in the dirty linen basket. While the washing machine did its stuff, she sat down and had a coffee and checked her email.

There was a copy of her travel details from the travel agents Tim's company used. They would be flying business class on QANTAS from Heathrow, departing at 8.00 PM on Wednesday and arriving in Sydney at 6.00 AM on Thursday. There was a refuelling stop in Singapore. They were booked into an Opera House view king bedroom at the Sydney Harbour Marriott Hotel. A limousine service would pick them up from Tim's flat at 3.00 PM on Wednesday.

Sally was getting really excited about the trip. Her phone pinged. It was a message from Zoe to say they should be at her place by 3.00 PM for the BBQ. After making good progress with the packing, Sally phoned Tim and told him she would be around at his place about 2.30 to go to the BBQ together.

When she arrived at Tim's place, he was already outside having a cigarette. They headed to Zoe's flat via an off licence to pick up some beers and wine. Zoe's apartment was on the ground floor of an old converted regency mansion. She had an outdoor courtyard that was accessed via a gate at the back of the property. Sally led the way and when she entered the yard, she found Andy getting the BBQ going.

"I am really looking forward to a genuine Australian BBQ. I hear you live on them out there," said Sally.

"Pretty much true. Apart from the pies and beer," joked Andy.

"Can I crack open a tinny for you, mate?" said Tim in a terrible attempt at an Australian accent.

"That would be absolutely spiffing, old boy," replied Andy in an equally lousy attempt at an upper-class English accent.

Zoe came and joined them with the platter of meat for Andy to BBQ.

"I hear you are off to Sydney next week," said Andy, as he started on grilling the meat.

"Yep, arrive 6.00 AM on Thursday," replied Tim. "Staying in the Marriott at Circular Quay. My company has offices in Martin Place, which I think is pretty close."

"Yes, just a 5-minute walk up Pitt Street," replied Andy. "Make sure you catch a ferry from Circular Quay across to Manly while you are there. I am from Manly and even though I am biased, it is the best beach suburb in Sydney, miles better than Bondi."

"I will make sure we do," replied Tim. "Have you any other tips of what and where to go?"

Andy gave Tim a long list of his favourite places, bars, clubs and restaurants, which Tim added as notes on his phone.

Once the meat was cooked, they all sat down around a small table and tucked in. "These lamb chops are sensational," exclaimed Sally.

"You should try the steak, out of this world," added Tim.

"Looks like your BBQ skills are as good as you claimed," pronounced Zoe.

"Secret is in the marinades and resting of the meat," added Andy.

It did not take long for them to all finish off the BBQ food. Zoe then produced a surprise for Andy. She had made him his favourite dessert, a Pavlova.

"Hope it tastes right. I have never tried one but got the recipe off the Internet."

"Looks good," said Andy as he got stuck in. "And tastes even better. Thanks, Zoe, that is so sweet—no pun intended."

They all laughed and then Zoe said, "You were lucky to get the two weeks off work at such short notice," to Sally.

"They would not give me the time off, so I resigned," replied Sally to gasps from her friends.

"Honestly, it is no big deal. I was thinking of resigning, anyway. I have been there too long and was getting stale," added Sally.

Tim put his arms around Sally and kissed her on the cheek. He then whispered in her ear, "I love you."

Sally went bright red and was speechless. She did not see that coming. When she had gathered herself, she whispered 'Me too' in Tim's ear.

"What are you two love-birds whispering about?" said Zoe.

"Nothing, all good," said Sally.

They all stayed outside in the courtyard, talking and drinking until the sun started setting and suddenly it became a little too cold. Tim had to go up to London early the next day, so he and Sally left and went back to his flat.

Chapter 12

Sally was woken up by the sound of Tim having a shower. She did not need to go to work, so she stayed curled up in bed. When Tim returned, he said, "Sorry but running a bit late, so need to rush. You stay there as long as you like. I have left a spare key on the kitchen table. Help yourself to whatever you want and see you tonight."

He kissed her quickly and then left the bedroom. Five minutes later, Sally heard the front door slam closed. She dozed for another 30 minutes, then got up and had a shower herself. She found some coffee pods in the kitchen and made herself an expresso.

She sipped the coffee and, feeling energised from the caffeine, decided to walk back home via the seafront to get some fresh air and exercise.

When she arrived at her flat, she finished packing and created a list of things she needed to buy. With her list complete, she headed out and up to the Churchill Square shopping mall. She purchased some new underwear so she could avoid exposing Tim to some of her worst bottom of the drawer back up knickers. She also bought a few medicines and some makeup.

Finally, she went to the bank to get some Australian money. She always felt more comfortable with some cash in her wallet as a backup to her credit cards. The bank had a multi-currency ATM that gave US and Australian Dollars as well as Euros. When she went to get her money out, she was delighted to see her balance was over one hundred and twenty thousand pounds. Her payoff was already in her account. She withdrew two hundred Australian dollars.

Back at her flat, she made herself a salad sandwich for lunch and sat down at her kitchen table with her laptop. She had decided to check up on her hacker, so she went to his Facebook page to see the state of the abuse he was getting. To her surprise, she found that his Facebook page had been deleted. She looked up all his social media accounts from his passwords document and found they had all gone.

She checked his email account and that was gone as well. She went to the cloud area that Simon's program stored the info it extracted from his computer and found that no new information had been added since Friday. His online presence had disappeared entirely. Sally went to her own Facebook page, but she could not log in with her original password. She had noticed from her hacker's password list that he used the same password for lots of his accounts, so she tried that.

It did not work either, so she went to the Facebook account recovery page and filled in the form. She spent the rest of the afternoon lying on her sofa watching TV. A guilty pleasure she had not enjoyed on a workday for many years. At 6.30 PM, Tim phoned to say he was on the train with a work friend and they would be going to The Lord Nelson for a beer and burger if she would like to join them. The Lord Nelson was an old traditional pub near the station and one of Sally's favourites so she accepted and said she would meet them there at about 7.00 PM.

Sally booked an Uber and arrived at the pub a little early and before Tim. She ordered a pint of her favourite local beer and sat down at a table. Tim and his friend arrived about 5 minutes later. Sally was expecting one of Tim's rugby playing and beer drinking friends, but instead, he was accompanied by a tall, slender woman with long blond hair.

"Hi Sally, this is Tina from work."

"Hi, Tina, nice to meet you," replied Sally.

Tina sat down and Tim went to the bar to get them both a drink.

"Have you worked together long?" asked Sally, making small talk.

"About five years, but we have only really become friends since my husband and I moved to Brighton and I have bumped into Tim on the train," replied Tina.

"Is your husband joining us as well?" asked Sally.

"Unfortunately, not. He is an actor and is away in Devon filming a movie at the moment."

"Sounds exciting," responded Sally, eager to learn more.

"Not that exciting. He is little more than an extra. I think he has two lines in this one, so better than usual."

Tim returned with two more pints and handed one to Tina.

"I love Harvey's Bitter," said Tina as she downed half the drink in one.

"What do you do at the bank?" asked Sally.

"I am a Dark Web Surveillance Office," replied Tina. "I look on the Dark Web for early signs of data breaches or other information that may impact a company's share price and tell the likes of Tim, who uses the information in their trading."

Sally knew that the Dark Web was a kind of parallel Internet where everything was anonymous and used to trade all sorts of illicit goods, including usernames and passwords. She meant to find out more, as it had always intrigued her but had not got round to it.

"Wow, sounds fascinating," said Sally.

"Can be, but mostly depressing," replied Tina. "I get to see the very worst in humanity on there. People are offering children for sexual abuse, murder on demand, all the worst drugs and pornography. You name it and you can buy it with enough bitcoins. Legality does not come into it."

"Tina is having her 30th birthday party at The Ivy in the Lanes in 3 weeks and has invited us both along," said Tim, changing the subject.

"Wonderful," said Sally. "I have been dying to go there. Thank you so much."

"You are welcome," replied Tina, who then knocked back the rest of her pint, got up and asked, "same again all round?"

They both nodded and Tina went to the bar. They had three more pints and a burger each before they all decided they had a better head home.

Chapter 13

The next day, Sally left Tim's place shortly after he had left for work and headed into the city centre. She was fascinated by what Tina had said about the Dark Web and wanted to see for herself. She knew that it would be too dangerous to use her own laptop to connect as the Dark Web was saturated with sites that would load viruses that, like the one she had used, could steal information from your files. Better to use a new clean machine with no personal data on it.

She found a good cheap laptop in a pawn shop in the North Laines and took it back to her flat. She wiped all the data from the machine's disk and memory, including the original windows operating system. She installed a copy of the Linux operating system on the laptop, as this was less prone to virus attacks than Windows. She then set up a VPN to connect to the Internet without revealing her real location and IP address. Finally, she installed a special Internet Browser called TOR that allowed access to sites on the Dark Web. Regular browsers were unable to access the Dark Web. She was all ready to go.

Sally spent the next 2 hours exploring the Dark Web and found plenty of the vile and repulsive goods and services that Tina had mentioned were advertised as being available. From what she had read about the Dark Web, Sally knew that although there were genuine websites selling drugs, guns and other illicit goods, there were many more scam websites.

The sellers on the Dark Web were totally anonymous. They had to be or the police would arrest them for selling illegal goods. When purchasing goods, you had to use bitcoins to pay, which again protected the seller's identity as there is no way to trace who gets your money. The many fake sites simply offered goods and services that they never intended to provide. They take the bitcoins from the buyer and give nothing in return.

The corner of the Dark Web she was particularly interested in was one that sold personal information. This could be a person's username and password, credit card details, driver's licence or passport number or even their medical records. She found that this information was available amazingly cheaply. She found a file of 200,000 user records stolen from a hotel booking site available for the Bitcoin equivalent of 10 pounds. She paid the bitcoins and was then able to download the file. She struck lucky; the site was not a scammer.

She opened the file in a text editor and found a set of email addresses that were used as the usernames on the hotel booking site, together with each user's password. The value of this data was not in using it to access the hotel booking website. Many people use the same passwords for multiple sites, so the value is to use the combination to access another site such as Facebook.

As a test, Sally tried a few combinations on Facebook. It only took three attempts before she had success and logged into a Simon Wilson's Facebook account. She resisted the temptation of posting something embarrassing.

Her phone buzzed and she picked it up to see a message from Tim. He was leaving work early and would be home by 3.00 PM. She replied that she would see him then. They had agreed that she would take all her stuff around to his flat that evening and then stay over until the car picked them up to take them to the airport. She put away her new laptop and started to get all her luggage together for the trip. At 2.30, she wheeled her suitcase out of her flat and went to Tim's flat.

Tim arrived back just after 3.00 PM as promised and Sally helped him with his packing. Once it was done, they headed out into the city and grabbed a few last-minute items for Tim to take with him. It was nearly 6.00 PM by the time they finished, so they decided to stay in the city and grabbed a quick drink, followed by some fish and chips. Tim said it would be their last chance for two weeks. After they arrived back at the flat, they watched a movie and had an early night.

Sally woke at 7.00 AM and got up immediately. She had decided to get up and get some fresh air and exercise before breakfast. Unfortunately, she had no luck persuading Tim to join her, so she headed out on her own. She went for a brisk walk along the seafront to Brighton Marina and, on the way home, picked up some freshly baked croissants and coffees for her and Tim's breakfast. When she got inside the flat, she found Tim still in bed, but the smell of the coffee and croissants was enough motivation for him to get up and join her in the kitchen.

"These are so good!" exclaimed Tim as he ate the first mouthful of his croissant.

"What is the plan for today?" asked Sally.

"After I have finished my coffee, I am going to shag you senseless," replied Tim.

"Assuming you will take 8 minutes to drink the coffee, then that is only the next 10 minutes taken care of," teased Sally.

"Very funny," replied Tim and then added, "seriously though, I do fancy a bit of rumpy-pumpy and then we should shower and start planning the itinerary for our trip. I have to work a fair bit, so we need to make the most of the time we have together, as well as find things for you to do."

"Rumpy-pumpy sounds good," replied Sally. "Much prefer that to being shagged senseless."

Sally got up and performed a sexy striptease in front of Tim and then headed naked very slowly towards the bedroom. Tim quickly drowned the last of his coffee and followed her in.

At about 10.00 AM, they both sat down to plan their trip. "At the BBQ, Andy gave me a list of things he recommended and I put them as Notes in my phone," said Tim as he looked at his phone screen. "He also said we should get in contact with his sister when we are there. She could be company to you when I am at work."

"Yes, Zoe mentioned that as well. She said she had only met his sister on FaceTime but seemed really nice."

They worked out the plan of what to see together and what Sally would have to see on her own or with Andy's sister. They then used up the last of the food in Tim's flat for lunch and cleaned up the flat, so they were ready to leave. Right on time, the doorbell rang and their airport chauffeur car was outside at 3.00 PM. They climbed into the Mercedes saloon and settled down on the leather seating for the trip to Heathrow.

The trip was speedy, with surprisingly little traffic to delay them. By 5.00 PM, they had checked in and were heading for the business class lounge. The lounge had two levels, with the lower one being a restaurant and the upper a bar and large open space with different seating to suit what the passenger wanted. They grabbed a cocktail each from the bar and found a couple of large comfy chairs to sit down and relax in. They later had a meal down in the restaurant and before they knew it, their flight was boarding.

The flight itself was uneventful and they landed in Sydney just 5min late. After clearing immigration and customs, they emerged into the arrivals hall. They had a chauffeur-driven car to take them to their hotel and a dark-suited driver was waiting with a sign showing Tim's name. They made themselves known to the driver and followed him to another Mercedes saloon that took them to the hotel.

Chapter 14

It was a bright sunny day in Sydney and the view over the harbour framed by the Sydney Harbour Bridge and Sydney Opera House from their hotel room window took Sally's breath away. "My God, what a view," she exclaimed as she entered the room.

"That is what you call a million-dollar view," added Tim in agreement.

They quickly unpacked and had a shower to freshen up. They were both keen to start exploring the city, so they headed out of the hotel.

The hotel was just a few metres from Circular Quay, which is the central hub for the ferries used by the locals as their preferred way to travel around their harbour city. They walked along the collection of wharves towards the Opera House. Sally noticed that a large ferry sitting at one of the Wharves had Manly displayed on the departure board.

"That must be the ferry I will need to get when I go and meet Andy's sister. She lives in Manly."

Once they had passed the ferry terminal, they strolled hand in hand along the water's edge towards the Opera House. It was only a 10-minute stroll before they were right outside the unique and beautiful building. They both stood and stared in silence at the remarkable façade.

"I cannot believe I am actually here. I have seen the building so many times on TV and have always dreamed of visiting it," said Sally.

"Same here and it is even more beautiful in real life," added Tim. "Let's go to the box office and try and get tickets for something while we are here."

"Great Idea. We cannot miss the chance to go inside and see something."

There was a small queue at the box office and while they waited, they read the programme of events for the next two weeks. The opera house had two main auditoriums. A Concert Hall for music and a theatre for opera and ballet. There were also three smaller venues.

In the program of events, they found that the opera Madame Butterfly was playing in the theatre. There were several different concerts, but the one that caught their eye was the Last Night of the Proms, with the Sydney Symphony Orchestra. When they reached the ticket window, they were disappointed to find the opera was sold out but delighted that a few tickets were available for the concert. So they purchased two tickets for the next Tuesday.

They walked out of the Opera House and into the Royal Botanical Gardens that were just next door. Even though it was winter in Sydney, the temperature was still 21 degrees and it felt much hotter in the bright sunshine. They explored the gardens for a while, then laid down on one of the large areas of lush grass to enjoy the sun and rest. After about 20 minutes relaxing, Tim said, "Fancy grabbing some lunch."

"You read my mind," responded Sally.

"I am sure Andy recommended somewhere near here," replied Tim, looking at his phone. "Here it is, Botanic House."

They got up and went in search of the restaurant. It was not complex as within a few minutes. Sally noticed a signpost with Botanic House directing them. They were given a lovely window table overlooking the lush gardens. The restaurant had a tasting menu, so they went for that. The food was Asian with Thai and Japanese influences and tasted divine.

"Wow, if that is the standard of food in Sydney, then this trip is going to be a real culinary treat," said Sally.

After lunch, they walked back to their hotel. The jet lag was starting to kick in and they both felt tired and lightheaded, so they grabbed a couple of hours' sleep. They were awoken by Tim's phone. His new boss welcomed him to Sydney and invited them both to join him for lunch at his house on Sunday. Tim was obliged to accept, so he did and his boss gave him the address.

They decided to spend the evening at the hotel and try and get their body clocks aligned with their new time zone by staying up until 11.00 PM and setting the alarm for 7.00 AM the next day. They managed to stay up until 11.00 PM and went to sleep quickly but were both wide awake by 5.00 AM. It was still dark outside, so they stayed in their room and ordered some breakfast.

"How about we contact Andy's sister and if she is free, then go over to see her on the ferry," suggested Sally.

Tim agreed, so Sally sent her a message from her phone. Almost immediately, the phone pinged back with her reply. "Just off for a surf but be free from 9.00 AM, so message me when you are on the ferry and I will meet you at Manly Wharf SYL Jules xx."

At about 8.00 AM, they left their room and went down to the concierge desk to check out the times of the ferries and how to get tickets. The concierge was accommodating.

"There are two ferry services to Manly. The slower government-run ferry goes from Wharf three every 30 minutes. The next one will be at 8.30 and takes about half an hour to get to Manly. There is a faster private service that runs every 10 minutes from Wharf two and only takes 18 minutes. I would recommend the government ferry for better views if you are not in a hurry—no need for tickets. You can pay on either by just tapping your credit card at the gate. It costs 8 dollars each way."

They thanked the concierge and headed out to catch the 8.30 ferry.

They reached the Wharf just as the ferry arrived from Manly on the reverse run. They tapped their card and went through the barriers to wait on the Wharf. The Wharf itself was a floating pontoon and it bobbed around in the slight swell, making Sally feel slightly queasy. They watched as hundreds of commuters disembarked from the two decks of the ferry and headed off to work in the city.

Once the last of the passengers from Manly had disembarked, one of the ferry crew's hands opened the gates, blocking them from boarding the ship. They headed to the top deck and then to the front of the ship or rather the end of the vessel, facing towards Manly. The ferry design cleverly allowed it to travel in either direction, so it had two front ends, complete with wheelhouses. There was an outside seating area and they picked the best seats with a clear view of the harbour.

Sally sent a message to Jules to say there were on the 8.30 ferry and she replied that she would meet them at the Wharf at 9.00 AM. The half-hour journey across the harbour to Manly was magical and they even had a pod of dolphins swim alongside the ferry for part of the time as they crossed the entrance to the harbour called The Heads.

As they approached Manly, they could see sandy beaches on either side of the Wharf, with a few people sunbathing and swimming on each. The beaches underwhelmed Sally. They were small and the water looked flat. Andy had raved about how much better it was than Bondi. She had seen Bondi Beach on the TV and it beat this, hands down. She hoped he had not exaggerated everything else he had told her about his hometown.

As they walked down the ramp to disembark, they could see a pretty brunette girl waving at them. They headed towards her and she introduced herself. "Hi, I am Julie Blake. Call me Jules. You must be Sally and Tim."

"Yes, lovely to meet you and thanks so much for offering to show us around."

"No problem. Follow me and I will show you the beach first."

"I have seen them from the ferry and, to be honest, they are not as great as Andy described."

Jules laughed out loud and explained, "These scraps of sand are not Manly Beach, but just the edge of the harbour. Follow me this way."

They crossed a main road opposite the Wharf and then headed down a wide pedestrianised street called the Corso, that was full of cool shops and pubs. At the end of the Corso, they reached the real Manly Beach. It was a gloriously long and wide white sandy beach with the aquamarine Pacific Ocean glinting in the winter sunshine. There were great waves that morning and the beach had plenty of surfers gliding in and on the waves.

"Wow, that is more like it," said Sally.

"Manly is on an Isthmus!" proclaimed Tim.

Sally looked puzzled. "You know, a strip of land with the sea on either side. That is why there are beaches at each end of the Corso," explained Tim.

They walked down to the sea and paddled in the water as they strolled up the beach towards the Manly Life Saving Club at the south end. "This area is called the South Steyne, named after the area near the beach in Brighton, UK, where you come from," said Jules.

They left the beach via the boat ramp and joined a winding footpath along the shore. The path took them to a beautiful sandy cove. "This is called Cabbage Tree Bay; it is a marine park and the snorkelling here is phenomenal."

Next to the sandy beach was a café called The Boathouse. Jules suggested they grab a coffee and they eagerly agreed. They found a table by the window and sat down. A waitress soon came and took their order. On the vacant seat next to where Sally was sitting, she noticed somebody had left a copy of the Sydney Morning Herald newspaper. She was intrigued by one of the headlines on the front page and picked it up. When she read the story, she was flabbergasted.

"My God. I don't believe it," she exclaimed.

"What's wrong?" enquired Tim.

"There is a story here about a local guy who has been arrested as an Internet scammer. It is the guy I outed on Facebook. Here is his name, Spencer Howard."

"What! You did that to Spencer?" shouted Jules.

"You know him?" asked Sally.

"Kind of. He went to school with my younger brother. Everybody feels very sorry for him. He was a nice guy but an idiot. He lost his job and, in desperation, responded to one of those ads that promise you can make $10,0000 a month working from home that he saw on a surfing website. He stupidly followed the instructions they gave him. Not sure he really understood he was doing something bad."

"Apparently, he hardly got paid anything. The organisers took the money in bitcoins and gave him a pittance. He was about to give up and stop doing it when the federal police raided his home, took his computer and arrested him."

"Even if he was an idiot, he still committed the crimes so deserved to be brought to justice," said Tim, to defend Sally.

"Sure and I am not defending him or saying Sally was wrong to expose him, but the real villains here were the people recruiting people like Spenser and getting them to do their dirty work."

"I agree," said Sally and added, "Do you know the website he saw the advert on?"

"Sure, we all use it," said Jules. "It is called Surf Sydney."

"Thanks, I will look into it and see if I can help bring the real crooks to justice as well," said Sally.

They left the café and continued their tour of Manly with Jules. The next part was a hike into Sydney Harbour National Park that took them to the top of one of the headlands that formed the harbour entrance they had crossed on the ferry earlier. From North Head, they could see the whole harbour and city laid out in front of them.

"What a magnificent city this is," said Sally.

They found a lovely Italian cafe nearby, where they continued to enjoy the views over lunch. After lunch, they followed bush trails that gave other views of the whole strip of beaches that go north up the coast from Manly.

"How many beaches are there in Sydney?" asked Tim.

"Including the harbour beaches, there are 156," replied Jules and then added, "But none with pebbles, I am afraid." She explained how Andy had told her about Brighton Beach.

The bush path eventually took them back to Shelly Beach and Cabbage Tree Bay and they walked back from there to the main beach. They had a quick drink in the New Brighton pub on the Corso before they thanked Jules for the tour and headed back to their hotel on the ferry.

Chapter 15

They were again wide awake very early on Sunday morning and ordered breakfast in their room, as it was still dark outside. Once dawn had broken, they headed out and got some fresh air. This time, they walked away from the harbour into the Central Business District. Tim wanted to find out where his offices were for the next day so he would not get lost and be late.

The offices were really easy to find in a pedestrianised plaza just a 5-minute walk up the street from the hotel. They carried on exploring and found themselves in the tourist area of Darling Harbour. They found a free seat in the sun near a children's playground and sat down and soaked up some rays. Time was getting on and they were expected at Tim's boss' house, so they headed back to the hotel and got changed.

Tim's boss was called Wilson and he lived with his wife and one small child in a suburb just north of the city called Roseville. They had decided to get the train as he said his house was only 5 minutes from the station. The trains did not run directly from Circular Quay, so they had to make one change, but nevertheless, the journey was straightforward and quick. Sally loved the fact that the Sydney Trains were double-deckers. She had never really considered the concept before.

Roseville station was a small suburban commuter station and was deserted on a Sunday lunchtime. They walked the short distance to Wilson's house and rang the doorbell. A tall leggy blonde woman answered the door and introduced herself.

"Hi, I am Izzy and you must be Tim and Sally," a small child appeared and hid shyly behind its mother's leg. "And this little rascal is Popsie," she added. They said their hellos and followed Izzy into the house towards a deck at the back where Wilson was already working on getting the BBQ fired up.

"Hi, Boss," said Tim.

Wilson turned around and said, "Tim! Great to meet you face to face at last and this beautiful creature must be your wife?"

"Just his girlfriend," added Sally and introduced herself.

They made polite small talk for a short while, but it was not long before Wilson and Tim were talking about their work. "Come and help me in the kitchen and let's leave the boys to talk shop," suggested Izzy.

Sally eagerly agreed and followed Izzy inside.

"How long have you and Wilson been together?" asked Sally.

"Only two years, I fell pregnant within just a few months of us starting to date. We got married as soon as Izzy was born. What about you and Tim?"

Sally blushed and admitted they only met the previous week.

"Wow, fast work girl, already got him to bring you to the other side of the world. How did you meet?"

"Sounds embarrassing now, but it was at a speed dating event. I only went to keep a friend company but met Tim and we really clicked."

"Do you have a job, Sally?"

"I did have one as a web developer but had to resign to get the time off to come over here."

"You must have been keen to come then."

Sally avoided going into the exact circumstances and replied, "Was a bit fed up with the job anyway and this sounded such a great opportunity. Do you have a job or are you a full-time mum?"

"I had to go part-time after Popsie was born, but I am a business analyst at the bank where Wilson and Tim work."

"So that is how you met."

"Yes, he pulled me into the foyer coffee shop with promises of unlimited flat whites," joked Izzy.

Sally helped Izzy prepare some salads and when they returned to the boys on the deck, Wilson had finished cooking the meat. They all sat down and enjoyed their lunch. Wilson produced some delicious Australian Chardonnay that he had purchased from a vineyard in the Hunter Valley just north of Sydney.

"You must go up to the Hunter and do a tour of some of the vineyard cellar doors while you are out here," suggested Wilson.

"I would love to if you give me some time off," replied Tim.

"Might have to wait until you move out permanently," replied Wilson, only half-joking.

They managed to finish off three bottles of the wine before they left. Once back at the hotel, the effect of the wine and the early start meant they were exhausted and went to bed by 7.00 PM, skipping dinner.

Chapter 16

They both woke as dawn was breaking and the sunlight lit up the room. In their exhausted state the night before, they had not closed the curtains. Tim showered first. Then, while he was dressing for work, Sally had a quick shower herself. They then went down to the hotel restaurant to graze on the breakfast buffet. After breakfast, Tim left directly for his office and promised to phone Sally at lunchtime and arrange to catch up.

Sally returned to their room and had a long lingering shower to refresh herself. She made herself a coffee using the in-room machine and got out her laptop. She wanted to try and find the advert that Spenser had responded to and got him involved in the scamming. She went to the Sydney Surf website and looked at the adverts that it was showing her. She was not interested in the actual adverts, but the ad delivery platform used to decide which adverts would be presented.

The platforms gathered information about people when they used websites or mobile apps and used the data to create a profile of each user and match them with advertisers. The biggest ad delivery platforms are Google and Facebook, but the one on the surfing website was an independent one and got its data from elsewhere. The data on Sally was currently not much more than her location as it just had some generic Sydney specific ads. She turned on her VPN connection and picked a server in New York to spoof browsing from there. The adverts all changed to local New York businesses.

It was time for Sally to start building a profile on the ad server that would hopefully match the profiles the company, that suckered in Spenser, was targeting. She began by looking at some men's health and men's clothing sites to establish her sex. She browsed some appropriate fashion sites that would appeal to twenty-something.

She next started searching for personal loans and credit cards with low credit rating requirements. Finally, she went back to the Sydney Surf site to check the ads. They were less generic and were aimed at young men with money issues, but most were for sites offering buy now pay later on men's fashion.

She tried various other websites to try and enrich her profile but with no luck. The ad was no longer being served or she could not get her profile to match what they wanted. She was about to give up when the answer suddenly came to her in a flash of inspiration.

She dug out the USB stick she had with the data from Spenser's computer. She copied the ad server cookie from Spenser's browser cache data to her browser and tried the surf site again. Bingo, there it was, "Earn $10,000 per month using the internet from home."

She clicked on the link and was taken to an online form to complete. The form required an email address, phone number and a Facebook ID.

She left the hotel and went in search of a supermarket. She found one about four blocks away and went in and purchased an Australian SIM card and a cheap Android smartphone. While she was out, she found a sushi bar and picked up some kingfish sashimi and a salmon sushi roll for her lunch.

Back in the hotel room, she put her lunch in the mini bar fridge, then got out her laptop and retrieved the list of hacked account names and passwords she had purchased. She wanted to find a Facebook profile she could hijack to use on the online form. She wanted one that was based in Australia and also was a female about her age. She thought it might be a tough ask, but one of the first email addresses she found was for a kylie.watson888@ozziemail.com.au and when she tried the account on Facebook with the matching password, she was in.

"Yessss!" she shouted in celebration. Seconds later, there was a knock at the door. She opened the door expecting it was somebody telling her to keep quiet, but the maid came to clean the room. She let the maid do her work and took her laptop and headed down to the lobby.

She found a table and ordered a coffee and muffin from the waitress. She opened Kylie Watson's Facebook profile and looked at her profile and posting history. Kylie was 22 years old, was a sales assistant in a department store and lived in Melbourne. Her profile picture was not of her but a picture of a cat. She had no photos of herself in her photos, just a few landscape pictures and more of her cat.

She had not posted for over six months and so was obviously not an active user. The profile was just about perfect. Sally changed the password and hijacked the account. Next, she set up a new Gmail email account in the name of Kylie.

She took out the new phone and set that up with the PAYG SIM she had purchased. Finally, she went back to the online form for the get rich quick offer and completed it. She finished her coffee and muffin and went back to the room.

She saw that the bed had been made as she entered the room, so she assumed the maid had finished. She checked the bathroom and found that it was refreshed with new towels. Her phone pinged and it was a message from Tim. "All going very well. Joining a new team for lunch. Will message you later and perhaps we can meet for a drink and then dinner at 5.00 PM?"

Sally replied straight away, "Sounds good. See you later."

It was too early for lunch, so Sally left the hotel to get some exercise. She walked back to the Botanical Gardens, but this time carried on past where they turned off to the restaurant on Saturday and ended up at a small headland and a sandstone carving called Mrs Macquarie's Chair.

She read the nearby tourist plaque 'The chair was carved out of a sandstone rock ledge by convicts in 1810. Specially commissioned by Governor Macquarie for his wife Elizabeth, who was known to love the area, this is one of the best vantage points to view the sights of Sydney Harbour'.

It was indeed a glorious view and she sat down to rest, enjoy the sunshine and harbour views. She then returned the way she came back to the hotel. In her room, she ate her lunch and then was still feeling some jet lag, so she had a short nap on the bed.

Her phone rang at about 4.30 PM and woke her up. It was Tim. She confirmed that she would meet him outside his offices at 5.10 PM. At 5.00 PM, she left and made the short walk up to Tim's Offices. She waited inside the lobby of the massive skyscraper that contained the offices of Tim's bank. She soon saw him get out of the lifts and come across to meet her with a kiss. "How did things go?" asked Sally.

"Brilliant," replied Tim. "Fantastic team and some interesting projects."

"Sounds like you have already decided to take the job," said Sally.

"Never thought about it like that, but if things still look as good at the end of next week, then I think I will."

They headed towards a sizeable busy bar that one of Tim's colleagues had recommended. It was already busy with groups of office workers enjoying an after-work drink. It had a very corporate vibe about the place and, to Tim's disappointment, a very limited selection of bland gassy beers. Neither of them particularly liked the place, so they had one drink and left. They headed towards the oldest part of Sydney, known as The Rocks.

Here they found a charming old sandstone pub that was much more to their taste and, much to Tim's delight, it sold a scarce thing in Australia; hand-pulled beer. The less gassy beer slipped down very easily and before long, both of them had managed to consume 3 pints. They decided they had better get some food. Tim noticed on the pub blackboard that Monday was Pie Night. They ordered two more pints and a steak pie with mash and mushy peas each.

"Andy said that Aussies love their pies and this one is so good," remarked Sally.

"I agree," said Tim as he finished his. "One more for the road."

"Yes, why not," replied Sally.

Tim went to the bar and returned with the drinks. "I forgot to tell you earlier, but I mentioned to Wilson that we were going to the Opera House for the concert tomorrow night and he said to make sure we booked the pre-concert dinner in the Bennelong Restaurant. Apparently, it is right inside the Opera House and is an experience in itself. It was fully booked, but Wilson managed to get our corporate entertainment team, who are big clients of the restaurant, to get us two tickets as a favour to him."

"Wow, that is fantastic and so kind of him."

They finished their drinks and then walked back to the hotel. The hotel bar was open and looked inviting, so they treated themselves to a brandy each as a nightcap and then headed up to their room. "Have you ever had sex upside down before?" said Tim in the lift.

"What do you mean?" replied Sally.

"You know, in Australia, we are upside down to people in the UK."

"You daft bugger!" said Sally. "And yes, we can have sex."

Chapter 17

Tim left for work at 7.30 AM the next morning, so Sally decided to treat herself to a lie in. She got up at 9.30 AM and went down for the breakfast buffet in the hotel restaurant. She resisted the cooked food and just had some fresh fruit and her favourite Bircher Muesli. The coffee they served in the hotel was not that great, so after eating, she walked down to Circular Quay and ordered a takeaway coffee from one of the specialist coffee shops she had noticed the day before. This coffee was sensational and she planned many return trips over the next week and a bit that she had left in Sydney.

When she returned to her room, she was pleased to find it had already been serviced. She sat down at the small desk and took out her laptop. In the Gmail account she had set up as Kylie, there was a reply to her application. Apparently, she had to undertake a video interview to check her suitability for the job. They wanted her to download a secure encrypted messenger app and send them a secure message to provide times when she would be available.

She now understood how Spenser had no trace of the contact with the group managing him on his PC. These types of messenger apps only store information in a secure encrypted cloud and then delete all the messages as soon as they are read. Before she responded, she needed to speak to her friend Simon in New Zealand again. She was only two hours ahead of his time zone so phoned him.

"Hi, Simon, Sally here. Thanks so much for that boobytrap program you found for me. Worked a treat."

"Hi, Sally, glad to hear. I was wondering how you got on. Have you developed insomnia? Must be the middle of the night in Brighton."

"I am actually in Sydney. I am over on holiday with my new boyfriend."

"Oh," said Simon in a deflated tone. "Guess I have missed my chance to sweep you off your feet, then."

"For the time being, at least," said Sally, trying to still keep some hope in Simon's mind so he would help her. She explained what had happened and how she needed to have something that would allow her to trap the person on the other end of the video interview.

"Look, I do not really have time to help you this time. I got the last program from a contact I have on the Dark Web. I will give you their details and you can go direct. I assume you can use the Dark Web?"

"Yes, of course," replied Sally. "Thanks for your help."

Simon said goodbye and hung up. A few seconds later, she got a message with a link to a website on the Dark Web. Sally regretted not bringing out the other laptop she had set up in Brighton for accessing the Dark Web. She would just have to create another one.

Sally found the nearest pawn store on Google Maps and headed there on the tram from Circular Quay. She found just what she needed for $300 and took it back to the hotel. It only took her an hour or so to strip the PC and set it up as a clean machine for use on the Dark Web. Her phone pinged with a message from Tim. "Be back about 5.30 to get changed and head to the restaurant. Get your glad rags ready."

She replied with a thumbs up and love emojis. Sally ordered some sandwiches and tea on room service and, while she waited for them, headed to the Dark Web site that Simon had given her. The site listed a mind-boggling array of illicit programs to commit a whole range of cybercrimes from identity theft, ransomware, spyware and things that allowed you to control specific features of other people's computers. There was a knock on the door and her lunch arrived.

She continued browsing the site and did some research on various cybercrime sites on the regular web. She knew that the criminals running the scam job were probably very sophisticated in their understanding and use of technology. It was not going to be easy to trick them into downloading a virus.

She was 99% certain they would use a VPN like she did to hide her location. She had found a program that hijacked the VPN server and used that to load viruses without the user knowing something was amiss. She expected the PCs they would use would be clean machines like her Dark Web machine and contain no data of use in themselves. She knew the device would have a webcam and microphone, so she planned to load a virus that would allow her to control those.

She was happy she had a plan and had found the tools to make it work. She paid for the illicit software using bitcoins and downloaded it. She replied to the job application email, saying she could do the interview anytime the following day.

Time was getting on, so she had a shower and got ready for the trip to the Opera House. She had just finished her makeup when Tim returned. He also showered and then changed into his favourite Hugo Boss sports jacket and chinos. They headed out and walked to the Opera House and the restaurant.

The Bennelong Restaurant was spectacular. It is situated inside the Opera House with massive windows giving a stunning panoramic view of the harbour. They were lucky to be seated next to the window, so they had the best uninterrupted views. It was now dark and the harbour and city somehow looked even more beautiful with the millions of lights that sparkled everywhere. The food managed to live up to the standards set by the views. Wilson had told Tim that the executive chef was one of the best in Australia.

After the meal, they made their way to the concert hall. Each seat had a small flag attached, either a Union Jack or the Australian Flag. There was also a short program with the music and the lyrics to some of the songs. The concert seemed to be divided into two halves. The first was a more conventional selection of classical pieces. The second was a rabble-rousing selection of the British prom favourites, such as Rule Britannia, with a couple of Aussie favourites, including Waltzing Matilda, thrown in.

They both loved the concert, particularly the finale, when they sang along with great gusto and waved their flags with everybody else as the streamers and confetti fell from the roof. They were both really buzzing as they left the Opera House and decided to go down to a large outside bar near the Opera House and right on the water's edge. While they were enjoying the drinks and chatting about what a great time they had, Sally's phone buzzed. The video interview was set for 10.00 AM the next day.

Chapter 18

The next day, they both went down for breakfast together at 8.00 AM and then Tim headed off to work. Sally returned to the room and got everything set up for the video interview. She put the do not disturb sign on the door and moved the desk in the room to a place where the video camera did not show anything that would give away the fact, she was in a hotel room.

She would take the video call on the secure machine she set up for the Dark Web. She did not want anything on her own laptop to give her away. To make things easy for herself, she had set up an automated script that would take control of the VPN server, infect the user's machine with the virus and then start streaming their video feeds to a secure cloud storage site she had established. All she needed to do in the call was get the other person's IP address and type it in. Once she was happy that everything was set up, she sat and relaxed on the sofa to clear her head.

Just before 10.00 AM, she returned to the desk and opened the secure messenger app on her machine. At precisely 10.00 AM, the app made a buzzing sound and a blue orb on the screen pulsated to indicate an incoming video call. Sally accepted the call and was then astonished to find she knew the caller. It was the goth whose picture she had captured with the original booby trap she had snared Spenser with.

Nevertheless, she remained composed and said, "Hi, I am Kylie."

The goth responded, "Nice to meet you, I am Sarah."

Sally doubted that was her real name and while they started the interview with a few standard questions, she set to work on her trap. She opened a Command-line window on her machine and typed in a command that gave her the IP addresses of other computers connected to hers.

Assuming the goth was using a VPN, then this would be the address of the VPN Server. She typed the IP address into her automated script and then executed it. She had a link to the cloud storage open on her main laptop and was delighted to see that a video file was streaming to it already. Her trap had worked.

She carried on with the interview for a few more minutes. The goth was asking her about how she felt about working all day on the Internet. Sally interrupted her and said, "Sorry, Sarah, but I have changed my mind and am no longer interested in the job. I don't think that I could sit in front of a PC all day. I want a more active job."

"Fair enough. Let's not waste any more of each other's time then," replied the goth and hung up.

Sally waited for an hour or so before checking back on her secure storage. There were now two more videos. She watched them and found they were simply a couple more interviews. She hoped something more exciting and revealing would emerge over the next few days.

Sally also had one more trick up her sleeve. The illicit software she had installed allowed her to remotely start up the camera and microphone on the goths PC without her knowing. She tried this now and saw a new video stream appear in the cloud storage. When she watched this, she saw that the goth was no longer in front of her PC, which gave her a view of where she was working.

The PC camera showed her a view across the room and out of a window on the far side. It was dark outside, so she must be in the northern hemisphere. She was about to turn the camera off when the goth came back into the room. She took out a phone and made a call. She was speaking in a language Sally did not even recognise, let alone understand. The goth finished the call and left the room again.

Sally turned off the camera and retrieved the video of the call from the cloud storage. She separated the section with the phone call and created an audio-only file of what was said. She sent the audio file to an online translation service she found that instantly translated and sent text file to her email of the conversation in English.

The translation tool had identified the language spoken as Romanian. The text of the translation was, "Tell him he must come to Ramnicu Valcea and we have a big party. Lots of money here and fun to be had."

Sally Googled Ramnicu Valcea and found *Three hours north of Romania's capital city of Bucharest, into the mountains and rural towns of the eastern European country, lies the city of Ramnicu Valcea. It looks like an idyllic mountain oasis, but around the world, it has a troubling nickname 'Hackerville'.*

Sally had never heard of the place, but the more she read about it, the more astonished she became. It was a prosperous place based solely on the proceeds of the hundreds of cybercriminals who all called it home.

Sally was pleased with her morning's work. She had successfully infiltrated the goth woman's privacy and was confident she would harvest more information over the next few days to nail the bitch. Sally decided to celebrate with another one of the fab coffees she had the day before and headed down to Circular Quay. The winter sunshine in Sydney made it seem like a summer day in Brighton, so she took her takeaway coffee and sat down on the lawns outside the Museum of Contemporary Art that was right next to Circular Quay.

After the coffee and sunshine fix, she decided to explore the museum itself and enjoyed a blissful two hours exploring the exhibits and grabbing lunch in the museum's café.

Back in her hotel room, she was just contemplating an afternoon siesta when to her surprise and horror, Tim came back to the room in a terrible state. He was sobbing his eyes out. He hugged Sally and blurted out, "I did nothing wrong, I did nothing wrong, but the bastards won't believe me."

Sally sat Tim down and tried to calm him down. He pulled himself together and Sally made him explain what had happened. "I was in the office and talking to one of the team and heard somebody on the other side of the office call my name. I turned around to see who it was but did not realise that Catherine Watson was standing right behind me. I ended up bumping into her chest. She shouted out, 'Stop fondling my breasts, you pervert', and ran off out of the office."

"Everybody saw it was an accident and laughed it off and we all got on with our work. About two hours later, the head of HR came down and asked me to go to his office. He said that Catherine had made a formal complaint of sexual harassment to them and considered talking to the police about charging me with sexual assault."

"I said it was a simple accident and not a premeditated sexual assault and I had a room full of witnesses who I am sure would back me up. He said they did not need witnesses as the whole incident was caught on security video. He then showed me a clip and what it showed was not my recollection of the incident at all. In the video, I was clearly rubbing her chest with my hands. I did not do that. I just bumped into her."

"What did Wilson say?" asked Sally.

"That is the worst bit. He was probably under orders from HR, but he said he no longer wanted me for the Sydney role and I should return to the UK immediately."

"This is all, so unfair," said Sally. "Surely, they must let you prove your innocence."

"The video evidence was pretty damming. Even some of the team who saw it live said they were no longer so sure I had just bumped into her."

"What does this Catherine woman do at the bank?" asked Sally.

"Same as me, really. In fact, she was the main other candidate for the job they offered me."

"Are you sure she has not set you up?"

"It did occur to me, but I have no proof and as I said, the video is damming. To make things worse, I have had my security pass cancelled, the team has been told not to speak to me. HR has cancelled our hotel room booking after tonight and booked us on the first flight home tomorrow."

Chapter 19

The airline limousine service from Heathrow Airport dropped Sally off at her flat first and then took Tim back to his place. Her first priority was to have a refreshing shower, as she felt grubby after the 22-hour flight. After the shower, she put her dirty clothes in the washing machine and popped down to the local convenience store for a few essential groceries. When she returned, she made herself a cup of tea and sat down to reflect on everything that had happened.

In some ways, she was pleased Tim had lost the chance of the job in Sydney. After the first two days, she became increasingly concerned that he would take the job and they would become estranged. She felt really sorry for Tim due to the way he had lost his chance. She was convinced there was something dishonest going on and Catherine had set him up. She started to hatch a plan to find out. She took out her phone and sent a message to Tim. "I love you so much and we will sort this mess out—Sally xxx."

She took out her laptop and searched for Catherine Watson's Facebook profile and soon found it. She was pleased to see that she was an active user and had not hidden her friends list. She extracted the list of friends and copied it to a USB stick. While she had her laptop open, she logged into the secure cloud storage where the goth's webcam videos were streamed to.

She found four more videos. Three were just interviews with prospective victims of her scam, but the other seemed like a personal call. She could not understand what was being said, so she again extracted the audio and sent it to her online translation software. After about 10 minutes, she got an email with the transcript in English. It was again somewhat garbled, but she saw the phrase, "Tell him Sofia Halep is keen to meet." Sally smiled to herself. Now she knew her name.

Sally spent the rest of the morning trying to find online references to Sofia Halep with no luck. She was obviously not as stupid as the majority of internet users who leave a rich trail of their personal details all over the web. She then remembered one of the services she had seen advertised on the Dark Web that claimed to be able to get hold of official records such as medical, police and banking details of individuals. She got out the laptop she had set up for use on the Dark Web and soon found the site again. She requested all records for Sofia Halep from.

Ramnicu Valcea age 20 to 35. She was required to pay 50% of the fee in advance, but the value of the bitcoins required was little more than 20 pounds. She gave the Gmail account she set up for Kylie as the reply address for the report. While she was on the Dark Web, she also purchased some more collections of stolen account names and passwords. The first one she bought turned out to be an empty file, but the other looked genuine.

She was now starting to feel tired and a bit lightheaded from the jet lag. She avoided the temptation to go to sleep, as she knew that would mess her body clock up for days. Instead, she decided to go out and get some fresh air. She sent a message to Zoe, "Back sooner than planned. R U free to catch up now."

She got an instant response. "What the hell happened! See you at the Meeting Place in 20 minutes."

Sally got to the Meeting Place café before Zoe, so they ordered their usual coffees and grabbed a seat in the sun. Zoe soon joined her. "What has happened? Did you and Tim fall out?"

"No, nothing like that. We were having a great time together." Sally went on to explain what happened with Catherine and Tim's boss, sending them straight back home.

"Does sound very suspicious, particularly if she was pissed at not getting the job. Surely Tim's boss would see that and at least give him the benefit of the doubt while they investigated things."

"I thought so as well, but apparently, the video from the security camera was damming."

"But you said Tim did not think it represented what he thought had happened."

"Yes, that is what he said straight afterwards, but he is still really upset and confused by the whole thing. I think he is just numb and no longer really understands what happened."

"Have you heard of Deepfakes?" asked Zoe.

"No, what are they?"

"It is when they used Artificial Intelligence technology to produce fake videos. Andy was telling me about it the other day. A friend of his works for a company that produces them."

"So, you think Catherine tampered with the video to make it look like Tim groped her when all he did was bump into her as he said?"

"I don't know, but just putting the theory out there."

"It is an interesting theory. Thanks, Zoe."

They finished the coffees, then took a stroll along the seafront before going their separate ways back to their flats. When Zoe arrived back, she called Tim. He had given in to his jet lag and gone to bed, but her call woke him up. They agreed she would go round and see him in about 15 minutes.

When Sally arrived at Tim's place, he had just finished a shower to freshen up. While he dried himself and got dressed, Sally made them both a cup of tea. When Tim joined her, she told him about Zoe's theory. "Could be something in it. I certainly know I did not do what it looks like I did in that video. There has also been another development and not for the better."

"What is that?" said Sally sounding worried.

"The head of HR in London told me not to plan to go into the office on Monday but has scheduled a video call with me at 10.00 AM tomorrow."

"That does not sound good," agreed Sally.

"I suspect that at best they will be suspending me or, at worst, sacking me. They might as well sack me. To be honest, once something like this is on your record, you are finished in the corporate world."

"All the more reason. We must clear your name and prove that you were set up."

"I agree, but the problem is how?"

"You must insist they provide you with a copy of the video. Hopefully, we can then show it is one of those deep fakes and clear your name."

Sally also told Tim about another plan. She had to find out a bit more about Ms Catherine Watson.

"Is that legal?" asked Tim.

"Not strictly, but there is no reason why anybody will find out."

Chapter 20

Sally returned to her flat after she and Tim had enjoyed a takeaway curry and some wine at his place. Before she went to bed, she started on the next part of her plan to uncover Catherine's deceit. She wrote a program that scanned the list of Catherine's Facebook friends against the stolen user ID and password lists she had purchased on the Dark Web to find matches. It was a pretty heavy task for her laptop to complete, so she planned to run it overnight.

The next morning, she was delighted to see that five of Catherine's friends had a user ID and password in her stolen credentials files. She could not wait to try and see if any of them used the stolen password on their Facebook accounts. Twenty minutes later, after trying them all, she was feeling deflated as none of them had. She was about to give up and try and think of a Plan B when a thought occurred to her about one of the passwords.

A friend called Clare Reeves had a password on the stolen accounts list of ClareR03. She knew that many people used the same password but, when prompted by a website to change it to a new one, just added an extra one to the number at the end. She decided to work back and logged into Clare's Facebook account using ClareR02 and it worked.

"Yippee," squealed Sally. She decided to work quickly and checked for previous Facebook Messages between them. There were quite a few but nothing very recent. Nevertheless, she gathered two things from them. Firstly, they had pet names for each other. Clare was Chops and Catherine was Pussy. The second was that Chops' birthday was coming up in 2 weeks. She sent a message to Catherine.

"Hi Pussy, I am having a party for my birthday and hope you can come. I have set up a website with all the details, including a pressie list (hint, hint). Please go there and RSVP. Love Chops xxx www.partyplannner.com/ClareR."

The link took the user to a website Sally had set up that contained another one of the naughty viruses she had purchased on the Dark Web. This one was like the one Simon had found for her before but was a much more recent version. In the fast-moving battle between hackers and antivirus developers, the potency of a virus usually is only valid for a few days before it is blocked on all machines that have current antivirus software installed.

Sally had promised Tim that she would go back to his flat to be there when he had his video meeting with the HR manager in London. She had a quick shower and headed over. She picked up some coffees and croissants on the way. She arrived by 9.30 and sat down to enjoy them with Tim at his kitchen table. "How did you sleep last night," asked Sally.

"Terrible," replied Tim. "With the jet lag and the worry over this Catherine thing, I hardly got a wink."

"You do look tired. After the call, I will give you a nice massage and see if that helps relax you."

"That would be great. Thanks, Sally," said Tim.

Just before 10.00 AM, Tim logged into his work laptop and set himself up to conduct the video meeting from his kitchen. Sally sat out of the shot but could see and hear everything. The HR manager called Tim at 10.00 AM on the dot. He was a big burly guy in a suit that was far too small for him and he was bulging out of it in a way that Sally was worried it might explode any moment. She could not help but giggle.

"What was that noise?" said the HR guy.

"Sorry, Angus, but just the cat wanting some food. I will just put her outside," said Tim and then got up to pretend he was doing so. He actually went over to Sally and whispered, "Naughty girl" into her ear.

When Tim returned to his chair, Angus said, "Look, Tim, there is no point in beating about the bush. Your behaviour in Sydney was reprehensible and will not be tolerated by this bank."

"Hang on," said Tim. "You speak as if I have admitted to what Catherine accused me of, but I still protest my innocence. The most I am guilty of is accidentally bumping into her."

"How can you possibly take that line when we have the whole thing on video?"

"I am glad you mentioned the video, as I want to challenge its legitimacy. I believe it has been fabricated using AI technology called Deepfake."

"What rubbish. The video was provided by our physical security team in the bank. I hope you are not concocting some kind of conspiracy theory that they are working with Catherine to frame you. I know Steve Wilson, the head of security in Sydney from when he worked in London and he is as straight as they come."

"If you are so sure it is genuine, then what is the harm in letting me have a copy to check it?"

"I am not wasting any more of the bank's time and money and your pathetic attempt to wriggle out of facing the consequences of your disgusting behaviour."

"Surely, I have the right to some kind of independent enquiry."

"You have no rights here. You are dismissed with immediate effect for gross misconduct. A formal letter is being sent by email within the hour. You should be grateful that my HR colleague in Sydney persuaded Catherine to not take your sexual assault to the local police."

"She would not take it to the police because then it would be properly investigated."

"I have heard enough of your nonsense. Goodbye, Tim."

With that, the video call was over.

Sally went and gave Tim a big hug. "The way that arsehole treated you was an absolute disgrace. You would be treated more fairly by the North Korean secret police."

"I agree. They will just not even listen to anything other than the narrative that Catherine gave them."

"Don't worry. They will not beat you on this. My plans to expose Catherine are already progressing. Just waiting for her to bite."

"Let's hope it is soon. I am not sure how much more of this I can take," said Tim.

"Let me give you that massage I promised," said Sally.

They both undressed and went into the bedroom, where Sally gave Tim the best massage he had ever had. "That must be one of your legendary ones," teased Tim afterwards. "The first one you gave me was a bit lame, to be honest. Now I know what you are capable of. I hope there will be more like today."

"If you play your cards right," replied Sally. She then got up and showered to remove the massage oil from all over her body.

Sally decided it was best if she stayed with Tim for the rest of the day. After lunch, she persuaded him to join her for a walk along the coast to a small village called Rottingdean to the east of Brighton. They got a bus back and dropped into the Lord Nelson for some beers and burgers for dinner. Tim asked her to stay the night and she readily agreed in the hope it would relax him and help him get some much-needed sleep.

Chapter 21

The following day, Sally left early to return to her flat. Tim got some sleep the night before but still had a restless night and decided to stay in bed. Sally was keen to check up on the traps she had laid to get Catherine and Sofia.

On checking her secure storage, she was delighted to find all sorts of files had been harvested from Catherine's PC, so she had obviously clicked on the party link that downloaded the virus. At least, half of the files were jpeg files. Sally scanned through the pictures and there was little of interest. There were also many PPT files that were slide packs for work presentations. These were of no interest to Sally. Sally hoped to find copies of Catherine's emails, but there was nothing. She was not using this PC for any email use.

There were also several spreadsheet files. Sally looked at these with low expectations but then found something intriguing. One of the spreadsheet files was password protected. Hoping the password was pretty simple, she used a password cracker to test the file against real words in a dictionary of common passwords. The program only took 5 minutes to crack it. The password was 'password'.

If the password had been a long set of random letters, then it may have taken weeks, months or forever to crack. *'People are so stupid,'* thought Sally. This thought was amplified ten times when she discovered the spreadsheet contained all Catherine's work and personal IDs and passwords. "You silly cow," said Sally out loud. Sally next called Tim and asked him, "Have you still got your work laptop?"

"No, they sent a courier to collect it yesterday. Why do you ask?"

"Does not matter. I hope to have some good news to share with you later. I will let you know when and come round and explain then."

"Sounds good," said a slightly confused Tim.

Without one of the bank's machines with the correct security certificates, Catherine's work credentials would be useless, so she concentrated on the personal accounts. The first one she opened up was her Google account. Nothing was interesting in the emails, but when she looked on the Google Drive storage, she saw a file uploaded three days ago called assault.mp4.

She immediately opened it and was delighted to see it was indeed a copy of the security video. She was shocked when she watched the part where Tim rubbed Catherine's breasts. It did look like he had sexually assaulted her. She put any doubts she momentarily had to the back of her mind and looked at Catherine's other accounts.

The spreadsheet was not entirely up to date as several passwords, including her Facebook account, did not work. She did get into Catherine's Twitter account and although it had not been used much; she was following a SteveWilson909. She checked his profile and it said he was a security specialist.

Sally sent a message to Zoe asking her to get Andy's friend's name and contact details who knew about Deepfakes. She then went to see if there was a reply to her query on Sofia in the fake Gmail account she set up in Clare's name. She was pleased to see a response and attached was a 20-page PDF containing Sofia's bank account statement, medical record, passport and driving licence.

Sally was stunned that getting such documents was so easy. She paid the remaining balance due in bitcoins to the hacker. She packed up her laptop and an overnight bag and headed round to Tim's flat.

Tim was in the kitchen fixing himself a brunch when Sally arrived. "Making myself a BLT. Do you fancy one as well?" asked Tim.

"Sounds great, yes, please," said Sally. She then sat down at Tim's kitchen table and got out her laptop. Tim finished making their sandwiches and bought them over. "Guess what I have got," said Sally as she turned her laptop to face Tim and then played the video.

"That's it!" exclaimed Tim. "Where did you get it from?"

"A naughty little virus sent it to me from Catherine's personal Google Drive. Interestingly, it was uploaded to the drive 30 minutes before you met with the HR guy in Sydney."

"Have you checked if it is one of those Deepfake things Zoe told you about?"

"Not yet, still waiting for the contact details of Andy's friend from Zoe. I also have some other interesting information. Catherine follows Steve Wilson, the Sydney security guy, on Twitter. He never Tweets, so why would she do that unless they had some kind of personal relationship?"

"The plot thickens," said Tim. "What do we do next?"

"We need to find more proof of a relationship between Catherine and Steve. That with the proof that the video is a fake should be enough to nail the bitch."

Tim was smiling for the first time in days. "Thank you so much, Sally. I don't know how I will ever be able to repay you if you get me out of this."

They finished their lunch and then Sally got a message from Zoe. "The friend of Andy is called Ursula. Her mobile is 0776343672. She is expecting your call."

Zoe immediately called her and she answered on the second ring, "Hi, Ursula here."

"Hi Ursula, I am Sally, a friend of Andy."

"Yes, he said you might call. It is about a Deepfake?"

"Yes, that is right. My boyfriend is being framed with a video we think has been altered using Deepfake technology and hoped there are ways that we could prove it is."

"Yes, that should be fairly simple. I'm in Sales rather than the technical side, but if you want to send me the file, then I will get one of our tech guys to have a look."

"That would be wonderful. My boyfriend is pretty stressed by this whole thing and we are super keen to get an answer ASAP so he can get some sleep again. Could we pop down now and bring the video and get your tech guy to have a look and tell us straightway?"

"OK, hang on a minute," said Ursula and they heard her shout out, "Steve, can you spare 30 minutes this afternoon to do me a favour?" They heard Steve say he could and Ursula returned to the call.

"Yes, we can do that. We are based in the Brighton Media Centre in Middle Street. Unit 12."

"Great, see you in about 30 minutes?" replied Sally.

Middle Street was in the central area of Brighton and a walking distance from Tim's flat, so Sally slipped her laptop into her rucksack and they headed off. Brighton Media Centre was in an old converted mew that must have once been used for the horses of the rich who lived in some of the nearby Regency mansions. They found Unit 12 and pressed the intercom on the door.

"Hi, Sally and Tim to See Ursula," the door buzzed and they went in.

A pretty woman with a pixie haircut welcomed them in and said, "Hi, I am Ursula. Nice to meet you."

Sally guessed she was about 22 years old. "Thanks so much for helping us out."

Ursula led them into a large open plan office and then into a small meeting room where a geeky-looking guy was sitting at the desk. "This is Steve, our Deepfake expert."

"What do you use Deepfake for?" asked Tim.

"Nothing nasty," replied Steve. "We just make funny fake videos of people as a unique gift idea."

"It is selling well," added Ursula. "If somebody likes say *Star Trek*, then we can get an episode and place them in it. It is so realistic; nobody would know it was not them."

"We also do a fair few Deepfake sex tapes," added Steve.

"We do not need to go there," said Ursula in a stern voice. "Where is this video you want us to look at?"

"It is a kind of sex tape," joked Sally and then explained the whole story.

Steve took a copy of the video, opened it up on his PC and ran a program to analyse the file. "How long have you worked here, Ursula?" asked Sally as small talk while Steve did his stuff.

"Nearly ten years," said Ursula, to Sally's surprise.

"You do not look old enough to have worked here that long."

"I am 36 years old, just lucky to look a lot younger."

"Wow, you are lucky. I would pay a fortune to look as good as you at 36."

"So you know Andy through his flatmate Zoe?" said Ursula.

Sally was taken back by Ursula calling Zoe a flatmate, but before she could probe further, Steve interrupted, "Definite fake. Come over and look at this."

They all gathered around Steve's screen.

"Look at the woman in the pink dress who is walking along the back of the office. She is moving at a constant pace, but she is frozen during the sequence that Tim gropes Catherine's breasts. She starts moving again as soon as the false groping finishes. Also, look at this close up of Tim's hands during the groping. They are not moving naturally at all but look what they are, just a loop of his hands moving up then down."

"Brilliant, thanks so much, Steve," said Tim. "You may have saved my life."

"No problem," replied Steve.

Ursula's phone then rang and after a brief conversation, she said, "Sorry, guys, but need to dash. Steve will show you out."

Sally and Tim returned to his flat. Tim's mood had improved enormously. "What do we do now?" asked Tim enthusiastically.

"We need to be careful as we did not legitimately obtain the video file. There is no point in getting your job back and then us being jailed for hacking."

"Have you a plan, then?"

"I think our best bet is to show that there has been a relationship between this Steve Wilson and Catherine. That would be enough for the bank to look more closely at the video or at least let us have a copy for analysis."

"Did you only find the Twitter Following link?"

"So far, but I am sure I can find more. Make me a coffee and I will start now."

Sally started by browsing Catherine's Facebook page to see if Steve was a friend. She was pleased to see he was. She scanned the public posts to see if there was anything that revealed the nature of their relationship. Unfortunately, there were very few public posts and most were very old. It was frustrating that she did not have Catherine's Facebook password. With more hope than expectation, she tried 'password', which was used for the spreadsheet but to no avail. She next logged in to Facebook as Clare Reeves to see what posts were shared with her friends.

This provided a much richer selection and one picture of Catherine had Steve Wilson tagged as well. Steve was a fair bit older than Sally had anticipated. '*He must be in his mid-fifties at least,*' thought Sally. Catherine was a beautiful twenty-something, so the romantic relationship she anticipated seemed unlikely.

She looked more closely at the picture. It was taken at a 50th birthday party for somebody called Anne Watson in 2018. She looked at Anne Watson's profile and amongst the numerous public posts were several more with her, Catherine and Steve. There were also many with Anne and Catherine as a schoolgirl and later a student, including the graduation picture of Catherine with Anne and Steve present and posing for the proud parents shot.

"She is Steve's daughter," exclaimed Sally.

"What!" said Tim in disbelief.

"Look at this graduation shot. That grey-haired bloke is Steve Wilson."

"Bugger me. He must be. Odd they have different surnames."

"Not necessarily her biological father. Maybe her mother kept her old name or never married."

Sally was still browsing Anne's Facebook profile and suddenly shouted out, "Yesss! That is great news."

"What now?" asked Tim.

"Julie Blake is a friend of Anne Wilson."

"Who is Julie Blake?" asked Tim.

"You know, Andy's sister Jules from Manly."

"Let's phone her and get the full story," said Tim.

"Bit late in Sydney right now, but I will send her message and see if she is still up."

Sally sends a message to Jules. "Hi Jules, need to catch up—we are back in Brighton—interesting story. Ping me when you are free and we can have a video call."

They decided to pass the time with a short trip to the pub at the end of the road. It was a lovely sunny afternoon and a cold pint in the beer garden was just what they both fancied.

The pub was deserted in the middle of a weekday afternoon, so they almost had the place to themselves. They took their beers and went out to the garden and found a table in the shade. The first beer never touched the sides. While Tim went inside to get them each another, Sally checked her messages. She was delighted to see a new email from her friend Lucy Cunningham from Los Angeles.

"Hi Sally, now coming back to Brighton for a visit on Friday. Sorry for the late notice but hope, the offer to sleep at your place is still good. Let me know and I will text you when I am on the train from the airport. Due to land at 2.00 PM."

Sally replied straight away. "Of course you can stay, really looking forward to catching up. Love Sally xxxx."

Tim returned with their drinks and after drinking the next one at a much more civilised pace, they headed back to Tim's flat. They picked up a pizza on the way and spent the rest of the evening watching movies.

Chapter 22

Sally was woken up by the sound of her phone buzzing on the bedside table. She picked it up and saw it was Jules calling. She answered the video call and sat up in bed. "Oh, sorry, I have woken you up," said Jules. "I should have waited until later but was desperate to find out what has happened."

"No problem, really keen to speak with you as well." Sally explained what had happened with Tim and how she was trying to prove Catherine and Steve faked the video. "So, how well do you know Anne Watson?"

"I used to work for her in her coffee shop. She is a lovely woman, but her daughter Catherine is a real hard-nosed bitch. So, it does not surprise me that she would try and do such a thing."

"What is the story about her relationship with Steve Wilson."

"Anne's husband and Catherine's biological father died when Catherine was just a baby. Steve was a friend of Anne who stepped in to comfort her after the loss and never left. Anne and Catherine always referred to him as Catherine's dad."

"Do you know where Steve works?"

"Not sure, but I think it is for a bank and he and Anne moved to London for a few years after Catherine finished school so he could take a job in the company's London office."

"He is definitely the guy who produced the video then," said Sally.

"But why would he commit a crime like that? Surely not to just help his stepdaughter get a promotion. I never met Steve, but when Anne talked about him, he sounded a lovely, kind and gentle man."

"You said Catherine was a hard-nosed bitch. What made you say that?"

"Whenever she came into the Café, she acted like lady muck. Ordering staff around and criticising everything. Anne also confided in me once that Catherine bullied her for money and threatened to disown her if she did not provide cash for her to spend on lavish luxury clothes and accessories."

"What a horrible thing to do. Do you think she used the same threat to get Steve to do her dirty work?"

"It is possible. I tell you what. I will pop into Anne's café tomorrow and gently see what I can find out. I cannot believe Anne would let a thing like this happen or let Catherine get away with it."

"That is brilliant, thanks so much and call me as soon as you know anything, no matter what the time."

"OK, will do. Speak tomorrow."

Tim had slept all through the call and was snoring away next to her in the bed. She poked him in the ribs and said, "Wake up, lazybones."

She let Tim come round slowly and went off to prepare some breakfast. Tim came out and joined her and she told him all about what Jules had said.

"We are getting closer to nailing the bitch. I cannot wait to make those vile HR wankers squirm when we do expose her."

"Now we know that Steve is her father, then we probably have enough to go back and appeal, but let's wait until we see what Jules can add from meeting with her mother."

Sally noticed a new message pop up on her phone from Ursula. "Sorry I had to rush off yesterday. I meant to give you the name of a Deepfake company I know in Sydney. They are called Ocean Media. If anybody made it, then it was probably them. I hope it helps."

Sally immediately went to the website for Ocean Media. They did indeed advertise the production of Deepfakes and they were based in the Sydney CBD not far from the bank. Sally went to the LinkedIn business networking site she used and searched for all the employees of Ocean Media.

There were only seven people and one of the names rang a bell. The name was Stefan Rosebottom and it amused her when she saw it before somewhere. She searched for the name on Facebook and there he was. She went to his friends list and it was not much of a surprise to see the name, Catherine Watson.

"We have got her hook line and sinker now," exclaimed Sally and told Tim about the new connection she had just found.

Tim wanted to go and visit one of his rugby mates who was having a birthday lunch in a local restaurant. Sally did not fancy a boozy lunch, so said she would leave him to it and he could ring her that evening if he were in a fit state to do anything. Sally returned to her flat and decided she would go for a run to the gym. She had too many days with little exercise over the last week.

After her gym session, Sally felt invigorated and decided to turn her attention back to Sofia Halep. She opened the PDF of the official documents she had purchased. The bank account was in the Romanian Currency, the Leu. She had 230,000 RON, which Sally checked on Google and found was worth about 40,000 pounds. This was hardly a fortune but still a healthy sum to have in a cheque account.

She suspected that Sofia's real worth was held as bitcoins. Sofia's medical records revealed nothing of much interest. She had an operation to alter the appearance of her nose about three years ago, but that was not an uncommon thing. Sally decided that the most useful thing about the documents was that they allowed her to commit identity fraud. She had enough documents to satisfy most of the identity checks set up behind online banks and other financial institutions.

She was familiar with the services of her old employer, so she went to the Anglo Credit website and applied for a credit card in Sofia's name. It would be a nice surprise for Sofia when it dopped through her letterbox. Having confirmed that the credentials all worked and Sofia had a good credit rating, she applied for 25 more cards and a few bank loans for good measure. This would cause Sofia plenty of grief in trying to unwind everything and probably messing up her credit history. It was, however, only a token gesture. Sally needs to find a better way to get back at Sofia.

Sally was feeling hungry so phoned Zoe and arranged to meet her at a local sushi train place. After lunch, Sally and Zoe went down to the beach to top up their tans and had a quick dip in the cold sea. After drying off in the warm sunshine, they found a table at one of the beach bars and ordered a jug of Pimms. The sun and alcohol made Sally feel sleepy, so she made her apologies to Zoe and headed back to her flat for a siesta after an hour.

Five hours later, Sally woke up to find most of the evening was gone. She checked her phone, but there was no message from Tim, so he was probably asleep in a drunken stupor as well. She called him and eventually, Tim answered. He sounded terrible.

"How are you?" asked Sally.

"Feel awful, had a real skin full at lunchtime."

"Just woken up from my siesta as well. How about I come around and make us some dinner? You will feel better with some food inside you."

"Do not feel much like it at the moment, but you are right. See you soon."

Sally went to Tim's flat via the supermarket and made them some Fajitas for dinner. She put in plenty of chillies to get the endorphins going and make them feel better. After dinner, they sat up late and binge-watched a new crime series on one of their streaming services.

Chapter 23

Sally had just got up when Jules called her. Tim was still asleep, so she went into the kitchen to take the video call. "Hi, Jules, how did it go?"

"Incredible, Anne thought something was up as Steve had been quite anxious recently but had refused to tell Anne why. After I told her about the video, she immediately phoned Steve and confronted him directly about it. He caved in straight away and admitted that Catherine had hatched the whole plan to discredit Tim and get his new job. She blackmailed Steve into providing the video extract from the security camera, getting it faked and making it appear as a legitimate copy."

"How did she blackmail Steve?"

"Turned out he had an affair in London that Catherine knew about. He thought Anne did not know. In fact, Anne did know but chose to let sleeping dog lie as they were returning to Sydney, anyway."

"Has Steve confessed to the bank about what he had done?"

"Apparently, yes. Tim should expect a grovelling apology soon."

"That is fantastic. Thank you so much for the help."

"No worries, just buy me a few beers in Manly when you come back."

"We will book the best restaurant and give you more than a few beers."

"I look forward to it. Must go as cooking dinner."

Sally ran back into the bedroom and woke up Tim. He was overwhelmed when he heard and burst into tears of happiness and relief. Sally hugged him and he carried on sobbing and shaking for a little longer before pulling himself together.

"Wow, what a week this has been! My nerves are in tatters but thank god it seems to be over and things can get back to normal."

While Tim got dressed, Sally made some breakfast. When Tim came through, he was holding his mobile phone and said, "Just got a message from

Angus. He wants me to meet with him at the office in London tomorrow at 9.00 AM."

"Let the grovelling begin," joked Sally.

"Not so sure a bit of grovelling is going to be enough," said Tim. "They have behaved appallingly towards me in this whole saga. I want to hear what they have to say about compensation. If I took this story to the press, then the bank's reputation would be in tatters."

"You are right, Tim, screw the bastards," said Sally.

After they had breakfast, they both fancied getting some fresh air. Tim said he knew a great place for a walk with a lovely country pub nearby for lunch. The walk was on a part of a long-distance path called the 'South Downs Way' in the National Park to the north of Brighton. Tim drove them to a car park high up on top of the downland near the long-distance path.

From up on the hills, they had panoramic views of the English channel across to France on one side and the lowlands of the Sussex Weald towards London on the other. They walked for several miles along the top of the downs but then had to descend into a valley as the Cuckmere River carved its way through the chalk hillside.

In the valley was the village pub that Tim had mentioned. They sat out in the garden and had a Ploughman's lunch each and a couple of pints of their favourite Sussex Best Bitter. After lunch, they followed the river down to the sea. From this point, they could look back up at the hills and the white chalk cliffs of where the South Downs met the sea.

The walk back was uphill to start with and a real slog but once on top of the Downs again, they enjoyed the stroll along the ridge to the car park. By the time they got back to Tim's flat, it was early evening. They were both tired from the long walk, so Tim ordered some takeaway from his favourite French restaurant to be delivered. Over dinner, they talked about their plans for the next day. "My friend Lucy from the States is arriving tomorrow afternoon and will be staying with me for a few days," said Sally.

"OK. I have the 9.00 AM meeting with Angus, so I had better get the 7.15 AM train to ensure I have plenty of time to get there. Difficult to plan the rest of my day without knowing what he will say."

"Call me as soon as you know anything."

"Of course, I will. Assuming I come back, then shall I come round and meet your friend in the evening."

"That is what I hoped. I will cook the three of us dinner and you can stay over."

"Sounds like a plan to me."

They tried a bit more binge-watching of the new crime drama they had started but were both too tired to watch much. They went to bed just after 10.00 PM.

Chapter 24

The next morning, Tim got up early and left to get his train to London while Sally had a lie in. She eventually got up just after 10 o'clock and left to go back to her flat. Sally had still not heard from Tim at 11.00 AM so she sent him a message, "How did it go?"

She cleaned her flat and then went to the supermarket to restock with food. When she got back, it was 1.00 PM and still no response from Tim. She was getting worried, so she sent him another message, "Please call me." A few minutes later, he did. "I was getting worried. What happened?"

"The bastard Angus had no intention of grovelling and just said that in the light of developments, they would reconsider my position. I went apeshit and called him a fat, pompous pratt. I also threatened to go to the press with my story and expose the corruption in the bank. He was furious and pinned me against the wall, grabbed my neck and called me a nasty piece of shit that should never have been given any job at the bank, let alone Head of Desk in Sydney."

"Wow, what happened next?"

"Luckily, the meeting room had a glass side and some of the other staff saw what was happening so came in and wrestled Angus away from me. I said I was calling the police and he said I could do what I liked, but I was never getting my job back. One of the people who rescued me found a General Manager to tell her what had happened. She told Angus to go and cool down and then let me tell her the whole story."

"What was her reaction?"

"She was horrified and called her manager, who then called the CEO. About 30 minutes later, I was in the office of the bank CEO and he did plenty of grovelling. I have just got out from the meeting with him."

"Did he give you your job back?"

"He offered, but I refused it. This whole thing has left a nasty taste in my mouth and I do not want to work with this company anymore. So instead, I negotiated a severance package if I signed a non-disclosure agreement covering the frame up and their subsequent behaviour."

"What did you get?"

"Two million pounds."

Sally stopped breathing from the shock and could hardly speak. "Fuck me, that much?"

"Yes please and yes," replied Tim. "I will be getting the next train back and will come round to your place about 6.00 PM if that is OK."

"Perfect, see you then."

Sally could not get her head around the amount of money they had paid Tim to keep quiet but then realised it may sound enormous to her, but to a multinational bank, it was loose change. She then started to get excited for Tim. With that amount of money, his options in life suddenly became so much more attractive. She made herself some lunch and waited for Lucy to say she had arrived.

At about 3.00 PM, she had a message from Lucy to say she was on the train from Gatwick Airport to Brighton. The whole journey only took 30 minutes so Sally knew Lucy would not be long. She sent a message back to say she would meet her on the station concourse by the platform exit gates. She took a leisurely walk to the station and arrived just before the airport train pulled in. She soon saw Lucy pass through the ticket barrier and rushed up to greet her.

"It has been far too long. So excited to see you again."

"Me too. I cannot wait to hear what you have been up to."

"If you came two weeks ago, it would be pretty dull, but things have got a lot more interesting recently."

"Cannot wait to hear the juicy details," said Lucy.

Lucy had a heavy suitcase, so they got a taxi from the rank outside the station and were back at Sally's flat less than 10 minutes later. Lucy had bought a bottle of vodka in the duty-free shop after landing and so they opened that and mixed it with some orange juice and ice. They sat in Sally's lounge with their drinks and Sally told Lucy all about her recent adventures with meeting Tim at the speed dating, the trip to Sydney, Catherine framing Tim and how they exposed her.

"So when will I be able to meet this Tim guy?" asked Lucy.

"He is coming round for dinner tonight."

"Perfect, cannot wait."

"So what have you been up to?" Sally asked Lucy.

"Did you know who I used to work for in LA."

"Not really, just that it was with some IT geeks for some kind of government dept."

"I actually worked for the NSA."

"The NSA that is full of American Government cyber spies?"

"Kind off, but mostly about stopping cyber-crimes. I was pretty impressed with how you managed to snare Catherine, although if I still worked for the NSA, I probably should report you to GCHQ."

Sally briefly considered sharing what else she had been up to in the hacking world but decided she would not just yet.

"Who do you work for now?"

"I have started my own company of Red Hat Hackers."

"What is a Red Hat Hacker?"

"We help companies who are attacked by malicious hackers and stop the attacks and then go after the attackers and destroy them."

Sally was so excited. That is precisely what she was trying to do. She could resist no longer and told Lucy the whole story of her Facebook being hacked, how she set up the false payment sites, exposed Spenser, then went after Sofia.

"Wow, that is all brilliant stuff. The false payment site was really clever. I might use that myself."

"How can I complete the job and get Sofia properly rather than just the annoying identity theft I have thought of so far?"

"You have two options. The first one is to report her to the Romanian Cyber Security police. They are keen to crack down on people like Sofia and would lock her up straight away, given your evidence. The other option is to provide you with some very powerful and nasty software that my company has built. You will not find anything like this on the Dark Web."

"Once a single PC is infected with this virus, it seeks out all other computers that ever connect to it and infects them. When we think we have infected most of the computers involved in the hacker's group, we trigger a detonator and the virus destroys every computer. They are literally fried. The virus causes the processor to overheat at the same time as turning off the cooling mechanisms."

"Second is tempting, but I think option one might be more productive in the long run."

"I agree. Give me all the information you have on Sofia and her activities. I know a guy in Bucharest who works with the Romanian Cyber Security team, so I will send it to him."

"That would be great," said Sally and got up to refresh their drinks. When she returned, she changed the subject away from hacking and asked Lucy, "So have you got anybody special in LA."

"For ages, the answer would be no, but like you, my luck has changed recently."

"Tell me more."

"I met Antonio through work. He works for one of our clients as a lawyer. Every time we met, I felt a kind of connection with him. Difficult to put into words but almost like we had known each other in a past life or something. Anyway, after one meeting, we were the last two left in the room after it finished and he said, 'Do you feel it as well?' A weird thing to say, but I knew exactly what he meant and said Yes. He invited me out to dinner that evening. We had a magical time and I ended up staying over at his place. I feel so right with him."

"That is wonderful, Lucy. I am so happy for you."

"I have a confession to make. My trip over is not just for our catch up. Antonio had a conference in London so I came now so we could spend some time together. I hope you do not mind, but I will probably go and stay with him in London when the conference finishes on Sunday."

"Of course not, just so pleased you have found somebody special."

At that moment, Tim breezed into the room and 'Hi, you must be Lucy, I am Tim'.

"Hi, Tim, Sally has been telling me all about you. How does it feel to be rich?"

"Much better than being an unemployed office groper," joked Tim.

They all laughed and Tim grabbed himself and a drink and joined them on the Sofas.

"I know it is a bit soon, but have you any idea what you want to do next?" asked Lucy.

"Not exactly, but I have decided on two things. Firstly, I want it to be with my beautiful, intelligent new girlfriend."

"You have a new girlfriend already," exclaimed Sally.

"I meant YOU. We have only been together two weeks, so I think that counts as a new."

Sally laughed and said, "I knew what you meant, just teasing."

"And secondly, I want to work for myself. I have had enough of the corporate world."

"Sounds like a good plan to me," said Lucy. "I love working for myself rather than a big govt department."

Lucy explained to Tim what her company did and how she had set it up with a few friends. "I am the only real hardcore geek amongst the founders. One other guy from NSA joined us, but one of the others is a Sales and Marketing specialist and the last founder is a sleeping partner who just invested some money."

Sally left Tim and Lucy to carry on chatting and she went into the kitchen to cook dinner. She cooked a seafood carbonara followed by a chocolate mouse and cherries with ice cream. When the food was ready, she called Lucy and Tim into the kitchen to eat.

After they had all sat down, Tim said, "I have been talking to Lucy and have come up with a brilliant idea. Lucy wants to expand her company so we will start a sister company over here in London. I will provide 80% of the capital for a 40% share. Lucy will provide the other 20% and her advice for 30% and we propose you get the other 30% for being the CEO."

"You have shown you have a real flair and passion for this kind of work. It will be great fun working together," added Lucy.

"What do you get out of it?" she asked Tim.

"I want to be a venture capitalist and invest my money in start-ups. As an investment banker, that is what I am qualified to do. You and Lucy will be my first start-up. It will help me get started and I get to work with my favourite person in the whole world."

"Thanks, Tim. I am very flattered," said Lucy.

They all laughed and then Tim said, "Seriously, Sally, are you up for this?"

"I would love to," said Sally and gave Tim a big kiss.

The End

One for You

Chapter 1

"Hi, Steve, it's Alex—how are you?"

"Not bad, mate—can't speak now, though, just putting the kids to bed."

"Fancy a beer later?"

"Sorry, but Sue is cooking a special meal and then we are planning on streaming a movie."

"Never mind, perhaps Friday?"

"Sue's mum is coming down from Manchester so will not be around this weekend. However, I will give you a bell next week."

"Yeah, do that."

"Bye."

"Bye."

"Hi Pete, it's Alex—how are you?"

"In the shit—got a bit pissed with some of the lads from work last night. You know how it is. I went for a quick pint at 6.00 PM and ended up staying all night. Clean forgot we were supposed to go round June's mum's for tea. My mobile was out of juice so she couldn't get hold of me. She's convinced I did it all deliberately and is spitting nails."

"I take it you're not on for a beer tonight then."

"Not sure I will ever be let out again!"

"OK, best of luck."

"Yeah, see you, mate."

"Hi Alison, it's Alex. Is Tom around?"

"No, sorry, he's working late."

"Tell him I phoned and, if he fancies a beer later, to give me a ring."

"OK, Alex, will do."

Alex knew she had no intention of passing the message on—at least until it was too late.

"Thanks, Alison."

"No problem, bye, Alex."

Alex could take no more rejection, so he resigned himself to another night alone in his flat.

He was about to sit back and surf the streaming sites for entertainment when he remembered he had still not got his sister's birthday present and it was only three days away. So he got out his laptop and logged on to Amazon to try and find the cookbook that she had told him she wanted. Before he got to search for it, an advertisement in the 'recommended for you' section caught his eye. "*How-to pick-up Horny women 100% Guaranteed.*"

Alex was initially slightly perplexed and insulted at how the site had determined this would interest him. It sounded like a book to appeal to absolute losers. Nevertheless, curiosity got the better of him and he clicked through to get more details.

"There are thousands of horny women out there who will sleep with YOU. All you need is the key. Phil Curtis has this key and he has used it to sleep with over 500 different women. He is now prepared to share this secret key with you in his new book *How-to pick-up Horny women 100% Guaranteed.* Phil and his publishers are so confident of his technique that they will refund your money if you have not slept with at least one horny woman within 30 days of receiving the book."

Next to the description was a One-Click Purchase button. Alex only hesitated for a moment before clicking. Seconds later, his email inbox pinged as the confirmation arrived. Alex went back to the task at hand and searched for the cookbook for his sister. A second ping a few seconds later confirmed that the purchase was also now complete.

Alex phoned his sister to find out what plans she had for her birthday and when he could give her the present.

"Hi, Sis, it's Alex here."

"Hi, Alex, I was about to phone you. I am having a small family birthday party on Saturday if you are free. Nothing fancy, just a few drinks and some take out Chinese—My Favourite!"

"That would be great. What time do you want me to come round?"

"About seven if that is OK."

"Perfect."

"Great, see then."

Alex's sister was two years older than him. She lived in Shoreham, a small town just along the coast from Brighton, with her husband Pete and their two children, Simon and Emma. Susan was Alex's only living close relative. He had no other siblings and both his parents were dead. He only met up with Susan on special occasions and celebrations, but she looked after her younger brother and called him regularly to check how he was. She also tried to fix him up with suitable girlfriends.

Unfortunately, Susan's concept of suitable did not match very well with Alex's ideal date. Susan wanted Alex to settle down and have a family like her, so the relevant dates consisted of broody 30-year-olds who stayed in to save for a deposit on a house.

Alex was not against having a family and buying property but wanted to have more fun first. He was only 28, so he thought he had at least five more years of fun due to him. He had a few girlfriends, but his social life mostly revolved around going out with his mates. Unfortunately for Alex, they were now starting to have families and serious relationships. That meant they socialised a lot less and he was often left to feel like Johnny No Mates.

Alex was looking for a girl who wanted to have a relationship but was not overbearing and clingy. He wanted to start slowly and casually and see how things went. He had no specific requirements but there needed to be a connection between them. The speed dating seemed a great way to see if that existed without wasting a whole evening. If there was a connection with somebody and they clicked, he thought he would know within the first couple of minutes.

Chapter 2

Sophie carefully unpacked her bag of groceries and put the contents in their allotted places. Sophie liked things neat and tidy. Every cupboard in her kitchen had a precise purpose and the contents of each were perfectly arranged. The last item to be put away was a small bag of flour, which she placed in the baking section of the cooking ingredients shelf of the dry goods cupboard.

Sophie was 32 years old. She lived alone in her tiny attic flat in a converted Victorian mansion in central Hove. She had no pets and very few friends. Both her parents were dead and she had no siblings. Sophie spent most of her time outside work on her own. She did not mind too much as she mainly was perfectly content in her own company but more recently had started to pine for a more fulfilling life.

Sophie worked as an economist for a large investment bank in the city of London. She commuted to work every day from Hove Station, which was not far from her flat. She had moved to Hove from Clapham three months before, hoping that she would establish that more fulfilling lifestyle. Sophie was not a very tolerant person and when she tried to socialise in Clapham found that, in her opinion, all the people she encountered were complete wankers.

Her attempts to build a social life in Hove had not taken off. This was primarily due to her making excuses based on all the stuff she had to do to sort out her new flat. She was now running out of those excuses and planned to build her new social life that weekend. She had signed up for a Yoga class in the hope of making friends with some nice chilled out other women.

Sophie found the alpha females she encountered in London unbearable. She had also signed up for a walking group that went on hikes in the nearby South Downs National Park. The first of these was on Sunday. Most daringly, she had also signed up for a speed dating event the following Tuesday eve at the art centre around the corner from her flat. She had seen the poster when she walked past and, in a moment of rare decisiveness when it came to her social life, signed up online as soon as she got back to her flat.

The first Yoga class was due to start in an hour, so Sophie went to her wardrobe to seek out some suitable Yoga gear. She found a nice loose-fitting t-shirt and some old yoga pants she had forgotten she had. She slipped these on, tried a few poses in front of her mirror to make sure she could move easily and did not look too hideous. Check passed.

She grabbed a quick snack and headed out to the class. The Yoga studio was a converted shop and about a 15-minute walk from her flat. She had allowed 30 minutes so arrived too early. She killed 10 minutes with a quick walk around the block and then went inside. She was immediately approached by a smiling blonde woman wearing a crop top and tight yoga pants.

"Hi, I am Tabatha, the Yoga instructor. You must be Sophie, our new girl."

"Yes, that's right. Nice to meet you."

"Have you done any Yoga before or are you a complete beginner?"

"I tried a few online video classes without much success, so just about a complete beginner."

"No problem, this is a beginner's class and we will take things nice and slowly, so I am sure you will soon pick things up. This first-class with be the toughest and you will probably get confused a few times but stick with it."

"I have paid for six classes so that I will stick with it for at least that long."

"That should be plenty of time to turn you into a proper Yogi. By the way, have you got your own mat?"

"No, sorry, did not think about that."

"No Problem, you can use one of those on the pile at the back but wipe it down before and after you use it. Most people prefer to bring their own."

"Thanks, I will get one before the next class."

The Yoga studio was a simple open space with a wooden floor and plain white walls. It was beginning to fill up with other students and Sophie assessed each as they entered the room.

She was pleased to see that they were primarily women of about her age and most looked a little shy and intimidated—none of the forceful alpha females she had detested in Clapham. A petite brunette girl with pointy features and a small nose ring came and took the space next to Sophie. The girl smiled gently at Sophie, who responded by introducing herself.

"Hi, I am Sophie. I am new here."

"Hi, Sophie, nice to meet you. I am Alice. I have been a few times but pretty new as well."

"How have you been enjoying it?"

"Struggled a bit at first but getting there now. I kind of joined to get out and meet people as new to the area but now starting to enjoy the Yoga."

"I am new to the area as well and joined for much the same reason. Perhaps we could go for coffee and chat after class?"

"Yes, that would be fun."

At that point, Tabatha called everybody to face her and get into their 'Downward-Facing Dog'. Sophie's 45min of torture had begun.

After class, Sophie and Alice went along to the coffee shop next door to the studio. They both ordered their flat white coffee and sat down at a table in the window.

"That was hell!" exclaimed Sophie.

"I felt the same after my first class," responded Alice. "Don't worry, it gets easier really quickly, I promise."

"So, how long have you been in Brighton," said Sophie, deliberately changing the subject. She was already thinking of writing off the money she had paid for the following five classes.

"I came down from Manchester about six weeks ago. I got a job as a UX designer with a small start-up based in the Lanes."

"What the hell is a UX designer?" replied Sophie.

"Sorry, a bit of IT jargon. UX means User Experience so. Basically, I design the screens of the iPhone app we are building."

"What does the app do?"

"Not allowed to say too much as it is still under wraps, but basically it lets you see all the people who stalk you on the web."

"Who has been looking at my Facebook posts?"

"Exactly and all your other social media posts and any websites that feature you as well."

"Sounds fascinating and scary. How are you enjoying Brighton?"

"Work is great and the city is fantastic, but to be honest, I am pretty homesick for family and friends in Manchester."

"Well, I hope we can become friends and help each other settle down and make our new lives here."

"Sounds Fab," said a grinning Alice.

Sophie was also grinning. Things were going to plan. Her new life was starting to come together.

Chapter 3

Andy woke with a severe stabbing pain in his neck. He sat up and rubbed the area that hurt in a desperate attempt at getting some relief. It helped a bit but not enough, so he got up on his feet and made some exaggerated head movements. This seemed to do the trick and the pain subsided. Unfortunately, the neck pain was an occupational hazard for what Andy did. He was a couch surfer. His bar work did not pay nearly enough to rent his place or even a room of his own, so he slept on friends and friends of friends' couches.

Andy was from Australia and was in Brighton at the start of a working holiday to see Europe. He had been in Brighton for four weeks so far and had got himself a job as a barman at the Bath Arms pub in the Lanes. Andy had spent the first week staying with an old Aussie girlfriend, but that had got messy when her new boyfriend had found out they had a past and he was not the gay friend she had claimed. So he was now staying for 'just a couple of days' on the sofa in the flat where a couple of his work colleagues at the pub were living.

He planned on staying in Brighton and working at the pub until he had saved enough for the airfare to Ibiza, where he planned to get his next job. So far, he had spent most of his earnings on having fun outside work, so he guessed he would be in Brighton for a few weeks more. Not that he minded. He was having a blast.

Andy found that the social scene in Brighton suited him perfectly. There were fantastic clubs, a load of pubs and an endless supply of gorgeous young women from the city universities or, like him, doing causal work in the hospitality industry. With his good looks, friendly, outgoing personality and chilled Aussie attitude to life, he was a big hit with the local women and the large gay community.

Andy had a shower and, when he returned to the living room, found one of his flatmates, Colin, sitting on the sofa.

"Can you do me a favour, Andy?"

"Sure, Col, what is it?"

"I have signed up for a speed dating event next Tuesday and would like you to come along and keep me company. So I have arranged for Susie to swap shifts with you at the pub."

"Let me stay until the end of the week and you have a deal."

"As long as you are out by the weekend."

"Great, where is the speed dating event held and what time does it start?"

"8 o'clock in the Old Market Arts Centre."

"Fancy a beer beforehand?"

"Sure, let's leave at 7.00 PM and have a couple of pints at the Farm Tavern first."

"Sounds good."

Colin got up and went back to his bedroom. Andy sat down on the sofa and browsed the social media apps on his phone. He noticed a post from Toni, one of his old girlfriends back in Sydney. She had tickets for an AC/DC concert at the Olympic Stadium and could not go, so she was offering them for sale.

Andy suddenly felt very homesick. He would have loved to take the tickets and go to the gig and go with his mates. The next post he saw was from one of his mates and showed him with a couple of other guys skiing in an Australian Ski resort called Thredbo. Australia is not known for its skiing, but many locals flock to the Snowy Mountains from Sydney and Melbourne between June and August each year.

There was an Australian tradition for families to club together, build Ski Lodges in the Snowy Mountains and share these to provide a cheap way to get on to the slopes. Andy's grandparents helped build a lodge in the 1950s and it was still in his family today. When he was a small toddler, he took regular trips to the lodge and had some wonderful times with his friends and family on the slopes.

The snow was not that reliable but became much better over time as more snowmakers were added. An additional benefit of learning to ski on often slush or ice was his fantastic technique. When he could ski on the groomed powder in Japan and the USA, he was a ski star and ate up all the black runs with no problems. He mentally added a trip to one of the European ski resorts to his plans for the winter. The next post he read was from one of his old girlfriend Toni's mates.

"IMPORTANT—DO NOT BUY TICKETS FROM TONI—Toni has had her account hacked. She has not got any AC/DC tickets. It is a scam."

Wow, that was a close thing. If he had been at home, he would have jumped on to buy the tickets as soon as he saw Toni's post. He momentarily wondered how the scam worked but dismissed the thought and moved on to the next post.

The post was from one of the barmaids he worked with at the Bath Arms. It showed her in her bikini on Brighton Beach. Andy had gone to the beach once since he arrived in Brighton. He had been completely stunned when he saw it.

His experience of beaches was all about white sand and the aquamarine sea like the Pacific Ocean beaches back in Sydney. The sight of the vast expanse of pebbles and brown looking sea of the English Channel took him by complete surprise and he ended up laughing out loud. His local friend, with who he had gone to the beach with was not impressed.

"They are just large grains of sand," the friend claimed in defence of the pebbles.

Andy was not convinced and had decided that Brighton Beach was a place he would visit just that once.

Chapter 4

Ursula was 36 years old but looked no more than 25. She had short black hair in a Pixie cut and a slim nubile body. She was lounging on her sofa and smoking a roll-up cigarette. She was trying to decide whether to go out on a date she had that evening or bail now and make her excuses.

The date was with one of the managers from work. He had been pestering her for weeks and had finally been successful thanks to his offer of a ticket to accompany him to a charity ball at the Grand Hotel. Ursula loved large glamourous events and she knew that the charity ball was one of the most sophisticated and glamorous events the city had.

The problem was that she did not like the manager very much and it was foolish to encourage him by accepting. He had a reputation as a groper, but there had been rumours that he had another girl sacked when she refused his sexual advances after an expensive dinner date. If the date had been with anybody else, she would have been so excited at this moment and be sorting her makeup and dresses to look her very best.

Her phone buzzed to indicate a new message. She looked at the screen and could not believe her luck. The message was from the manager she was supposed to have the date with. He said he had been taken ill and could not go, but the tickets were at the door in his name and she could use them both. Ursula let out a squeal of delight. She sent a message back to say how sorry she was and thank him for the tickets. Her head was suddenly spinning with everything she needed to sort before the ball started at 7.00 PM. Not least was who to go with.

The first name that came into her 'head' was her ex-boyfriend, Phil. They had dated for over five years and split up amicably three years ago. She phoned his number and had her fingers crossed.

"Hi, Phil, Ursula here."

"Hi. Ursula, how are you?"

"Good, thanks; just lucked out and got two free tickets for the charity ball at the Grand tonight. Do you fancy coming with me?"

"Wow, I always wanted to go to that. The problem is, Kim would kill me."

"Why?"

"I have not told you before, but she is extremely sensitive about my relationship with you. She does not understand how we are just friends and are both happy with that. She thinks it is only a matter of time before I dump her and get back with you."

"I can see your problem. You should have told me before and I could have reassured her. I like Kim and think she is good for you."

"Too late for tonight, though. If I went, she would go mad and no reassurance from you would do any good. Why don't you ask Bob if he is free?"

"Not that desperate yet," replied Ursula.

Bob was Phil's best friend. Bob was a nice enough guy and she would not mind an evening of his company over a couple of pints in the local. However, he was not the kind of date Ursula wanted for a glamorous night at the Grand. She was looking for a Daniel Craig type rather than a Johnny Vegas.

She racked her brain for alternatives and discovered she actually knew very few good-looking single guys. She had a shortlist of three that would be OK and tried the first two with no luck. The third option ticked all the boxes for a handsome, elegant gentleman to accompany her but was also gay.

Nevertheless, she called him and he was super excited to go with her and immediately panicked over getting his tuxedo pressed. So Ursula left him to it and arranged to meet him at his flat near the Grand Hotel at 6.45 PM. She concentrated on getting herself dressed up but also decided that she needed to get a new boyfriend. That speed dating thing she saw advertised might be a good idea.

Chapter 5

Alex was getting nervous about the speed dating event that evening. He was considering not going, but a voice in his head told him not to be a wimp and this was a chance for something great to happen in his life. He had a shower and then blow-dried his hair. He then shaved and splashed on some of his favourite Armani cologne. Alex had purchased a new shirt to wear for the event and put this on together with his trusty skinny black jeans. The venue for the speed dating was too far to walk, so he left in plenty of time as he had to get a bus.

When he arrived, he saw a couple of other people heading inside, so he followed them. He saw a table with the sign Boys above it and headed to that. He was given a small card with six numbers written on it and a box next to each number. He was told to add each date's name when he met them and tick the box off if he wanted to see them again. He was to put a cross in the box if he did not want to see them. He was to wait in the bar area.

The first date would start at 8.15. The girls were seated in the main hall with a number on their table to indicate which date they were on the card. Each date lasted 10 minutes with a 5-minute gap in between. The date started when a whistle was blown and ended when a siren went off. The boys were to return to the bar between dates. You were free to end the date early if you wish, but in no circumstances could the date go on more than 10 minutes.

After the final date, you should post your card in the box on the registration table as you left. The organisers would collate the results and send an email with the contact details of the dates where both parties wanted to see each other again. The email would be sent to all participants by 10.00 PM. You would get an email even if you had no matches. All seemed straightforward, so Alex went through to the bar and got himself a bottle of beer. The other guys in the bar looked a bit nervous and mainly were sitting alone nursing their beers.

At precisely 8.15, a whistle sounded and all the boys put down their beers and headed into the main hall. Alex's first date was number 7. He found her table and was delighted to see an attractive young woman with short dark hair. He guessed she was a fair bit younger than him.

"Hi, I am Alex. Nice to meet you."

"Likewise, I am Ursula."

They both scribbled the other's name on their date cards. "I love your shirt," said Ursula. "Is it a Burberry?"

"Well spotted," replied Alex. "I just recently purchased it. They are my favourite brand."

"One of mine as well," replied Ursula. "Although my absolute favourite is Zimmerman. I have a lovely blouse of theirs. I wished I had worn it now instead of this skanky T-shirt."

"Whatever it is, you look fabulous in it," replied Alex. "You are so pretty. I love your Pixie cut."

"Ahh, that is very nice of you," said Ursula, warming to Alex by the minute.

"Are you a student or have you got a job?" asked Alex.

"I have a job as a sales executive for a digital media company in Brighton," responded Ursula.

"Cool, I work in digital media as well. I am a producer at Ace studios," said Alex.

"I know them. Good company," said Ursula. "What do you like doing out of work?"

"Masturbation and strangling small animals," replied Alex.

Ursula laughed out loud, "I love Monty Python!"

Alex was relieved she understood his joke and they shared the same sense of humour. He was keen on Ursula. They chatted easily for the remaining few minutes and when the siren went off, Alex returned to the bar and put a big tick next to Ursula's name.

Alex's next date was on table number 2. The whistle sounded and he went through and found a very fit looking tanned girl sitting there. She was wearing a crop top and had the most amazing toned stomach.

"Hi, I am Zoe," she said, a little too stridently for Alex's taste.

"Alex," he responded.

"What are you looking for?" asked Zoe.

"What do you mean?" asked a confused Alex.

"What type of person were you hoping to meet tonight?" clarified Zoe.

"Nothing very specific but somebody I immediately felt I had a connection with," replied Alex.

"I am looking for a rich, good-looking man under 30 with a terrific physic and huge sexual appetite," said Zoe.

"I am not for you then," replied Alex. "I only fit 3 out of 4."

"Which one are you lacking?" replied Zoe.

"I only earn 50 thousand a year," replied Alex.

"Shame," said Zoe. "I can see you are good looking and would be keen to check out the other two."

Zoe was beginning to annoy Alex with her assertive, direct manner. "Sorry, but you missed my single criteria, but it was nice meeting you," replied Alex and got up and left for the bar.

Alex ordered another beer and sat down to wait for the next whistle. He took out his date card, wrote Zoe next to her box and added a cross. His next date was on table 9. She was a shy-looking girl with curly hair who smiled timidly as he sat down.

"Hello, my name is Alex."

"Hello, Alex. I am Rachael," she replied.

"Tell me an interesting fact about yourself," said Alex in an attempt to start up a conversation.

Rachael thought for a moment and then said, "I drink my own urine every day."

This was not the kind of fact that Alex expected or made Rachael seem more attractive to him.

"Why?" he responded.

"Well, it goes back to when I was a teenager and had terrible acne. None of the treatments the doctor prescribed really worked, so I googled cures and found that drinking your urine was one used extensively in China. So I tried it and it worked, so I have just carried on. I don't want to risk getting the acne back."

"Fair enough," said the dumfounded Alex.

"So what about an interesting fact about you?" said Rachael.

His stock reply about once being on the books of Brighton and Hove Albion seemed lame now, so he tried to think of something more dramatic.

"I can lick the end of my nose with my tongue," said Alex and immediately did so to prove it.

"A girl could have a lot of fun with a man who has a tongue like that," said Rachael. She then realised what she said and went bright red with embarrassment.

Alex laughed and added, "Play your cards right and you may be that girl."

They carried on flirting until the siren went off. Alex liked Rachael and added a tick to her box, but his real hope was to get matched with Ursula.

The following two dates were both reasonably dull. They made polite small talk, but neither appealed to Alex either physically or through their personality. There was zero connection. The last date was on Table 6 and Alex found a rather severe-looking blonde woman who was about his age or perhaps a little older.

"Hi, I am Alex."

"Nice to meet you, Alex. I am Sophie."

"What do you do for a living, Alex?" asked Sophie.

"I am a producer for a digital media company here in Brighton. What about you?"

"I am an economist for an investment bank in the city."

"Sounds high powered stuff," replied Alex.

"Sounds better than it is, mostly pretty dull. Your job sounds more exciting."

"Can be but like yours, mostly pretty dull. Do you commute to London?"

"Yes, just moved to Brighton from London. Travel is a bit of a pain but living here by the sea makes it worth it."

Sophie seemed nice but was being too serious, so Alex decided to spice things up.

"If you had to give up chocolate, Wine or Sex for a whole year. Which would you choose?"

Sophie looked Alex straight in the eye and for a moment, he thought she would tell him not to be so stupid, but then her face broke into a foxy smile. She said, "I saw what you did with your tongue when talking to the girl with the curly hair, so if the sex were with you, it would be chocolate."

Keeping full eye contact, Sophie then rubbed Alex's thigh under the table. Things had got a lot spicier than Alex planned.

"Which would you choose out of sex, beer and football?" said Sophie, cleverly adjusting the question to match Alex's tastes. Her hand went a little higher up his thigh and he could feel a bulge building in his underpants.

"If the sex was with you, then football. I suspect I would not have the energy, anyway."

Sophie's hand was now on his bulge and she was rubbing harder. Andy found himself breathing very heavily in an attempt to control himself. The siren sounded and Sophie took her hand away.

"It has been a pleasure making your acquaintance," said Sophie.

"The pleasure was all mine," replied Alex. He gingerly got to his feet and tried to hide his bulge with his hand as he made his way to the bar. There had definitely been a connection with Sophie and it made him both excited and scared at the same time. He ticked her box and then finished his beer before leaving and dropping the completed card in the box by the front door.

Chapter 6

Sophie was getting ready for the speed dating event. She picked out a simple white cotton blouse and a knee-length skirt to wear. She put them on and was happy with what she saw in the mirror. It had been a good week for Sophie. She had made a good girlie friend at her yoga class and enjoyed the company of the walking group she joined. All she needed now was a little romance in her life. She had created a list of the criteria the man would need to meet. Sophie liked to organise things and approach them methodically. The criteria were:

1. Has a proper job and career.
2. Clean and presentable.
3. Articulate and witty.
4. Taller than her and not overweight.
5. Rocked her boat (she fancied him).

She planned to award up to 20 points against each criterion and, if he scored over 75, would mark him as a match.

Sophie arrived at the speed dating venue and went to the girls' table to collect her card with its table number on it. Then, she went through to the hall and waited for her first date. A whistle sounded and the boys came through from the bar in the next room. Finally, her first date arrived and she sat down and introduced himself.

"Hi, I am Colin."

"I am Sophie. What do you do for a living, Colin."

"I am a barman at the Bath Arms in the Lanes. Do you know it?"

Colin just failed the first criteria and he was not looking to score very highly on Clean and Presentable, either. He was wearing a shabby jacket and a t-shirt with a stained collar. Sophie already had low expectations but carried on and replied, "I am new to Brighton, so not that familiar with the pubs yet. Would you recommend it?"

"Yeah, it's not bad and being in the Lanes is nice," replied Colin.

He now scored low on wit and being articulate. She definitely did not fancy him, so testing how tall he was and overweight became irrelevant. Sophie made a mental note to check that one out first on the next dates before they sat down. Sophie carried on making polite and very dull small talk until the siren went off and Colin left. She marked a cross next to his name on her card.

Next up was a boy called Pete, who was at least 10cm shorter than Sophie and had a serious beer gut. He also smelt and could bore for England. This event was not going as Sophie had hoped. Another cross on her card. The next boy was not much better.

His name was Norman and although he was about the same height as Sophie was, also carrying a beer gut and looked about twenty years older than her. He spent the whole of their time together trying to look down her blouse. Sophie was tempted to slap him and tell him to piss off. The only good thing about the date was when Sophie gazed across the room at the other tables and saw an astonishing thing. A guy in a lovely Burberry shirt sitting at a table one row across with a curly-haired girl put out his tongue and licked the end of his nose. Norman got no credit for this, so another cross.

Sophie decided to carry on and hope for better luck on her final three dates. When the next one arrived, she was glad she did. "Hi, I am Andy," he said. Andy was a tall, handsome guy with a gorgeous smile and a twinkle in his eyes. He already scored max points on two categories. "Hi, I am Sophie. What do you do for a living?" replied Sophie, with her stock opening line.

"I am travelling around Europe in my gap year, so just have casual work. Currently, I am doing bar work in the Bath Arms."

Not the answer Sophie wanted, but '*It could be worse,*' she thought. "I just met a guy called Colin who said he works there as well," replied Sophie.

"He is the reason I am here," confessed Andy. "He persuaded me to come along and keep him company."

"So you are not looking for a date?" said Sophie and prepared herself for more disappointment.

"I am single and a chance of a date with a gorgeous, intelligent woman like you is something I would never turn down," said Andy and gave her one of his winning smiles.

Sophie felt a little giddy but gathered herself and then said, "Thank you, kind sir, I am likewise inclined towards you."

"Then we should expect our fate to be further advancement of this mutually desirable liaison," replied Andy and collected max marks for wit and articulation. He had passed Sophie's test and got a nice big tick on the card.

Things went back downhill with Sophie's next date. A tall biker looking guy called Slash, of all things. He failed on everything except height and weight—a definite cross. Sophie was delighted to find her final date was with the guy in the nice shirt and long tongue.

"Hi, I am Alex," he said as he sat down.

Sophie had checked out his physique and it was just about perfect. Slightly taller than her and had no sign of a gut under his nice shirt. Top marks as well for clean and presentable. He smelt really good, Armani guessed Sophie. Sophie asked her standard opening question and was happy to find he had a proper job. Things were looking good. He then asked Sophie a very flirtatious question about giving up sex, wine or chocolate. She decided she liked Alex and might as well try and accelerate things. She mentioned she had seen his tongue trick and would not give up sex if she had a partner like him.

At the same time, she placed her hand on his thigh and squeezed it gently. For a moment, the poor guy looked petrified but then pulled himself together and Sophie asked him about giving up sex, beer or football. Sophie loved his answer and got a bit carried away. She moved her hand further up his leg and started rubbing his cock under the table. She could feel it responding and grow bigger.

Luckily, she was saved by the siren and withdrew her hand before she could consider her next step. She was tingling all over. Alex was a definite tick. She wanted to grab him and take him home now to finish what she had started. However, she decided that a little more decorum was more appropriate and after exchanging goodbyes with Alex, she put her card in the box and left to go back to her flat and wait for the matches email.

Chapter 7

Andy and Colin went for a pint before the speed dating in a nearby pub called the Farm Tavern. Colin got them both a pint of best bitter and they sat down at a spare table next to a couple of young women. One of the women asked Andy about his T-shirt, which said Manly Beach, the suburb of Sydney, where Andy came from. She was precisely Andy's type, slim tanned and with a sensational physique. She was wearing a crop top that showed off her flat toned stomach beautifully.

To Andy's delight, the woman invited him and Colin to join them. They enjoyed a fun conversation in which it emerged they were all going to the speed dating event. They agreed to meet back in the pub to compare notes after it had finished.

Andy and Colin made their way to the speed dating venue and collected their date cards from the boys table. They did not have time for a drink in the bar as the whistle for their first dates sounded before they could order. Andy went through and found the table number of his first date. "Hi, I am Andy," he said as he sat down opposite a shy-looking woman with curly hair.

"Nice to meet you. I am Rachael," she replied in a very soft, almost inaudible voice.

"Hi, Rachael, what do you do for a living?" replied Andy, to start a conversation.

"I am a rocket scientist," replied Rachael with a completely straight face. Andy could not help himself and laughed loudly. "It is not a joke. I really am," protested Rachael.

"Wow, I did not see that coming," said Andy.

"I work for BAE in Crawley," explained Rachael. "What do you do then, Andy?"

"Nothing at all exciting like you. I am over on a working holiday from Australia and mostly doing bar work."

"What will you do for a long-term job when you go back to Australia?"

"I have no idea. Part of the reason for coming over on this trip was because I could not decide. Maybe I should consider becoming a rocket scientist," joked Andy. "What do you do when you are not building rockets?" asked Andy.

"I love to go running up on the downs or cooking food for friends," replied Rachael.

Andy found Rachael pleasant enough, but there was no spark that meant he would want to see her again. They made more small talk for the remaining time and then Andy returned to the bar. He added Rachael's name and put a tick on the card. Not because he wanted to see her but wanted to know how many women wanted to see him.

Andy just had enough time to enjoy a swift beer with Colin in the bar before the whistle sounded for the next round of dates. Andy was delighted to find an absolutely gorgeous young woman with a pixie haircut waiting for him at the designated table.

"Hi, I am Andy."

"Ursula, nice to meet you."

"I love your Pixie haircut. Is it new?"

"Thank you, No I had it forever. Should probably grow it longer and try a new style."

"Don't do that. It suits you so well. You are gorgeous."

Ursula blushed and replied, "That is so kind of you, but I think you may need your eyes tested."

Andy smiled broadly and replied, "I have perfect vision and great taste, so I know real beauty when I see it. So do not underestimate how great you look."

"Next, you will tell me I could be a model."

"I am not dumb enough to trot out that old line. I sincerely mean what I said, but I can see it is making you uncomfortable so let's change the subject. What do you like to do for fun?"

"Masturbation and strangling small animals," replied Ursula, stealing the line from her previous date. Andy was obviously not a Monty Python fan, as he had a look of shock and bewilderment on his face and had been rendered speechless by her reply.

"It is a joke, from an old Monty Python sketch," explained Ursula. "I like dancing and fine dining."

"Oh, I see. I thought I had found a beautiful weirdo for a moment. I love dancing as well, although my culinary tastes are probably not in the 'fine' category."

"What would your favourite meal be, then?"

"A proper Ozzie BBQ with snags, shrimp and some good lamb kebabs."

"Sounds good to me, dreaded you saying a big mac or some other junk food."

"No way. Hate processed food. Where do you do your dancing?"

"My favourite club is Dynamo Bongo in Kemp Town. Have you been there?"

"Not had much of a chance to explore the nightlife in Brighton yet. I have been waiting for the right guide."

"Looks like this is your lucky night," said Ursula with a big grin on her face.

Andy really fell for Ursula, so he added a big tick next to the box with her name when he was back in the bar.

Next up for Andy was a reasonably attractive blonde woman who looked slightly older than him and had a solemn expression on her face. The woman's name was Sophie and she immediately quizzed him on what he did for a living. Andy could see she was not impressed by his answer. Andy flirted with her a little, without much genuine enthusiasm. He added a tick for Sophie, anyway.

Andy had three more dates and all went OK. He rolled out his full charm offensive for each one and they all seemed to fall for it, but he was not inclined to see any of them again. Andy still put a tick against each of their names. Andy decided Ursula was definitely the one for him.

Chapter 8

Ursula arrived at the speed dating venue just in time to get to her table before the first whistle blew.

The first date was with a good-looking guy called Alex. Ursula loved the shirt he was wearing and he was very complimentary about her, but she was perturbed when he asked her if she was a student, thinking, "Shit, how old does he think I am—A student!"

Ursula knew she looked young for her age, but for somebody to think she was only about half her true age was a bit too much. She briefly considered admitting her actual age but decided to go along with things and see how they developed first. She liked Alex's style and sense of humour and decided he was possible, so she added a tick next to his name on the card.

Next up was a great-looking guy called Andy with a smile that made Ursula swoon every time he turned it on. He told Ursula how beautiful she was, which made her feel both euphoric and embarrassed at the same time. She was even more embarrassed when she re-used Alex's old Monty Python line and Andy did not understand it, but after that, she relaxed and enjoyed flirting with Andy and she felt there was some real chemistry between them.

Given what happened before with Alex over her age, she was a little anxious about how old Andy thought she was. He only looked about 23 or 24, so there was a pretty large gap. She decided it was better to come clean and asked Andy, "How do you feel about dating older women?"

He replied, "If they are as gorgeous as you, then I am very cool about it. Why did you ask? You must be about my age or even a bit younger."

Ursula was not sure where to take the conversation next. For good or bad, Andy changed the subject and asked her about her favourite nightclubs. Ursula put the age issue to the back of her mind and flirted with Andy as strongly as she dared. She could tell from his demeanour that it was working and she was pretty confident she would get a tick on his card. After the siren sounded and Andy left for the bar, she put his name and a tick on her card.

Next up for Ursula was a horror date with a lanky biker with greasy hair and the most boring conversational skills she could imagine. Not only did he only have one topic (bikes), but he made that sound the most boring topic in the world. "The best bike, I think, is a Triumph, but I cannot remember which one is best. I once thought that Ducati might be better, but now I do not think so."

His name was Slash and he droned on and on like that for the whole date while Ursula stared blankly across the room.

The next date was a smartly dressed balding man. He sat down and introduced himself.

"Hi, my name is Ian."

"Nice to meet you. I am Ursula."

"I am 38 years old. Hope you do not mind asking, but how old are you? You look like you could be too young for me."

"Don't worry, Ian, I am 36 years old."

"Wow, that is fantastic news."

"Not so much for me. I would rather be 24," joked Ursula.

Ian laughed and replied, "Good for my hopes of meeting a suitable partner. How have things gone for you so for you this evening?"

"Mixed bag so far," said Ursula. "One definite NO and one YES, although he seemed very young and I think he also thought I was a lot younger than I am. How about you?"

"First date did not turn up, so I sat alone at the table hoping she would come in later but never did. The second date said I looked like her grandfather. Hence my sensitivity over age."

"Oh dear, sorry to hear that. I hope your luck improves."

"Certainly seems to with you," said a smiling Ian. "What do you like doing for fun?"

Ursula resisted trotting out the Monty Python line again and played a straight bat. "Fine dining and dancing."

"Awesome, same here," beamed Ian. "Have you tried the new Michelin starred restaurant in The Lanes? I went last week and then onto Dynamo Bongo for a good bop."

"Sounds like my perfect night out," replied Ursula.

"Perhaps you could join me for a repeat next week," said Ian, pushing his luck.

"Let's see how the rest of tonight works out. If we both match and want to, then sounds great," replied Ursula. She thought Ian was promising but did not want to limit her options with two more dates to go. She could also not get the feeling Andy had awoken in her out of her head. She had not felt light-headed and euphoric with Ian.

Sadly for Ursula, her last two dates were terrible. The first said he was 22 but looked about 12. Ursula doubted he had passed puberty as he had a high squeaky voice and no body hair she could see. The final date was just vile. He was a scruffy-looking slob who stank of stale tobacco. His opening line was, "I am not messing around here. I am looking for a good fuck later and you can be the lucky lady."

Ursula told him to piss off, which, to her relief, he did.

Chapter 9

After the speed dating event had finished, Alex returned to his flat. He opened a beer from the fridge and played some music while waiting for his email with the matches. At 9.40 PM, his phone pinged as the email arrived. Alex was delighted he had three matches from Ursula, Rachael and Sophie.

The match that excited him most was Sophie, but he was also a little scared of what he was getting into, given her outrageous behaviour at the speed dating. He briefly considered contacting Rachael, as she seemed friendly and timid and was very keen on him. Or should he contact Ursula? She was stunningly good-looking but perhaps a bit young. It was no good. He had to see Sophie; he found her so exciting and could not miss the chance of some real fun.

Alex phoned Sophie's mobile but was disappointed that it just went to voicemail. When the beep went for him to leave a message, his mind went blank, so he just hung up. He briefly considered giving up and phoning Ursula or Rachael but then thought that he may have been a bit quick off the mark and maybe Sophie needed time to get her email and consider her responses. So he grabbed another beer and turned the music up. He would try again in 30 minutes.

After about 15 minutes, his phone rang and he looked expectantly at the number, hoping it was Sophie, but it was not. A quick check against the email showed that the number was Rachael. Alex let the call go to voicemail. A couple of minutes later, he got a message saying he had a new message. He called the voicemail service and heard the message from Rachael. In her soft, timid voice, she said, "Hi Alex, this is Rachel from the speed dating. So pleased you liked me and would love to meet up. Call me back so we can arrange when and where."

Alex was about to phone back when his phone rang again and this time it was Sophie.

"Hi sexy, it is dirty girl here, so pleased you want to carry on where we left off."

Alex was immediately turned into a bag of nerves and replied, "Oh, Hi Sophie, I phoned you earlier but got no reply."

"I did not recognise your number than as I had not received my email. So what are you doing now? Want to come round to my place?"

"Where is your place?"

"Flat 5, 17 First Avenue in Hove."

"Not very far, so I will be there in 15 minutes."

"Can't wait, see you soon."

Alex was now physically shaking with nerves. He was not sure why he had agreed so readily to go round but just seemed drawn in by Sophie. Her flat was only around the corner from his, so he left and walked to it.

Alex rang the bell for Flat five and was buzzed in. The flat was on the second floor, so he had to walk up the grand Victorian staircase to reach her front door. When he arrived, Sophie was waiting with the door open. She had a mischievous grin on her face and was wearing a very revealing lace nightie. "Fancy a nightcap?" asked Sophie.

"Large Brandy, if you have some."

"Have a great bottle of Armagnac in the kitchen."

Sophie disappeared to get his drink and Alex had a chance to take in his surroundings. The flat was very neat and tidy. Hardly anything seemed out of place and all was spotlessly clean. Sophie returned with a massive glass of Armagnac for each of them and beckoned for Alex to join her on the sofa.

"You must think I am a real slut. I do not know what has come over me tonight. I just got carried away. I am normally pretty straight-laced and a bit boring."

Alex was flabbergasted and deeply relieved by Sophie's change of tack. "To be honest, you were a bit OTT. I was a bit scared of what I may have got myself into."

Sophie laughed and then said, "How about we do a re-set and slow things down?"

"Does that mean I am not getting a shag tonight, then?" joked Alex.

"It will just need to be a slow one," said Sophie and clinked her glass against his. "Cheers."

"Bottoms Up," replied Alex and Sophie obliged.

They stayed on the sofa drinking their Armagnac and chatting for about an hour and found they had a fantastic rapport between them. After they had both finished their second glass, Alex moved in closer to Sophie and started kissing. Pretty soon, they were undressing each other and headed to Sophie's bedroom.

The next morning, they woke early and had sex once more before showering and heading to Sophie's kitchen for breakfast. "I cannot believe how wonderful things are going. It seems an age ago that I was that poor nervous guy entering the speed dating event."

Sophie kissed Alex gently on the lips and said, "I am so happy I went as well. Everything I hoped for has all come true." Sophie looked at her wrist as her smartwatch vibrated with an alert. "I need to leave in 10 minutes to get the train to work. I will phone you later and perhaps we can see each other tonight."

"That will be great. I need to get moving for work as well, so speak later."

Alex gave Sophie one last kiss, then gathered up his stuff and left.

Chapter 10

After the speed dating had finished, Andy met up with Colin and they headed off back towards the pub where they had agreed to meet the two girls they had met before the event. Sally and Zoe were only just leaving themselves, so they called across to them and they all walked back to the pub together.

Once inside the pub, they got their drinks and sat down to compare notes on the event. Zoe asked how many ticks they each put down for other people. Zoe admitted that she only ticked the last date, so she had done at least once but was not really interested in him. Colin said he had only ticked one and that he already knew Rachael was his dream woman. Sally pretended to be affronted as she had ticked Colin's box and one other. Andy knew that Sally must have only ticked Colin's box as a sympathy vote, as she was way out of his league. Andy admitted, "I ticked all the boxes," and added, "any port in a storm."

Zoe seemed confused, so he explained that he was currently couch surfing and needed somewhere to stay, so shacking up with one of the girls from the speed dating would help him out. To his astonishment, Zoe blurted out, "You can stay with me."

Andy could not believe his luck and so, despite not particularly liking Zoe, replied, "Wow, that would be fantastic," he then added, "I would much rather stay with you than any of the girls at the speed dating."

At that moment, their phones started to ping as their results emails came in. Andy was pleased to see he had a complete set of matches and all the girls' details. However, Zoe was not happy when he announced this and warned him not to contact any of them. Andy was not so sure yet that he would comply.

After they had finished chatting, Sally and Colin were keen to get home and fix up meeting their matches. Zoe asked Andy if he wanted to stay for another drink in the pub or go back to her place. Andy said, "How far away is your place?"

"Not too far, just off Norfolk Square," replied Zoe.

"Cool, let's go there then," said Andy.

It only took them 15 minutes to walk to Zoe's flat. Once inside, Zoe asked Andy if he wanted a drink. "A beer if you have one, please," replied Andy. So Zoe got his beer and a cold white wine for herself and sat down next to Andy in her lounge. "Nice place you have, Zoe," remarked Andy. "Is it a one or two-bedroom place?"

"Just one bed and no sofa," replied Zoe with a grin. "You will have to earn your keep to stay in my bed or sleep on the floor."

"What kind of work is involved in earning my keep?"

"Pleasuring a randy young woman mostly but also some cooking and cleaning."

"I am not much good at two of those things?"

"I hope they are the ones I am hoping."

"Want to try me out?"

"What now?"

"Sure, I will go and clean the kitchen and cook you an omelette."

"Oh, I was hoping to test the other duty?"

"Might be more fun." They took their drinks and headed into Zoe's bedroom.

The next morning, Andy woke before Zoe. He was pretty sure he passed the test, judging by the screaming and trembling he had induced from Zoe the night before. Andy kissed Zoe on the forehead and told her he was going to shower and then fix some breakfast. Zoe just purred and went back to sleep.

Zoe emerged just as the coffee was ready and Andy poured her a cup. "That was the best ever," said Zoe and kissed Andy on the lips.

"I take it I will not have to sleep on the floor then," replied Andy.

"I need to clarify one thing, though," said Zoe. "We are going to be a proper couple and you are not just a lodger with benefits."

Andy was not sure he wanted to get into a serious relationship, but he now liked Zoe and needed somewhere to stay, so he went along with her wishes. "Of course, that is exactly what I want," he replied, then kissed her. After breakfast, Andy said, "I need to be at work by 11.00 AM, so I will leave now and go back to Colin's to get my stuff and bring it back here. I will then just have time to get changed and head off to work. I am only doing the lunchtime shift, so we can then spend the evening together."

"That sounds great," replied Zoe and Andy headed off to Colin's.

"Hi, Colin," shouted Andy as he let himself into Colin's flat.

"Hi Andy," replied Colin. "How did it go with Zoe?"

"Great, I am moving in with her today. How did you get on with Rachael?"

"She has agreed to meet me tonight for dinner, but I am supposed to be working. Can we swap shifts and I will do this lunchtime instead?"

Andy knew how much his chance of a date meant to Colin, so he readily agreed, "No Problem mate, least I can do." Andy got out his phone and called Zoe, "Hi Zoe, listen, I need to switch shifts and work tonight but and now free all day, so will come back with my stuff this morning and we can spend the day together if that is OK?"

"No problem, sounds better," replied Zoe.

Andy got his stuff together and was about to leave when his phone pinged to indicate a new message. The message read, "Hi Andy, this is Jo from the speed dating. Just to make sure you know, I am keen to hook up if you are. Just let me know where and when we can meet."

Andy was conflicted. He would be stupid to mess up the good thing he had started with Zoe but wanted to keep his options open. He replied immediately, "Hi Jo, love to meet up, but something has come up and will not be around for a few days, so that I will get back to you later."

Chapter 11

After the event, Ursula went back to her flat and waited for her email. She was pleased to see that she had three matches. She had matched with both Alex and Andy and although she thought them both gorgeous, was worried what their reactions might be once they knew her age, particularly Alex, who thought she was a student.

She decided that Ian was her best bet and although he was not the fit young hunk of her dreams, he was not bad looking and seemed intelligent and fun. She decided she would not make any first moves and see what hand fate dealt her. Ursula grabbed a glass of red wine and settled down to watch another episode of the Scandi noir series she was currently binge-watching.

Ursula was halfway through the episode when her phoned buzzed and she could see from the incoming number that it was Ian calling. She immediately answered and Ian said, "Hi Ursula, Ian here. So pleased we matched and would love to take you out on that dream date we talked about."

"That would be wonderful."

"I took the liberty of checking when they have a table so in the hope you would be keen, I have booked for 7.00 PM tomorrow if that works for you. Razor Edge is on the decks at Dynamo Bongo later that night. He is great."

"I love him as well and tomorrow is good. Where shall we meet?"

"How about 6.30 PM in The Bath Arms? It is really near the restaurant."

"Fantastic, see you then."

"Bye."

Ursula poured herself another glass of red wine and settled back to watch the end of the Swedish crime show.

Now, she had the date with Ian set up. She was warming to the idea of dating him rather than one of the young bucks. He was taking her to a Michelin starred restaurant and the best nightclub in Brighton. That was her kind of date. She felt thrilled and contented with her lot and was so pleased she had made an effort and gone to the speed dating.

Chapter 12

Sophie still had a grin on her face when she got to work. Her boss' PA guessed precisely why when she went past her desk to meet him. "Had a good night then Sophie, you naughty girl."

Sophie grinned even more and replied, "Good morning as well. Thanks, Sam."

However, Sophie's boss was not so perceptive and said, "Wipe that stupid grin off your face and concentrate, please Sophie."

Sophie left her office building at lunchtime to grab a sandwich to eat in a local park. She was eating the sandwich and watching some children feed the ducks in the park lake when Alex phoned. "Hi Alex, how are you? Still good for this evening?" said Sophie.

"Good and thanks for a fantastic night. I am afraid I am not going to be able to make it tonight as there is a bit of a family crisis and I need to go and look after my sister and her kids."

"Sorry to hear that. Nothing too serious, I hope."

"Not sure yet. My sister's husband has disappeared. He seems to have just vanished some time yesterday. He left for work in the morning as usual but never turned up. His phone is turned off and nobody who knows him heard or knows anything. Just weird and my sister is distraught."

"She must be. Best of luck and let me know when you know what is going on."

"Will do, must go."

With that, Alex hung up. Sophie suddenly felt totally deflated. A few minutes ago, she was on cloud nine and could not wait to get home and get her hands on Alex again. Now she would not see him this evening and did not know for how much longer. Sophie also had a slight doubt about his story about his sister.

Could it all be a lie to avoid telling her he did not want to see her again? Was it a way to put her on hold while he tried out some of the other dates he matched with last night? Sophie's brain was in overdrive with bad thoughts. She threw the rest of the sandwich into a rubbish bin and returned to work.

Sophie left her office at 5.15 PM and got the train back to Hove Station. Her phone pinged while she was on the train. She looked at the screen to see a new message from Alice, who she had met at the Yoga class. "Hi Sophie, I am at a loose end this evening and wondered if you fancy catching up. R U free at 7.00 PM for dinner and wine at my place?"

She was delighted with the offer. Just what she needed to avoid sitting at home brooding over Alex and his excuse. She replied immediately, "Sounds wonderful. See you at seven; love Sophie xxx."

The train was not delayed for once and Sophie had plenty of time to get home, change and get to Alice's place by 7.00 PM.

Alice had a flat in a converted Victorian terrace near Hove Library. The apartment was much larger than Sophie's and was beautifully decorated with all sorts of quirky pieces of art adorning the walls and shelves. "Wow, where did you find all these fabulous pieces?" said Sophie as she picked up and inspected a small sculpture.

"They are nearly all pieces I made myself."

"They are astonishingly good. So how come you work as a UX designer? Surely, you could be a professional artist with this kind of talent."

"You are very kind, Sophie, but I do not think they are that good. I just make them for my own pleasure."

"I am telling you seriously that they are outstanding. You must let me get a friend who has a gallery in Soho to look at them."

"No, really, I am happy to make them for my own pleasure. Anyway, what would you like to drink? I have made some of my favourite cocktail, Cosmopolitan."

"My favourite as well. That would be fab."

Alice gave Sophie her drink and they moved into the kitchen to chat while Alice cooked dinner. "Hope you like fish," said Alice.

"Love it. What have you got?"

"I saw a lovely line caught Sea Bass on the fish stall by the beach and could not resist it."

"Wow, that sounds awesome. I love Sea Bass."

"I will grill it and serve it with an Asian salsa and New Potatoes. Have made some orange and truffle ice cream for afterwards."

"Sounds delicious," said Sophie.

"Are you going to the Yoga again on Saturday?" asked Alice.

"Not really made my mind up yet. I cannot say I much enjoyed the first class. The only good thing about it was meeting you."

"You should at least stick with it for the classes you have pre-paid for. I promise it gets better. Saturday will be my fifth class and for the first time, I am looking forward to it. I would look forward to it even more if I knew you were coming."

"That is very sweet of you. I promise I will give it at least one more go."

"Perhaps we could have coffee afterwards again?"

"Yes, that sounds nice," said Sophie.

Alice was almost finished grilling the fish and Sophie helped set the table while she plated up.

"There is a bottle of Pinot Grigio in the fridge. Open it and pour us both a glass," said Alice.

Sophie did so and then they both sat down and enjoyed the delicious fish. "This is honestly the best piece of fish I have ever eaten and that includes in Michelin starred restaurants," said Sophie.

"You are too kind," said Alice, blushing.

Sophie was even more impressed by the orange and truffle ice cream. "That is the best thing I have ever eaten. Full stop."

Alice blushed even more and poured them some more wine. However, there was only enough for one glass, so she opened another bottle. Sophie then helped Alice clean up and stack the dishwasher. Afterwards, they took the glasses of wine into the lounge.

"This has been a wonderful evening. I was feeling pretty stressed and anxious at work and this was just what I needed to unwind a bit," said Sophie.

"If you are stressed, then let me give you one of my aromatherapy massages."

"That sounds divine. Are you sure?" said Sophie.

"I would love to. Come through and I will do it on the bed."

Sophie followed Alice into her bedroom. Alice heated some oils in her diffuser and the room soon smelled wonderful. She put a large bath towel on the bed and mixed some more oils for the massage. "Strip off and lie on the towel," said Alice.

Sophie was suddenly a little anxious about the whole thing but stripped down to her knickers and lay face down on the bed. She felt Alice climb onto the bed, straddle her and start the massage. Alice's technique was fantastic and Sophie soon forgot her inhibitions and dropped into a state of deep relaxation.

After about 15 minutes, Alice said, "Turn over now."

When she did, she was a little surprised to see that Alice had also stripped down to her knickers. Alice poured some oil into her hands and started massaging Sophie's legs. She then poured some oil onto Sophie's chest and rubbed her shoulders and then her breasts. Sophie found this last part sexually arousing and her nipples became erect.

Alice reacted by paying particular attention to the nipples and massaged them between her fingers. Sophie had always enjoyed when men did the same during sex and was now becoming even more aroused. Alice climbed on top of Sophie and started kissing her on the mouth. Sophie responded and they were soon in a passionate embrace.

An hour later, Sophie was lying naked next to Alice on her bed, wondering what had happened. The sex with Alice was incredible and she had multiple orgasms. She had never had any sexual attraction towards other women before and had not seen the prospect of sex with Alice until moments before it happened.

"Was that your first time with another woman?" asked Alice.

"Yes, how did you know?"

"I did not know, just guessing."

"Have you always been a lesbian?" asked Sophie.

"Never have been a full-on lesbian. I had plenty of straight sex and just a couple of times with another woman when it felt right. Tonight felt right."

"It felt right for me as well," said Sophie and she kissed Alice on her forehead.

They showered together and then returned to the lounge and finished the wine. "I hope what has happened will not get in the way of us also being friends," said Alice.

"Friends with benefits," said Sophie.

"I hate that expression, but I guess so. What I mean is that we can still be good friends first and if we both feel we would like to have sex again, then good, but if not, then that is OK as well."

"Sounds perfect," said Sophie.

"So I will see you at Yoga on Saturday and then we can go for coffee afterwards."

"Of course, but I have to go home now, as I have an early start tomorrow. See you Saturday."

Alice got up and saw Sophie out.

Back at her own flat, Sophie's head was spinning. What was going on in her life? Two days ago, it had been so long since she had sex that she felt she may become asexual. In the space of just over 24 hours, she had sexually assaulted an almost complete stranger in public, then lured him back to her flat to seduce him and then had lesbian sex with a woman she had only met once before.

Overnight, she had turned into a nymphomaniac. She decided she needed to cool things down. She needed to re-ground as slightly stuffy and serious Sophie of old.

Chapter 13

Alex was at work but still thinking about the night before with Sophie. He liked her so much he was scared. Not scared in the same way as when he thought she was some kind of man-eating nymphomaniac but scared by how much he liked her. She was beautiful, intelligent and independent. They really clicked both physically and emotionally. Could she be the one? Alex was interrupted in his thoughts by his phone ringing.

"Alex, it's Susan. I am so worried."

She sounded terrible and Alex replied, "What is wrong?"

"It's Pete. He never came home last night. I left messages on his phone all day yesterday, but he never replied. So I phoned his work and they said he never showed up for work yesterday morning, but he left here at the normal time."

"Have you reported it to the police?"

"Yes, but they just said not to worry. It happens all the time and there is nearly always some innocent explanation. They have put him on the missing persons register and will check the hospitals now but will not investigate any further until more time has passed."

"They are probably right. Probably nothing. How has he been lately?"

"Just the same old Pete. He never wears his feelings on his sleeve, but sure he was OK. We were discussing last night the prospect of taking the kids on a ski trip in winter."

Sue started crying and sobbed, "I don't know how I am going to cope without him. He was my rock."

"I will come right round. I will be there in about 30 minutes."

"There is no need."

"I am coming round to support you. End of story," said Alex.

He then phoned Sophie and explained he would not be able to meet up as planned and headed to his sister's house.

When he arrived at her house, his sister ran out to greet him. Still in tears, she hugged him and sobbed, "Thank you for coming."

"No problem. Where are the kids?"

"They are at school. They know nothing about Pete disappearing."

"Have you checked to see if any of Pete's things have gone?"

"The police got me to check and nothing seems to be missing."

"Have you checked with all his friends to see if they know anything?"

"His only real friend is Gordon and he is as baffled as me about what has happened. Gordon has been trying to find Pete as well and is checking with his work colleagues."

"This is so strange," said Alex, racking his brain to try and find any kind of rational explanation.

Just then, Sue's phone rang and she eagerly answered it. After a brief conversation with the caller, she hung up and said, "That was the police just to say that they have checked all the hospitals and there is no record of anybody fitting Pete's description having been admitted."

"Well, that is some good news," said Alex.

"But where is he then?" replied Sue and started crying again. Alex took Sue inside the house and sat her down in the lounge while he made them both a cup of tea. When he returned with the tea, he asked Sue if Pete had his own laptop or shared a family computer. "We share the one in the kitchen," said Sue.

"Do you know Pete's password?"

"It is pete123," "all lower case," replied Sue.

Alex logged in as Pete and, with Sue watching over his shoulder, looked through Pete's email inbox to see if there were any clues. Pete clearly hardly used email and everything was just junk mail. Alex opened the browser and looked at the browsing history. There were recent sites relating to the skiing holiday that Sue had mentioned and then many sites about football and, in particular, their local team Brighton and Hove Albion. Alex then noticed several sites visited about two weeks ago that were all about Sydney, Australia.

"Any idea why Pete was looking for information on Sydney?" asked Alex.

"No idea," replied Sue.

"Go and check if his passport has gone," said Alex.

A few minutes later, Sue returned with her and the kids' passports and proclaimed, "His is missing. Do you think he has left for Australia? That makes no sense and why would he not tell me he was going?"

"I have no idea, but I think you should call the police and tell them about the browsing and missing passport. They will be able to check if he did go."

Sue phoned the police and they promised to get back to her as soon as they had any updates.

Alex went with Sue to collect the kids from school. They had agreed that they would tell the kids that Daddy had to go away on a trip for work to buy themselves some time. Alex also decided to stay with Sue that night. Alex got some KFC for dinner, which was the kids' favourite.

After they had eaten, they put the kids to bed and Sue opened a bottle of wine for them to share. As they were drinking the wine, Sue got a call from the police. After a slightly longer conversation than before, Sue hung up and said, "He has gone to Sydney. He was on a flight that left from Heathrow yesterday afternoon. He should be landing in about 2 hours."

"Will the Australian police meet him and find what is going on?" asked Alex.

"There is nothing the police here or in Australia can do. Now we know he is not missing. They are closing the case. What Pete does and who he tells is his business, as long as it is within the rule of law."

"So they will do nothing."

"SFA," said Sue.

Chapter 14

Andy and Zoe had a lovely day spent at the Palace Pier. Zoe treated them to an unlimited rides ticket for the fairground at the end and they rode them all from the Log Flume, Big Dipper, Bumper Cars, Helta Skelter, Ghost Train and Wurlitzer. They then played on the Dolphin Derby and Andy won a giant teddy bear for Zoe. After that, they had some fish and chips in the pier restaurant and then found a karaoke contest in one of the bars. They entered and came second with a duet of Don't Go Breaking My Heart, the old Elton John and Kiki Dee number.

In the evening, Andy left Zoe at home and went to work in the Bath Arms. The pub was not that busy and he spent most of his time chatting with the other staff. At about 6.30, he was pleased to see Ursula, the beautiful young girl with the pixie haircut from the speed dating, come into the pub. She immediately went over and sat with an old balding guy who Andy assumed must be her father or possibly her boss. The balding guy came up to the bar for drinks, but Andy was already serving another customer, so he did not get the chance to find out.

About 20 minutes later, the balding guy left the table to go to the toilets, so Andy went over to speak with Ursula. "Hi, Ursula. I am Andy from the speed dating. Remember me."

"Of course I do and now I recall you said you worked here."

"Sorry, I have not called you yet. You were definitely my favourite, but one of the other matches phoned me first and persuaded me to see her. I did not want to cheat on you, so I thought I would let that run its course first. The good news is that the date was a disaster and I will not be seeing her again."

"Sorry, but you are too late. I am on a date with one of my other matches now."

"Surely not that old bald bloke. I thought he must be your dad."

"He is a lovely guy and not that old."

"Whatever, but if you change your mind and fancy hooking up, then just call me."

Andy took the empty glasses and headed back behind the bar, feeling frustrated and annoyed.

After the shift, he went back to Zoe's flat. She had waited up for him and was sitting in the lounge playing a game on her Xbox.

"How was work?" she asked.

"Pretty boring," replied Andy.

"Fancy a game," said Zoe, referring to the Xbox.

"How about a game of Hide the Sausage," said Andy.

"Sounds more fun."

They left the lounge to play their game in the bedroom.

Chapter 15

Ursula left work a little early, so she had plenty of time to get ready for her date with Ian. She had a long bath, did her makeup and then slipped into her favourite Zimmerman dress. She then called a taxi to take her to the Bath Arms, where she was to meet Ian. Unfortunately, the cab could not drop her outside the pub as it was in the pedestrianised Lanes area, so she had a short, uncomfortable walk on the cobblestones to the pub door. Inside the pub, she soon spotted Ian sitting at a table and joined him.

"You look fantastic," said Ian as he first saw her.

"Thank you. You scrub up pretty well yourself." Ian did indeed look pretty stylish in his Rick Owens outfit. Ian went up to the bar and came back with two glasses of Champagne.

"How was your day?" asked Ian as a conversation starter.

"Pretty average, to be honest. I hope to make a big sale today for us to produce a new music video for *Dog In The Snow*, but it fell through."

"Shame, good band. I like their stuff a lot."

"I never found out what you do for a living," asked Ursula.

"I was an IT project manager but recently have become a Scrum Master."

"That sounds much more interesting than an IT project manager but have I have no idea what it is. Is it something to do with rugby?"

Ian laughed and then said, "Nothing to do with rugby, just a new method for developing software called Scrum."

"So, really, you are still an IT project manager but with a new job title."

"You are a very perceptive woman."

They carried on chatting and were developing a good rapport when Ian said he needed to be excused and headed for the toilets. While he was gone, the barman came to collect their empty glasses.

Ursula was surprised and a little delighted to see Andy, the other guy she matched with from the speed dating. He made some excuse as to why he had not contacted her that Ursula saw through. She was not interested in being the second choice. When she mentioned she was on a date, Andy was very rude about how old Ian looked. Before Ian had returned, Andy left but not without one last attempt to get Ursula to go out with him.

To Ursula's great relief, the restaurant was very near the pub, so she did not have to walk far in her heels. They were given a great table in their own private booth. The waiter came and greeted them and gave them each a menu. Ian ordered two more glasses of Champagne. The food on the menu looked delicious but one thing about the menu, Ursula found odd.

"My menu has no prices on it," she said to Ian.

"It's not supposed to. Ladies do not pay for the meal."

"That is a very sexist attitude," said Ursula as she considered whether to take offence or not.

"I agree. It is a weird thing to do in this day and age. Shall I complain and get you one with prices?"

"Only if you want the lady to pay her share."

"Your company is enough payment," replied Ian.

Ursula squirmed and joked, "That is a relief. I thought you might want me to do a turn later."

"That is still an option I would like to keep open," replied Ian.

The waiter bought their Champagne over and talked them through the menu. They both decided it was too difficult to choose, so they selected the six-course degustation menu with matching wines.

The first matching wine arrived about 15 minutes later and the first course of food a few minutes later. The waiter announced the dish as he placed it in front of them. "Smoked carrot, washed rind, liquorice & sea buckthorn."

They both tucked in and looked at each other with wide-eyed expressions of delight. "Wow, this is good," said Ursula.

They had only just finished the matching wine from the first course when the second wine was served and a few minutes later, the second course appeared, "Raw Mooloolaba scallop, palm heart, white radish & sunflower," announced the waiter.

"I had this one when I came last week and it tastes even better the second time," said Ian.

"I have never eaten such elegant and delicious food," said Ursula.

The other four courses did not disappoint. They both agreed that it was one of the best meals they had ever had. After Ian had paid the bill, he suggested they walk to the nightclub. Ursula was not so keen. "I can only really walk a few yards in these heels. Can we get a cab?"

"No problem," said Ian and they walked the short distance to the nearest Taxi Rank. The nightclub was in the Kemp Town area of Brighton and only a 10-minute drive in the taxi, even with all the traffic and terrible one-way system.

As they approached the club, Ursula could see a long queue had already formed of people wanting to get inside. "Must be because Razor Edge is on the decks, usually pretty quiet on a Wednesday night?" said Ursula.

"Don't worry, we will not be queuing up to get in?" said Ian.

He went straight to the front of the queue and had a word in the head bouncer's ear. The bouncer immediately pulled back the rope barrier and ushered Ian and Ursula into the club.

"Friends in high places?" asked Ursula.

"My brother owns the place," replied Ian.

"Handy," said Ursula as she followed Ian into the VIP section of the club.

Ursula had a wonderful time at the club. Several local celebrities were in the VIP section and Ursula managed to get selfies with a footballer who had always had a crush on and an actor from her favourite soap opera. She also met some local musicians and took the chance to pitch her company for their music videos.

The guest DJ came on at 1.00 AM and did a 90-minute set. Ursula spent most of that time on the dancefloor and when they left at 2.45 AM were both exhausted. Ian got the bouncer to call them a taxi and dropped off Ursula at her flat.

"Thanks for a wonderful evening, Ian," slurred Ursula as she went to get out of the taxi.

"I hope it is the first of many more," said Ian, who then planted a kiss on her lips.

"Call me tomorrow," said Ursula and she got out of the taxi and entered her flat.

Chapter 16

Sophie's head was still spinning over the events of the two previous nights when she woke the next day. She got the train to work and during the journey, she continued to try and make sense of everything and decide what to do next.

She liked both Alex and Alice and wanted to make sure she remained close friends with them both. She also knew she wanted to have sex again with them both, but this latter thought was causing her most angst. She knew that Alice would be OK if she were bisexual but was not so sure if she would be happy if she knew she was having a heterosexual relationship with a man at the same time as having sex with her. She had no idea what Alex's reaction would be to her being bisexual.

Sophie did not know if being open with them both or keeping quiet and dating each as if they were in monogamous relationships with her was best. She decided she could not be deceitful, so the last option was out. Sophie decided that she would only have a sexual relationship with Alex and tell Alice they could only be friends from now on. She felt much happier and relaxed by the time she got to work.

She had a gap in her schedule at 3.30 PM, so she took the opportunity to call Alex and see the lay of the land with him. "Hi, Alex, it is Sophie here, just calling to see how things are going."

"Hi, Sophie, so good of you to call. Look so sorry about having to disappear after what happened on Tuesday night. I want you to know that I had a wonderful time and want to see lots more of you. All this is not any kind of excuse to not see you."

"That is great to hear, as I would love to see lots more of you as well. What has been going on with your sister and when will you be able to escape?"

Alex explained what had happened and that her husband was now in Sydney.

"That is so weird. He just left for the other side of the planet without saying a word to anybody."

"Seems like that is it. My sister is still a right mess, so I cannot see how I can leave her at the moment. However, her best friend has promised to come round on Friday and stay over, so how about we go out for dinner on Friday?"

"Sounds good. Come round to my place at 7.00 PM and we can find a place to eat locally on Church Road."

"See you then."

Sophie was relieved that Alex was still keen and her concerns about him having cold feet were misplaced. She spent the rest of the day in a much calmer frame of mind.

On the way home from the station, she picked up some takeaway Thai food and decided to have a quiet night on her own. Once home, she put the food in the oven to keep warm and changed into her pyjamas. She grabbed a glass of wine and then settled down to enjoy her dinner in front of the TV.

Chapter 17

Alex had slept on his sister's couch and was woken up at 6.30 AM by her kids wanting to play with Uncle Alex. He amused them with a game of I Spy while he prepared some breakfasts for everybody. The kids got their favourite chocolate flavoured cereal while he made some scrambled eggs on toast for himself and Sue. She came into the kitchen just as he finished preparing them. "Hi, Sis, how are you feeling?"

"Terrible. I hardly slept a wink of sleep. My head was spinning all night trying to fathom what was going on."

"Have some food and a nice cup of tea. It will make you feel better."

"I am not hungry."

"Please eat some. I have made it for you with chilli and tomato in the eggs just as you like."

"OK, I will try and eat some."

"I will take the kids to school, so once you have eaten the breakfast, you should go back to bed and try and get a little sleep. When I come back, we will work out what to do next to find out what the hell Pete is up to."

"You are so kind. OK, I will."

Alex took the kids to school and, on the way back, stopped at the local superstore to stock up on food and some treats. When he got back, Sue was asleep on her bed, so Alex left her. He phoned his work and let them know he would need another day of compassionate leave. Sue woke up after about an hour and joined Alex in the kitchen, where he was trying to find more clues from Pete's account on the family PC.

"Anything new?" asked Sue.

"Nothing on here, but I have another idea."

"What is it?"

"I have found a private detective agency based in Sydney that specialises in finding missing persons. I thought we could engage them to find Pete and tell us what he is doing."

"That sounds a great idea. If the police cannot help, it is our only option."

"I will send an email now and give them all the details and see what they say."

"Thanks, Alex, you have been a great help."

"Have you checked Pete's phone again yet? He must have landed by now."

"Checked it every 20 minutes since 2.00 AM and still not turned on. Suspect he has ditched his UK SIM and swapped for an Australian one."

"Yes, I thought that is a most likely option as well."

Alex wrote the email to the Australian detective agency and then persuaded Sue to go out for a walk with him along the seafront for some fresh air. While out walking, they stopped off at Café and both enjoyed a bacon roll and coffee.

When they got back, Alex was pleased when Sue said she was tired and would go and get some more sleep. When she had finished her siesta, she looked much better than she had since before Pete disappeared. Alex made her a cup of tea. "Glad you are feeling better," said Alex.

"I decided that I am not going to sit around and worry about what has happened to Pete. It looks like he has left me but never dared to tell me. To be honest, things between us have not been that great recently. Pete has been very withdrawn and has not really engaged with the family or me for months. I am not going to waste any more time on the selfish, cowardly bastard. I have decided to move on."

"Fantastic! That is exactly what you should do. Do you still want to do the private detective thing?"

"Yes, I still want to find the miserable bastard and give him hell. I have phoned Tina and she is coming round on Friday and staying over."

Tina was Sue's best friend who now lived in Southampton, about 2 hours' drive away along the coast. "That will be good for you," said Alex.

Sue left to pick up the kids from school and while she was gone, Alex was pleased to get a call from Sophie. They arranged to meet on Friday evening while Tina was looking out for Sue, although Alex hoped she would not need him around much longer, anyway. She seemed to be getting over the shock of Pete leaving remarkably well. Alex thought it must be primarily shock that he left and not that much regret on Sue's part.

161

Chapter 18

Andy had enjoyed their game of Hide the Sausage the previous night and was hoping to carry on playing the next morning, but Zoe was not in the mood. In fact, she was in a very cranky mood, so Andy left her to lie in while he went out for a run along the seafront. His favourite run was to head east to Brighton Marina and back, but he decided to head off in the opposite direction for a change this morning. He headed west along the seafront towards the port of Shoreham.

About halfway along was a recreational area called Hove Lagoon, with various water sports facilities and a famous café run by the DJ Fat Boy Slim. Andy was running past the café when he spotted Jo from the speed dating evening waiting outside for a takeaway coffee. He stopped and went up to her and said, "Hi Jo, I am back now. Sorry I had to stall you the other day but now keen to hook up."

Jo looked at him suspiciously. "Other girl not work out or are you cheating on her already?" replied Jo.

"You have got the wrong end of the stick, Jo. You were the only one that I matched with and it was only because my friend Colin, who I went to the speed dating with, was taken seriously ill that I did not call you right after the event."

"Sorry, what happened to Colin and is he OK now?"

"We were walking to the pub when he was suddenly bent over in agony. I called an ambulance and he was taken to the hospital for an emergency Appendectomy. Apparently, he was lucky and they caught it before the appendix burst, so he should be fine."

"Sorry for doubting you. I was looking forward to getting to know you better."

"No more time to waste, then. What are your plans for the rest of the day?"

"I have to complete an assignment for my Uni degree by midnight but should only take a couple of hours's work."

"Do you live near here?"

162

"Yes, just across the road. I was going to take my coffee home. Want to grab one and join me?"

"Sounds great."

Andy got himself a Flat White and headed back to her flat with Jo. When they got to the flat, Andy said, "Do you mind if I have a quick shower? I am very sweaty from the run."

"No, but on one condition," said Jo.

"What is that?"

"I can join you," said Jo and started to remove her clothes.

After the shower, they had sex and then another shower. Unfortunately, Jo got carried away in the second shower, so they had sex again, followed by a third and final shower. They then heated their cold coffees in the microwave and relaxed in Jo's lounge. "How come you have such a great flat?" said Andy looking at the sea views from her window.

"My parents bought it for me to use while I am studying at Sussex University."

"What year are you in?"

"This is my first year. The flat is nice but not being in the accommodation on campus means I have not made any friends yet. I was a bit lonely, so I decided to try the speed dating."

"Have you thought of getting a flatmate?"

"Are you interested then?" said Jo.

Andy was not fishing for this invite and was not sure what to say. It was a lovely flat, but he had only just moved in with Zoe.

"I am committed to staying where I am. The friend I live with relies on me for my share of the rent, so I could not dump her in it and move out."

"You said her. You live with a woman."

"Yes, but nothing going on. Her name is Zoe. She is a lesbian."

"Oh, OK then. You can stay over here whenever you want anyway," said Jo.

Andy's phone buzzed and saw it was a message from Zoe. "Where the hell are you?"

Andy told Jo, "That was a message from her. I promised to help her move some furniture for one of her lesbian friends and am late, so better leave."

"When will I see you again?"

"Soon," said Andy and he gave Jo a quick kiss and left.

Andy got some severe grief from Zoe when he eventually got back from his run. He told her he had got carried away and ended up running to Worthing and back, which was about 20miles. She started pretty dubious but then decided she was impressed by his level of fitness.

"I am knackered after 5 miles. Twenty miles is more than two-thirds of a full marathon. Have you ever done the whole marathon distance?" asked Zoe.

"I have done the Sydney Marathon twice," replied Andy and for once was not telling a lie.

"Wow, what was your best time?"

"The first time I managed 4:08."

"That is a seriously brilliant time for a first marathon. I am impressed. What happened in the second one?"

"I was pushing hard to break 4 hours and guess I overdid it at the start or was not fit enough as by the end I could only manage little more than a jogging pace."

"I was thinking of training for the Brighton Marathon next April. Apparently, it is a fast course, so perhaps you can try and beat the 4 hours here and we could train together," said Zoe.

Andy was keen to get her back on his side and readily agreed and they pencilled in a first run the following day. But, unfortunately, Andy had to work at the pub from 11.30 AM to 6.30 PM, so he rushed off and promised Zoe he would come straight home after his shift.

During the middle of the afternoon, an attractive brunette came up to the bar while he was serving another customer and blew him a kiss. He vaguely recognised her but was not sure how he knew her. After he had finished serving the customer, he went over to see her. "Hi there," he said.

"Sorry to surprise you like this bit. I was just passing and remember you said at the speed dating event that you worked here." Andy now knew why he recognised her but could not remember her name.

"Nice to see you again. Sorry, I did not get back to you."

"No worries, I had three other matched that did. I picked the best one and had one date, but it was awful. You were always the one I really wanted to ask me out."

"I had a similar experience but will not be seeing her again, so no reason why we cannot hook up."

"Great, what time do you finish?"

"6.30 PM."

"Great, I will come back then. My name is Annie, by the way, in case you have forgotten."

Andy was now thinking about what excuse he could use with Zoe. He could not say he was working, as she may well come down to the pub. He thought about re-using the story about Colin having appendicitis that he gave to Jo but decided that was too risky, as Zoe knew him.

He had a sudden spark of inspiration and sent a message to Zoe. "Sorry, but I have just remembered that I promised to help one of the guys to move flats after work tonight. He has hired a van and everything, so I cannot let him down. I will get back as soon as I can. It should not be that late. Love Andy xx."

Zoe sent back a sad face emoji and a love heart.

Annie returned to the pub at 6.20 PM, grabbed a stool at the bar and said, "I will have a gin and tonic while I am waiting."

"One G&T for the beautiful lady coming up," replied Andy.

When he had given her the drink, he asked, "What do you fancy doing tonight? I have an early start tomorrow, so I cannot be too late, I am afraid."

"How about coming back to my flat for a Pizza and a shag? My flatmate is out all evening."

"Perfect, my two favourite things," quipped Andy.

Andy left Annie's place about 10.00 PM and on the way back to Zoe's flat, his phone pinged. It was Ursula, the one match he really fancied and who had turned him down for the old bloke in the pub. When Andy got home, Zoe was still up and said, "How did you get on?"

"That bloke has so much stuff, it is unbelievable. It would have taken until 1.00 AM to move everything. I promised you I would not be too late, so I told him we will have to finish it after work tomorrow."

"That means you will be out all afternoon and evening tomorrow as well," sulked Zoe.

"I am so sorry, Zoe. I will make it up to you. I have taken Sunday off. Why don't you invite your friend Sally and her new boyfriend around and I will do a proper Ozzie BBQ for you all?"

"That sounds wonderful," said Zoe and kissed Andy.

Chapter 19

Ursula's alarm went off at 6.30 AM and she was in no state to get up. She had a splitting headache and could only just open her eyes to narrow slits. She turned the alarm off and went back to sleep.

When she woke up again, it was 9.30 AM and she felt just about well enough to get up. She immediately sent a text to her boss to say she was feeling unwell and would not be coming into the office until later, if at all. She then had a long invigorating shower, followed by fried bacon and eggs. This was her go-to recipe for overcoming a hangover and it worked as usual. By 11.00 AM, she was feeling good and briefly considered heading onto the office.

However, she had done enough unpaid overtime recently, so she decided to take things easy for the rest of the morning and go in later. She reflected on the time she spent with Ian the previous night and what fun she had. She sent a message to Ian, "Thanks for the fabulous evening. I had so much fun and hope we can see each other again soon. Love Ursula XXXX."

Ian replied almost immediately, "I had lots of fun as well. Fancy dinner at my place tonight?"

Ursula could think of no reason why not, so she replied, "Sounds great."

Ian replied with his address and said she should be there at 7.00 PM.

Ursula had a pang of guilt and so did spend the afternoon at work. She returned to her flat at 5.30 PM and got ready to meet with Ian. His address was a fair way from where she lived, so she booked an Uber to take her there at 6.40 PM.

When she arrived, she was impressed with the lovely Victorian terrace house that Ian lived in. She rang the doorbell and it was answered by Ian with a glass of Champagne in his hand for her. They both went through to the kitchen so Ian could finish preparing the food. Once the food was all prepared and in the oven, they went into the lounge.

"You have a beautiful house," said Ursula.

"When our mother died last year, I used my inheritance to buy this place and my brother bought his nightclub."

"Did you consider buying a business rather than a house?"

"Not really. Ian, my brother, is eight years younger. I am getting to the age when I wanted to put down some roots and perhaps start a family."

"I thought it was normally women who get broody in their late thirties, not men."

"Broody is a bit strong. I just want to have a settled life for the long term. What about you?"

"I guess my emotional age is closer to the biological age everybody thinks I am. I would have got a nightclub like your brother."

"You never worry about age catching up with you?"

"I am not desperate to have kids and there is still enough time for that. However, I sometimes feel lonely as so many friends have families now and socialise much less, but I would rather find some more single friends than join them in the family and kids club for now."

Ursula was beginning to think that Ian was after a lot more than her from their relationship. He seemed to want a lifetime partner and mother of his children. She wanted some fun and an occasional shag. Ian went back into the kitchen and called Ursula to come through a few minutes later to eat their meals. Ian had prepared a Beef Wellington and served it with some Argentinian Malbec wine. The food was but a bit stodgy for Ursula's taste. Maybe she had been spoilt the previous night at the restaurant.

After the meal, they returned to the lounge and finished off the Malbec. "I hope I did not put you off me earlier with all that talk about settling down. I am not about to get heavy. Let's just take things one day at a time and have some fun," said Ian.

"I was a bit worried, to be honest, but I like your suggestion." Ursula moved closer to Ian and stroked his hair with her fingers. He responded by kissing her on the back of her neck. But, unfortunately, Ursula hated being kissed there and pulled away from him. "Sorry, but I hate being kissed there. It makes my whole spine tingle," said Ursula.

"Never mind, I have an early start anyway, so let's call it a day," said an obviously offended Ian.

"If that is what you want, then fine," said Ursula and got up and left.

By the time Ursula arrived home, she was furious with Ian. The more she thought about what had happened, the more she felt that Ian had acted like a complete pratt. It was not the first time that a man had made the same mistake. They usually laughed it off and made a joke of the whole thing.

Ursula poured herself a large glass of wine and got out her phone. She found the contact details for Andy and sent him a message. "I have not stopped thinking about you since we met in the pub. My date was a miserable old bastard and a big mistake. Can we meet and let me make things up to you? Love Ursula XXXX."

It did not take long for Andy to reply, "That is wonderful. How about I come around to your place at 6.30 PM tomorrow?"

Ursula sent him her address and an OK emoji.

Chapter 20

Sophie had a pleasant but dull day at work and arrived home with Alex in plenty of time for her date. Alex arrived at Sophie's flat right on 7.00 PM as planned. He buzzed her flat and she said she would come down. Moments later, she opened the front door and greeted Alex with a big kiss on the lips. "Good evening, new boyfriend," said Sophie.

"Hi there, sexy," said Alex and took Sophie's hand.

They walked hand in hand up to the start of the nearby restaurant strip. They both liked the look of a Spanish Tapas restaurant and got a table in the courtyard out the back. They ordered a selection of Tapas and, at Sophie's insistence, a carafe of Sangria.

"I love Sangria. It reminds me of the long hot days on Spanish beach holidays when I was at Uni. Just one jug, then we will switch to the Rioja you spotted," promised Sophie.

"This is much nicer than I expected. Can stick with it if you like."

"How is your sister?" asked Sophie.

"Remarkably well. Now she is over the shock of Pete's disappearing act. She seems pleased he has gone and keen to build a new life."

"Do you suspect something was going on before and that is why he ran off?"

"Not sure and to be honest, I would rather let sleeping dogs lie and just be grateful that Sue is so positive."

"Have you hired the detective to find him, though?"

"Yes, Sue wanted to make sure he pays for his cowardice in sneaking off. I spoke to him this morning. He seemed pretty confident of finding him and will then keep him under surveillance for a few days and report back what he is up to."

"How exciting. Seems just like in a movie. Maybe he is KGB double agent."

"Knowing Pete, I doubt he is doing anything remotely exciting."

The first round of their Tapas dishes arrived and they tucked into the Chorizo in Sherry and Spanish Tortilla. "So you are free and do not need to stay at your sisters and more?" asked Sophie.

"Yes, she told me to leave. So, I collected all my stuff and took it back to my flat this afternoon."

"Can you stay over with me tonight?" asked Sophie.

"I was hoping that would be the plan," said Alex and he produced a toothbrush that he had put in his pocket.

"Now I think I am easy," said Sophie.

"Not at all. I am just a born optimist," replied Alex.

They finished the rest of their Tapas and had another jug of Sangria before heading the short distance back to Sophie's flat.

The next morning, Sophie got up first and was making breakfast when her phone pinged, "Don't forget Yoga at 11.00 AM."

It was a message from Alice. Sophie did not want to go, but she had promised Alice and did not want to let her new friend down. She finished making the breakfast and then called out to Alex, "Come on, lazy bones, breakfast is ready."

"Coming," shouted Alex and arrived in the kitchen a few minutes later.

"I have to go to a Yoga class at 11.00 AM, but it would be great if we could spend some time together after lunch," said Sophie.

"That works for me. I need some time to go home to clean up and do some shopping. The weather looks fab, so how about we go to the beach this afternoon?"

"Sounds fun. See you on the beach opposite the end of my road at 2.00 PM."

After eating breakfast, Alex headed back to his flat and Sophie got ready for Yoga. She left a little later than before and arrived just before the class started. Alice had kept a space on the floor next to her, free for Sophie to use. Sophie found the class marginally less painful than the first one but was not convinced she could endure a third one.

After the class, she went to the same café as before with Alice. "Told you it gets better," said Alice when she admitted it was not as bad as before.

"I will try and stick with it," lied Sophie.

"What are you doing tonight?" asked Alice. "I am at a loose end and hoped you would come around and we could watch a movie or perhaps play some board games."

Sophie decided she needed to tell Alice about Alex. "I would love to, but I have just met this new guy and will probably see him tonight. So perhaps we could do it next week."

"What new guy? How did you meet? Tell me all," said a very excited Alice. This was not the reaction Sophie expected, but she was pleased that Alice was excited for her.

"His name is Alex and we met at a speed dating event last week. We went out for Tapas last night and had a lovely time."

"What happened after Tapas?" asked Alice.

"What do you mean?"

"Did you stay at his place?"

"Actually, he stayed over at my place."

"Well done, Sophie. I hope it all works out for you. When can I meet him?"

"Thanks, Alice, that is very sweet of you. Not sure what our plans are yet but sure you can meet him soon."

"I have a brilliant idea. Bring him round to my place tonight. I will cook dinner and we can play some board games. I promise I will let you take him home for another night of passion afterwards."

"I am not sure. I will ask him and let you know later."

They finished their coffees and as they left, Alice said, "Let me know if you are coming round by 3 o'clock, so I have time to buy stuff for dinner and get it ready."

Sophie went back to her flat and got her beach stuff ready. Just before 2.00 PM, Sophie headed down to the seafront at the bottom of her road. She crossed the main seafront road and made her way to the nearest pebble beach. The tide was out and she quickly spotted Alex waiting for her in the shallow water at the edge of the sea. She joined him and they walked hand in hand along the sand that the low tide had exposed.

"I met my friend Alice at Yoga and told her about you. She is keen to meet you and has invited us both round for dinner tonight. She is a fantastic cook. What do you think?"

"Sounds like a great idea. Restaurants are always so packed on a Saturday."

Sophie got out her phone and confirmed with Alice that they would be around for dinner. After completing their walk up the beach, they found a spot to lay down their towels and enjoy some sunbathing.

Chapter 21

Andy had set the alarm for 6.00 AM so he and Zoe could go for their early morning run. Zoe was obviously not a morning person, but Andy coaxed her out of bed. They got changed into their running gear and jogged down to Hove Lawns on the seafront to do some stretching and warm-up exercises. "What is your best time for 5 miles?" Andy asked Zoe.

"I did 38 minutes in a charity run."

"That is pretty good. You are no slouch. Let's start with a pace of 9 minutes a mile and see how you go then."

"What would my marathon time be at that pace?"

"About 4 hours, but running at that pace for 5 miles and 26 miles is very different."

"I know, but I am a competitive bitch and want to beat your time."

"Challenge accepted," said Andy. "It is 5 miles to Shoreham, so let's run there and see how we are going."

"Sounds good," said Zoe and they both started running towards Shoreham. They ran alongside each other, with Andy setting the pace. Andy was pretty impressed with the way Zoe was able to keep up. They reached the high street in Shoreham in 45 minutes. Right on the pace.

"You did fantastically. How are you feeling?" Andy asked Zoe.

"I feel a bit tired but pleased with how the run went. I felt I had a good rhythm and was never out of breath."

"You had a great running style. Really efficient. So many runners waste energy with unnecessary body movements, but you were very smooth."

"Thanks, Andy," said Zoe with a big grin on her face. "What next? Do we run back?"

"Not quite. Do not want to overdo things and get injured at this stage, so we will walk halfway back, then jog the last half."

"OK, Coach," joked Zoe and they both headed back to Hove.

Back in Hove, they stopped at the Meeting Place Café and treated themselves to some breakfast. By the time they had finished eating, the sun was beating down and they both felt like a cold dip in the sea. So they stripped down to their underwear and dived into the waves. "Ice baths are all the rage, but this is even colder," joked Andy.

"You Ozzie wimp," teased Zoe.

They did not stay long in the sea and headed back to Zoe's flat for a hot shower. After that, they spent a chilled morning just listening to some music and reading before Andy had to leave for his shift at the Bath Arms. "Try and get back as quickly as you can," pleaded Zoe as he went.

After his shift had finished, Andy went around to the address that Ursula had given him. She answered the door in just a skimpy tee-shirt, so Andy knew what kind of evening he was about to have. At 10.00 PM, he made an excuse about needing to video conference his mother in Australia for her birthday and left. He arrived back with Zoe by 10.30 PM. "Sorry I was not back earlier. We went as fast as we could, but he had so much junk."

"You are back now. So let's snuggle up on the sofa and watch a movie together."

"Sounds great," said Andy, secretly relieved she did not want sex, as his equipment was probably worn out. Ursula was even more demanding than Annie.

They both fell asleep on the sofa before the movie had finished. Andy woke first and carried Zoe, still asleep, back to her bed. The alarm went off at 6.00 AM as they had not re-set it. Since they were both awake, they decided to go for another run. So they changed and again headed down to Hove Lawns.

"This time, I think we will try and run the whole ten miles to Shoreham and back, but I will vary the pace, so we do 2 miles at full pace followed by two miles at a slower pace and then back to full pace again. That way, we will build up your endurance without exhausting you."

"Sounds like a good plan, Coach," said Zoe.

They managed to do the entire 10 miles, but in the end, Zoe was still exhausted and did not feel like breakfast straight away. So instead, they went into the sea for their ice bath treatment. After the swim, Zoe lay in the sun to warm up and recover. Andy ran back to her flat to get them both towels and fresh clothes. After they had dried themselves and put on the new clothes, Andy asked Zoe if she now fancied some breakfast.

"That would be nice, but I would prefer to have some back at the flat. Let's stop at that little bakery near Brunswick Square and get some freshly baked croissants."

"Tell you what, you go back to the flat to shower and make the coffee and I will get the croissants," said Andy.

"That would be lovely," said Zoe and kissed Andy.

Zoe headed back to her flat and Andy headed towards the bakery. He picked up the croissants and headed towards Zoe's flat when he saw Jo run along the pavement towards him. She stopped and took out her earphones when she spotted him. "Hi Andy, just out for my morning run. When are you going to call me and meet up again?"

"I have been helping a mate move house and do some renovation work. Will be busy all weekend but could come round on Monday."

"That would be great. Since you left, I have been really lonely. Come around anytime, as I have no Uni classes on Mondays."

"OK, will be around about 11.00 AM then."

"Probably still be in bed at that time but guess that is OK," said Jo with a mischievous smirk on her face.

When Andy arrived back at Zoe's flat, she had already showered and the coffee was bubbling away in the Espresso maker. Andy had a quick shower and then joined Zoe for breakfast. "I am enjoying our running so much," said Zoe.

"Same here. You are a natural. Cannot wait to bring out your full potential," replied Andy.

"I also love how the running is bringing us closer together," said Zoe.

Andy smiled and changed the subject. "I will go and buy the food for the BBQ this morning. Do you think that lamb chops and steaks would be OK?"

"Sure, that would be good. I know they both like their meat," replied Zoe.

"Don't forget that I am doing a double shift today so I can have Sunday off. I will be working from 11.30 until we close," said Andy.

"I know," said Zoe. "I thought I would come down and sit at the bar. I could not face another night on my own."

"That is a good idea," said Andy.

Chapter 22

After spending a couple of hours on the beach, Alex and Sophie had a quick drink in one of the seafront pubs before returning to Sophie's flat. They chilled out for the rest of the afternoon, listening to some music and chatting. They then got changed and headed off to walk the short distance to Alice's flat.

Alice buzzed them in and was waiting at the door to her flat when they entered the building. Alex thought that Alice was just what he expected one of Sophie's friends to be like. She was about the same age as Sophie but a little thinner and shorter with a cute pointy nose and big blue eyes. She was also very excited to see them and kissed both Sophie and him before they had got inside the flat.

Once inside, Alice said, "I have made us all some of my special cocktails," and she disappeared into the kitchen and then returned with three glasses. "These are Cosmopolitans. Sophie and my favourite."

"My favourite as well," said Alex. They clinked glasses and sipped their cocktails. '*Wow, this is strong,*' thought Alex.

They carried on chatting and Alice refilled their cocktails. Alex was enjoying himself. The three of them really clicked and the conversation flowed effortlessly. Alice left and went to the kitchen to prepare their dinner. "I really like your friend," said Alex. "She is so much fun."

"Yes, she is. I have been so lucky finding you and her," replied Sophie.

"Does she have a boyfriend?"

"Pretty sure she is single. I don't think she has many friends in Brighton apart from me."

"Perhaps we should try and fix her up with somebody."

"Yes, that would be good. Do you know anybody?"

"Not off the top of my head, but let me give it some thought."

Alice called from the kitchen for them to go through to eat. Alice had made a Kingfish Ceviche.

"This Ceviche is unbelievably good," said Alex.

"Your cooking is fantastic again," added Sophie.

The main course was a roasted spatchcock served with Potato Dauphinoise and green beans.

Alex thought it was one of the best dishes he had ever tasted. "You are a cookery genius. This chicken is brilliant." The dessert of a chocolate Fondant with clotted cream had Sophie squirming with pleasure. "Can I pay you to cook all my meals?" said Sophie. "I love your food so much."

They all helped Alice clear up and then retired to the lounge. They all had another glass of wine and then Alice said, "How about a game of something? I have loads of board games. Why don't you pick one, Alex? They are all in that cupboard next to the bookshelf."

Alex went over and came back with a small box with 'Truth or Dare' written. "What about this one?" he suggested.

"I am not so sure," said Alice. "It is a bit rude. What about Risk or Monopoly?"

"They are boring. This sounds more fun," said Sophie.

"Don't say I did not warn you," said Alice.

Alice explained that there were three piles of cards, Questions, Dares and Forfeits. Each player took a turn to take either a question or a dare. They have to answer the question or do the dare. If they do not want to answer the question with the truth or do the dare, then they will be given a forfeit. The forfeits are like the dares but much worse. Sophie went first and took a question. "What is the last lie you told," readout Alice.

"That is easy," said Sophie. "I told Alice I would go to Yoga until my pre-paid sessions are done, but sorry Alice, I hate it and am not going anymore."

"I am not that surprised," said Alice. "I could see you hated it."

"I love Yoga," said Alex. "Can I have your lesson credits then?"

"Sure can. Shame to waste them," said Sophie.

"Look like we have a date next Saturday, then Alice."

"Cool, that will be great," said Alice.

Alex went next and took a dare card. "Show us your party trick."

"That is easy as well," said Alex and licked the end of his nose with his tongue.

"That is why I decided to go out with him," Sophie said to Alice.

"I can see how that long tongue could be very handy," replied Alice.

176

Alice went next and decided on having a question, "Who was the last person you had sex with?" readout Alex.

Alice went very red and looked at Sophie, who was also blushing. Luckily, Alex never noticed and Alice said, "I will take a forfeit."

"Really!" exclaimed Alex. "It cannot be that embarrassing."

"Just give me the forfeit," said Alice.

Alex read it out. "Massage the feet of the person on your right. That is you, Sophie."

Alice took off Sophie's shoes and gave Sophie her foot massage using some of the massage oil. Alex noticed that Sophie was really enjoying it. "Alice must be as good a masseur as she is a cook, judging by the expression on your face," said Alex.

Sophie just purred.

It was Sophie's turn to go next and she went for a dare this time. "Close your eyes and guess who kisses you. Take a forfeit if you get it wrong."

Sophie closed her eyes and Alex kissed her on the lips. To try and confuse her, he used an awful lot of tongue. "Easy," said Sophie. "I would recognise that Armani scent and giant tongue anywhere."

Alex followed and decided to take a question. "Which famous actress do you have a secret crush on?" readout Alice.

"That is such a lame question," complained Sophie.

"The answer is a young Helen Hunt," said Alex.

"My god, that is who Sophie looks like. I have been trying to think who she reminded me of since we met," said Alice.

"It has been mentioned before?" said Sophie.

"And I did tell you that you were my dream woman," said Alex.

It was Alice's turn next and she picked a dare. "Eat a raw egg," read out Alex.

"Shit, not that one," said Alice. "I always seem to draw that and there is no way I could swallow that slimy egg, Yuk. So I will have to take a forfeit."

Alex picked the next forfeit card and read it out. "Perform a lap dance for the person on your left."

"Do it for us both," said Sophie and snuggled up to Alex.

Alice started her lap dance and had soon removed her blouse and skirt to reveal a very sexy matching bra and panties. Alice writhed around in her underwear close to Alex and Sophie. Alex was getting very aroused and had a strange feeling that Sophie was as well. When Sophie reached out and kissed Alice, he did the same. Alice recoiled in horror and screamed, "What do you think you are doing?"

"I am sorry, Alice. I got carried away," said Sophie.

"Me as well. Sorry Alice, but you were so sexy," added Alex.

After Alice had calmed down, something suddenly dawned on Alex. Alice's dancing had definitely aroused Sophie and he asked, "Are you bisexual, Sophie?"

"Not until last week," replied Sophie and explained about her night with Alice.

"So it was me kissing you that made you recoil in horror," said Alex to Alice.

"Not at all. It was both of you doing it that freaked me. I would happily have sex with either of you, but the threesome thing makes my skin crawl."

"Would you be OK if I was had sex with Alice?" Alex asked Sophie.

"I would be fine if we were still having sex and I was also allowed to go with Alice."

"What about you, Alice?"

"It is all too weird for me," said Alice.

"Why weird, you and Sophie both get to have sexual partners for each of your preferences and I get to have sex with two women I find incredibly sexy. We also get to have fun together as three friends."

"Putting things that way, it sounds wonderful. I am willing to give it a go," said Alice.

"Me as well," said Sophie, "but I want Alice to do a private lap dance for me tomorrow night."

"And you can do one for me tonight, Sophie," said Alex.

Chapter 23

It was 6.00 PM and Andy was over halfway through his marathon double shift. The afternoon had been relatively uneventful. His recent exertions had left him feeling pretty tired, so he hoped the evening would be the same. He was looking forward to his day off tomorrow. At about 7.30 PM, Zoe came in and grabbed a bar stool. "Hi Zoe, good to see you. What would you like to drink?"

"I will have a large glass of Chardonnay, please. The good Australian one."

"Coming right up," said Andy and prepared Zoe her drink.

At about 8.30 PM, Andy was horrified to see Ursula enter the pub and come up to the bar. "Hi, Andy. I was at a loose end, so thought I might as well come and have a drink."

Luckily for Andy, he was serving at the other end of the bar, to where Zoe was sitting.

"I will be swamped so will not be able to speak with you much," replied Andy.

"No problem, just stop by when you can. Get me a glass of Prosecco."

Andy gave Ursula her drink. He was relieved there were no spare seats at the bar and she had to get a table near the door.

Things got more complicated 10 minutes later when Annie came in. "Hi Andy, though I would hang here tonight."

To make things worse, Annie sat at the table next to Ursula. Andy's head was spinning as he started to panic.

It nearly exploded 5 minutes later when Jo arrived as well. "Hi Andy. I thought it would be cool to come down and keep you company."

She could not find a spare table, so to Andy's horror, asked Annie if she could use the spare seat at her table. Andy's heart sank further as Annie agreed and Jo sat down.

"Fuck," said Andy under his breath. He knew it would now only be a matter of time before his cover would be blown. Out of the corner of his eye, Andy saw

179

Annie and Jo having an increasingly animated discussion that was punctuated by lots of staring across the room at him. He then saw Ursula join the discussion and all three women were then marching across the room towards him.

"You lying bastard, you can forget seeing me again," said Ursula.

"Or me, you rat," added Annie.

"I hate you," said a tearful Jo and then all three turned around and left the pub.

"What was that all about?" said Zoe, looking concerned.

"They were three of the women I matched with at the speed dating. I had been trying to get rid of them all week, but they would not take no for an answer. So, in the end, I agreed to meet them all tonight in here. When they each turned up, I told them again I was taken and that they could console themselves with the other two sitting over there."

"That was very clever. If they ever bother you again, then just let me know and I will sort them out."

"Thanks, Zoe," said Andy.

At that moment, Sally and Tim came into the bar. "Hi, Zoe," said Sally. "I was hoping you would be here." Sally pushed Tim, her boyfriend, forward and introduced him. Zoe invited them both to the BBQ that Andy was doing the next day at her place. They both accepted.

Chapter 24

Three weeks later

Sophie had invited Alex and Alice around to her flat for dinner. She was initially stressed about competing with Alice in the culinary stakes but had been much more relaxed once she decided to do her own thing and not produce a MasterChef style meal. Her own thing was around a Mexican theme and she had purchased most of the food in Marks and Spencer's food department.

She was sure nobody would know once she had taken everything out of the packaging and presented it in her crockery. She had also purchased plenty of the ingredients to make Margaritas. As a final touch, she found some giant sombreros for them to wear in a junk shop in the North Laines.

Alice had stayed with Alex the previous night. In the short time they had been in their three-way relationship, they had already developed certain routines. Alice and Alex both went to Yoga on Saturday morning, so they stayed at Alex's flat the night before. They all met up as a threesome on Saturdays and Sundays and Alex and Sophie usually slept together on Saturday night. They all went out together on Wednesday night to a local pub quiz. Sophie and Alice usually slept together after the quiz night.

Alex and Alice rang Sophie's intercom and she buzzed them in. She met them at her door and had their sombreros ready for them to put on. "Bienvenido," said Sophie. She led them through to her lounge and gave them both a Margarita to drink. As always, the three of them had a fabulous evening and Alice even complimented Sophie on her food. "I must confess that I cheated a bit on the food," confessed Sophie. "I got a little help from Mr Marks and Mr Spencer."

"Who are they?" asked Alex.

"You know Marks and Spencer, the department store that has a food hall," said Alice.

"It was so nice. I thought they must be the name of chefs."

They all laughed and then Alice said, "I love the relationship that the three of us have so much, but I have a problem."

"What is that?" asked a worried Sophie.

"A guy at work has asked me out," said Alice.

"Do you like him?" asked Alex.

"I have adored him ever since I started working there but thought I had no chance. He told me yesterday that he had split up with his girlfriend and so could now date me. Apparently, he always liked me as well."

"You should definitely go out with him if you feel that way," said Alex. "I was so lucky to have our relationship, even if only for a few weeks and we will still be able to be friends."

"What do you think?" Alice asked Sophie.

Sophie burst into tears. When she had composed herself a little, she said, "I love you, Alice and do not want to lose you. I am also grateful for the wonderful times we have had. I have been so happy over these last few weeks."

"I have loved it as well," said Alice, "but cannot help think it will never be a permanent thing and do not want to miss my chance with Rob."

"I understand and am just being silly and a bit selfish," said Sophie. "Go out with Rob and we can all carry on being friends."

"Unfortunately, without benefits," quipped Alex.

Chapter 25

Andy was relieved he had, at last, managed to unravel the mess he had created with his arrogance and voracious sexual appetite. He knew all along he should have told each of the other matches he was not interested in, but they were all so beautiful and keen that his pathetic willpower had no chance.

The woman he felt the worst about was Jo. She was little more than a child and the most vulnerable being in a new city with no friends. He eventually persuaded her to meet him so he could properly apologise. He took a girl called Eve he worked with at the pub and was also a student at Sussex University. Eve had promised to befriend Jo and integrate her into some social activities amongst the university student community who lived in the city rather than on campus. It had all worked well and Eve had told Andy that Jo was already dating a guy from the university rugby team.

He apologised to Annie, but she seemed to have quickly gotten over him and admitted to already seeing two other matches when she had sex with him.

Ursula was the most difficult to persuade to speak to him, but when she did, she shocked Andy by admitting she was 36 years old and should have known better than going around chasing randy schoolboys.

After her confession, she seemed less angry and even friendly towards Andy. Andy joked about fixing her up with one of his father's friends and then it suddenly occurred to him that his uncle Toby would be a great match with her. He was also 36, a great-looking guy and was working in London as an IT Developer. Ursula was reluctant to take the suggestion seriously until Andy showed her a picture of Toby sunbathing on Manly Beach. He had an incredibly toned body and boyish good looks. Toby and Ursula were now an item and Andy was in Ursula's good books.

Andy was relieved and astonished that Zoe never realised that he had been playing away behind her back and he hoped she never would. They had grown very close over the last few weeks and Andy admired her strength of character and the determination to improve in their daily running sessions. They were already planning on going to Australia for Christmas so she could meet his family. The love rat had been tamed.

Only Hope

Chapter 1

Tony was bored. Tony was always bored. Tony spent his entire life bored. He got up from his office chair and wandered towards the coffee vending machine on the other side of the open-plan office. He did not really want a coffee, but it was something to do. Something to ease his boredom, even if only slightly.

Tony had worked for Anglo Credit for 28 years. For the last 23 years doing the same job in the same office and for the last 15 years sitting at the same desk. No wonder Tony was bored. Tony's job was to deal with changes to customers' addresses when they moved to a new house. It was a tedious job.

Although Tony currently led a boring life, he had a plan to change all that. Tony was going to win the lottery. He would move to a fabulous luxury villa in the sun. He would travel the world and mix with the beautiful people. Tony had had the same plan since 1994. The only problem was getting that bit of luck needed to win the jackpot.

Tony wandered back to his desk with his vending machine coffee and sat back down. His mobile phone vibrated on his desk. He could see from the screen that it was his wife.

"Hi Fi, what's up?"

"Just checking what time you will be home tonight."

"About 5.30, same as always."

"Good, I need to go shopping but the garage phoned to say the car will not be ready until tomorrow. Can we drive to Sainsbury's when you get home?"

"Yes, that is fine. We can go straight out as soon as I get there."

"See you then."

Tony and Fiona had been married for 22 years. They had met when they both worked for Anglo Credit. Fiona got drunk on a night out to celebrate a colleague's birthday and had decided she would have Tony. He never stood a chance and at the end of the evening had been hauled back to her flat by Fiona, who demanded to be 'satisfied'. To be fair to Tony, he had performed this task rather well, which is why Fiona was keen to continue their relationship.

Over the subsequent months, she had often had second thoughts about the relationship. Tony was very dull and lacked any real drive and ambition. She had called the relationship off a couple of times but then could not help getting back in touch when she had 'needs'. Tony's ability to satisfy her needs was so much better than anybody else she had ever met. Tony was also a nice, dependable kind of guy, so when he proposed over dinner on valentine's night, she accepted, thinking she could do a lot worse. Fiona anticipated being able to shape Tony into a more dynamic and successful person.

Unfortunately, this proved to be impossible. Tony had the opposite impact on her and her ambitions and aspirations were paired down to match his. Despite the initial vigour of their sex life, they never managed to have any children. They both accepted this fact and, in line with their jointly passive approach to life, never sought medical help to find the reason and look for potential cures or treatments.

At precisely 5.30 PM, Tony pulled up outside his house and sounded the horn. Fiona opened the front door and gesticulated that she would be out in 1 minute. She reappeared with a clutch of re-usable shopping bags and got in the car. The supermarket was only a short drive and they were soon in the car park looking for a free space that was not reserved for the disabled, pregnant, elderly or dirty car owners willing to pay to get their car cleaned while they shopped.

They found a spare undesignated spot in the far corner of the vast car park and made the long trek to the actual shop. Inside, they followed their usual routine, with Tony following Fiona around with the trolley while she picked out what they needed. They always purchased the same things. They liked what they liked and did not want to try anything new. The only excitement came when the supermarket had run out of an item and they had to find an alternative.

This crisis would provide them with a topic to talk about and debate about what was otherwise a soulless and silent operation. There were no supply problems on this occasion, so they made their way around the entire supermarket and back to the car without speaking a word to each other.

Back home, Tony took the bags of shopping out of the car and through to the kitchen, where Fiona put the contents away into the cupboards. Tony went and sat in the lounge and watched the early evening news while Fiona cooked their dinner.

As it was Wednesday, they had grilled lamb chops, mashed potatoes and peas as the main course. For dessert, they had tinned peaches and cream. They had this identical meal every Wednesday for the last eight years, except when Xmas or one of their birthdays fell on a Wednesday. Over dinner, their conversation turned to the only subject Tony was ever interested in talking about.

"I was looking at some nice villas in the Maldives that we should consider after we have won the lottery," said Tony.

"How many villas do we need?" replied Fiona.

"Not sure yet, but when we decide, we should definitely look at these in the Maldives," responded Tony.

"OK, better put it on your list then," said Fiona.

Tony loved to plan what they would do with the money they would have after winning the lottery. He was constantly looking at luxury houses, cars and destinations. Tony had what was now a pretty dishevelled notebook that he used for what he called 'The Planning'.

Despite being disappointed every Saturday evening for the last 32 years, he remained optimistic that they would win the following week. They had had many minor wins, but these were not the life-changing events of winning the jackpot but simply helped fund future ticket purchases.

Chapter 2

The next day, Tony left for work as usual and arrived at just after 8.00 AM. When he reached his desk, he saw the room had been decorated with balloons and banners. The banners proclaimed it was 'Agile Launch Day'. '*What the fuck is that?*' thought Tony and he grabbed himself a coffee from the vending machine.

While he waited for the device to make his drink, a young woman with dyed pink hair came up to him and said, "Isn't it exciting?"

"What is exciting?" replied Tony.

"The Agile Launch."

"I don't know what you are talking about."

"Did you not read the newsletter or get briefed at your last team meeting?"

"I never read any of that nonsense sent out by HR and usually fall asleep at the team meeting or play Candy Crush and ignore what is said."

The pink-haired girl looked flabbergasted and deflated and said, "OK, suit yourself," before wandering off.

Tony was the most unmotivated and cynical employee any boss could have. His view on work-life was, "Just leave me to do my job well and let me ignore all your management bullshit."

He had zero tolerance for the trendy fads that regularly came and went, thanks to naïve managers who happily threw millions of pounds at the management consultancies that peddled them. Tony had seen many trends come and go over his long years and, in his opinion, he had been proved right about all of them, 'More Bullshit'.

The latest fad he would be ignoring was called 'Agile'. It involved re-organising the entire workforce as a large number of small teams called 'Squads' who managed their work in two weekly chunks of time called 'Sprints'. Tony had a meeting in his diary later that morning with his own Squad to start working in the new way. His manager had warned him that if he did not attend and participate enthusiastically, he would be at risk of disciplinary action.

However, Tony knew the new fad would disappear in a short time, so he was happy to go along with things in the meantime, anyway.

The Squad all met in one of the large meeting rooms at 11.00 AM. Tony knew nearly all the participants, as they were just the rest of his team, who processed the changes of addresses, but there were two other new members. One of them was the girl with the dyed pink hair he had met at the vending machine earlier. "Hi everybody," she said. "I am Emily and I am your Agile Coach."

The other newcomer was a thin guy in his late thirties who was trying to look young and trendy in a ripped tee-shirt and black jeans but, in Tony's view, made him look like a twat. "Hiya," he said. "I am Ian and I am your Scrum Master."

They spent the next 2 hours going through how their new way of working would operate. Tony kept quiet and passively went along with things to avoid any unpleasantness from his boss. However, some of the other team members were less passive. It was clear that Emily and Phil had their work cut out to make the team understand how things were supposed to work and, more importantly, why they needed to adopt such a complex way of working for such a straightforward task.

After the meeting, Tony went to the communal kitchen to have his lunch. As it was Thursday, he found that Fiona had put some ham sandwiches and some cheese and crackers in his lunch box. Lunchtime had the same kind of routine as their dinner. Tony loved routine. It made him feel safe and secure.

There were no more Agile meetings that day, so he could get on with the backlog of work from attending the morning meeting. He left work just after 5.00 PM and was home by 5.30 PM. Fiona was in the lounge, reading a book, when he got inside. "Hi Darling, have a good day?" said Fiona as they entered the lounge.

"Bloody awful morning. They have got some more of that management consultant's bullshit to roll out. Beggars' belief how supposedly intelligent, well-educated managers of the company fall for the same old snake oil stories year after year," moaned Tony.

"Don't get stressed, darling. Just go along with it until they give up like they always do," replied Fiona.

"Yes, you are right. But why should I care? As soon as the lottery comes up, I will be off anyway."

191

Chapter 3

Over the next couple of weeks, nothing changed in Tony's life. In fact, nothing much had changed in the last 20-odd-years. Then all hell let loose.

Tony left for work at precisely 8.03 as usual. He drove the short distance to his office and parked in the underground car park. He got into the lift to get to the floor he worked on. Somebody who had used the lift beforehand must have farted as it stunk—the worst kind of stale garlic and egg smell. The lift started going up and then abruptly stopped at the next floor and the door opened.

To Tony's horror, a young woman carrying a cycle helmet got in the lift. Tony felt so embarrassed. He knew she would think he had farted. He monetarily thought of explaining what had happened but decided it would sound like a lame excuse, so he kept quiet. The young woman's face screwed up in disgust as the full power of the smell got inside her nose. As she left on her floor, she gave Tony a horrible stare and called him disgusting.

Tony got out at his floor and made his way slowly to his desk. He did not have a great deal of self-esteem, so the incident in the lift had made him feel pretty low. He logged on to his computer and then went to get his first vending machine coffee of the day. Tony was just starting work when his manager Geoff, came to his desk. "Can you come to my office for a quick chat?"

They both went over to Geoff's small corner office and closed the door. "I have some news that you might think is bad, but I think might be for the best in the long term," said Geoff. "We are moving all routine admin tasks offshore to Vietnam to save money, so your job here in Brighton is redundant. Don't panic. We are not getting rid of anybody, but you will be required to re-skill."

"What do you mean by re-skill?" responded Tony.

"You will need to go on a course to learn new skills that will enable you to take up a new role. This is a great opportunity for you."

"What kind of new skills are required for these jobs?" asked Tony.

"Certain language skills are in great demand or technical skills like IT or graphic design."

"What if I do not want to learn new skills?" said Tony.

"There is an option to take nine months' severance pay as a tax-free lump sum," replied Geoff.

"I will take that," Tony said in a curt tone of voice.

"You are missing a great opportunity here. You will be trained for six months at our expense on full pay and at the end, you still have the opportunity to take the severance pay if we cannot find you a suitable job at the same or increased pay," protested Geoff.

"I don't care," said Tony. "I do not want to learn new skills. I like doing what I do."

"OK, your choice. I will get HR to draw up the forms for you to sign and get the severance pay," said Geoff, realising he was not going to change Tony's mind.

"Good and when do I leave?" said Tony.

"End of the week," replied Geoff.

Tony returned to his desk and realised he was in shock. His hands were shaking and he was starting to breathe very fast. He got up and left the building and headed down to the seafront to get some fresh air and clear his head.

Once he felt he had calmed down, he found a bench to sit on and reflect on what had happened. It was not a complete surprise. He had been conscious of the company moving functions to cheaper overseas locations for a couple of years now. He had hoped he would win the lottery before his dept was targeted and he could tell Geoff where to stuff his job. He did not regret taking the money and turning down the training. He was confident he would win the lottery soon, so there was no point in wasting his time learning how to do a new job. There was only one question he was still unsure about. Should he tell his wife?

He had secretly decided about five years ago that he would trade her in for a newer model when he won the lottery. He was prepared to give her the house and provide a reasonable income for her from his winnings, but he felt she would now be a liability in his new lavish lifestyle. She was not the glamorous and vivacious companion that he envisaged in his new life. He had already found a high-class escort agency that could provide him with a new suitable short-term companion until he found the genuine article in his new jet-set social circles.

He felt that if he told his wife, she would panic and nag him to get a new job before they ran out of money. He had no intention of getting a new job. He was confident the redundancy money would be enough to cover them until he won the lottery. He was way overdue on the big win.

Tony returned to work and then left for home at his usual time. When he arrived home, he found the house empty and a note on the dining room table from his wife.

Dear Tony,

I have decided to leave you. I no longer love you and now am not sure I ever did. I know that you no longer love me. Our life has become so dull and routine that I am starting to think about what the point of living is. I know that you pin everything on winning the lottery, but you must face up to the fact that it will never happen. I am not prepared to waste my life any longer. I am going to Australia to visit my sister and work out what I will do next. It will not be a life with you. I have told my solicitor to start divorce proceedings and I want half of the house and your pension. I wish you only the best for your future but do not want to share it. Do not try and contact me.

Regards
Fiona.

Tony was dumbstruck. He had absolutely no idea this was coming. Fiona had never made her feelings known to him. He knew she was getting a bit weary of his lottery win plans but thought deep down she shared his view that the big win was coming soon and their life would all change for the better. A voice inside his head said, "Don't worry, Tony, you wanted to dump her anyway once you win the lottery."

He acknowledged this was true, but at the same time, he felt deeply hurt that she had left him. Tony found himself bursting into tears and sobbing uncontrollably. She was wrong. He did love her.

After Tony had recovered slightly, he sat on the sofa in his lounge and tried to make sense of his day. He now had no job and no wife. All he had left was his hope of winning the lottery. He decided that if this was the case, then he had better make sure it happened. He usually spent 50 pounds on his lines of numbers for a Saturday draw. This week he would spend 5000 pounds. This was the maximum credit he currently had on his credit card.

Once he got his redundancy money, he would be able to increase the amount. He found his laptop and went to the lottery website and started maxing out his credit card. He felt much better with this done and decided to go and fetch himself some fish and chips for dinner. He put on his coat and walked to the local chippie at the end of their road. He had to pass an off-licence on the way back and decided to buy himself some beers to go with his supper. Tony hardly ever gets drunk, but he was now invigorated by his new sense of purpose.

After his dinner and beers, Tony sat in front of the TV and watched a film. The beers had relaxed him and he was feeling good about how things were turning out. Halfway through the film, Tony fell asleep. He woke up the next morning feeling terrible. He had a shooting pain in his back, a throbbing headache and bleary eyes. A long shower made him feel a little better, so he grabbed some cereal for breakfast and then headed in for his last day at work.

Tony's last day was as dull as all the others. His boss had sent out an email telling the rest of the department that it was his last day. It said he had decided to leave to pursue new opportunities elsewhere. Tony hated that kind of corporate HR bullshit and made it plain to everybody that came up and wished him the best of luck what he felt the actual story was.

"The bastards have thrown me on the scrapheap after 28 years of loyal service."

At 4.00 PM, his boss came out and told Tony he could leave now and he would escort him from the building. This annoyed Tony even more. "You make me sound like a bloody criminal," cried Tony.

"Not at all, it is so that I can collect your building security pass," protested his boss.

When Tony arrived home, he was struck by how silent and lonely it felt in his house. The time was only 4.30 PM and Tony did not know what to do with himself. He had no friends he could call and no genuine interest to pursue.

Suddenly, he felt very depressed and desperately missed Fiona. He remembered feeling better after his beers the night before, so he decided to go and get some more. In the off-licence, he also spotted a special deal on Whisky. He had never tried it before but had always wanted to, so he bought the litre bottle that was on special as well as 12 cans of lager. He decided he should probably get something to eat as well, so he went into the small Indian grocery next door and purchased a frozen Pizza.

Back home, he put on the oven to cook his Pizza. While it was heating up, he opened and drunk his first can of beer. It soon made him feel better and he wondered why he had never been a drinker before. Once the oven had reached cooking temperature, he put in the Pizza and drunk a second can of beer while it cooked. He consumed his third can when eating the Pizza and was then feeling good about things again.

Chapter 4

Fiona had not told Tony the whole story in her letter. She was going to Australia to meet her sister, but she was not going alone. She had met somebody new and intended to spend the rest of her life with him. His name was Pete and she met him several months before, when they had called a plumbing company to get their boiler fixed.

While Pete was fixing their boiler, she had offered him a cup of tea, which he gladly accepted. Over the tea, they started talking. Initially, just small talk about the weather, but then Pete mentioned his wife and kids. Fiona told Pete that she and Tony could not have children. Pete then surprised Fiona when he asked, "Are you happy in your marriage?"

Fiona replied, "Not really. Why do you ask?"

"Just wondered. I feel I am just going through the motions in my life. I love Sue and the kids but find my life so dull and unrewarding. It is the same thing every day and none of it do I find much fun."

"I feel exactly the same way," replied Fiona.

"The problem is that there is no way I can make my feelings known to Sue, as she would be distraught and that would make things even worse."

"I am sure Tony would simply not care if I told him."

Pete then seemed to suddenly realise that maybe he should not be sharing intimate details of his life with a stranger, let alone to one who is also a customer. "Sorry for talking like this to you. Sure you do not care about my troubles. I do not normally talk about things like this to my best friends, let alone somebody I have only just met."

"Sometimes it is easier to talk to a stranger and honestly, I do not mind at all. It is probably good for me to share my issues as well. Let's help each other."

"I would really like that, Fiona. You are such a good listener. I hope I can be of help to you as well."

They arranged for Pete to return later that day, when he had a gap in his work schedule. Pete started coming round every day at least once and some days he spent as much time with Fiona as he spent working. They both got great relief from sharing their frustrations with their current life and supporting each other to take action.

One afternoon Fiona was sharing her fear of being alone. "I think the main reason I have never left Tony is that I would be all alone in life. I am scared I would end up alone for the rest of my life and be one of those people they find dead in their house weeks after they actually die because nobody ever noticed them gone."

"I would be there for you," said Pete.

"That is kind of you, Pete, but you will probably get back with Sue or find a new girlfriend. Our relationship is not necessarily going to last that long."

"Why not?" said Pete, looking rather hurt.

"We are not having an affair or any kind of romantic liaison. We are just two people who find it easy to confide in each other and are supportive friends."

"I think you are a wonderful woman, Fiona. I would love to have a romantic relationship with you," said Pete, to Fiona's surprise.

"Sorry, Pete, but I did not see that coming. You have caught me off guard. Let me think about it."

After Pete had left, Fiona went for a walk to clear her head and consider what he had said. She could just not see him as her romantic partner. He was OK-looking and there was nothing about him she disliked, but there was also nothing she really liked. He had not once been even a little flirtatious when with her. So she decided that there was no future for them as a couple.

The next day Pete was due to come round at 10.00 AM and Fiona was nervous about telling him she did not think they should meet anymore. When she opened the door to let Pete in, she was surprised to see he was not wearing his usual plumber's overalls but an Armani tee shirt that was just tight enough to show off his muscular physique. 'He also smelt divine, Armani as well,' thought Fiona. He was carrying a beautiful bunch of flowers, which he handed to Fiona.

"Beautiful flowers for a beautiful woman," said Pete. "After I left yesterday, I realised there was no way you would be interested in me based on the way I have behaved so far. I was so wrapped up in my own problems and depression that I never gave your feelings any thought. It will never happen again."

"I don't know what to say," replied Fiona.

"Say nothing for now. I have called in sick and intend to spend the day with you to convince you we could have a future together. If by this evening I have not won you over, then we just go our own ways and no hard feelings."

"How can I refuse," said Fiona. "Where are we going?"

"France," said Pete, "plane leaves from Brighton airport in an hour, so hurry up."

Fiona quickly changed and then they drove to the airport just in time to catch the last boarding for their flight to Le Touquet. The flight in the small 12 seater plane only took 40 minutes and they were soon in a taxi from the airport to the luxury hotel where Pete had booked them into a couples spa session.

After the spa treatments, they had a wonderful lunch in a beachfront restaurant and walked hand in hand and barefoot along the beach. On the beach, Pete took Fiona in his arms and gave her a passionate kiss. Afterwards, he said, "You are a beautiful woman inside and out. The thought of spending my life with you makes me so excited. I will never take you for granted and will make sure that you will always be happy."

Pete then took her shopping and treated her to some lovely beach sandals that she spotted in a small boutique. After shopping, they stopped at a small bistro for cocktails and then got the plane back to Brighton. Throughout the whole day, Pete had been a completely different person to the miserable plumber that used her to moan about his wife. Instead, he was dashing, witty, romantic and unbelievably attentive. She would undoubtedly be prepared to have a romantic relationship with this Pete.

Back in Brighton, they returned to Fiona's house. Pete asked her, "Have I changed your mind about having a proper relationship with me?"

"If you really are the man I spent the day with, then yes, but I am not sure this is the real you and you are not just putting on an act."

"It is the real me that I want to be," said Pete. "I have been so ground down by the life I have with Sue that I became the boring unresponsive person as a defence mechanism."

"OK, I am willing to trust you and start a relationship, but it must be a completely fresh start for both of us. I am not going to be the other woman. You need to leave Sue and come with me to live somewhere else."

"Live where?"

"Australia."

"What!" exclaimed Pete. "How would that be possible? I could not even afford the flight, let alone pay to live there."

"My sister lives in Sydney and she is very well off. She has been trying to persuade me to leave Tony for years and is happy to let me use their holiday home on the northern beaches for as long as I wish. I also have some money that I inherited from my mother that I have hidden away. It will be enough to get us started until you can get a job out there."

"You seem to have all this worked out."

"I have wanted to do this for so long but never had the courage to go out on my own."

"OK, I agree," said Pete and took Fiona in his arms for a long passionate kiss.

Chapter 5

Tony woke with a terrible hangover; he had got a bit carried away and drank five cans of lager and made a big dent in the bottle of Whisky. Tony decided that his new drinking habit was not such a great idea after all. He briefly got up but felt so awful that he just took some paracetamol and went back to bed. It was not until 1.00 PM that he felt well enough to consider getting up.

Once up, he had a long shower and then made himself some breakfast/lunch. He did not feel like eating but had heard it was the best thing to do when you had a hangover. At about 2.00 PM, he started to feel slightly better so decided to go out and get some fresh air. So he drove down to the seafront and walked from the old west pier to the marina and back. He stopped on the drive back home at Waitrose supermarket and picked up some decent food.

He decided to have the slow-cooked lamb shanks with redcurrant sauce pre-prepared meal he had purchased, so he put it in the oven to heat up and prepared some mashed potatoes and green beans to go with it. The meal was delicious and he felt very pleased with himself. He started to think that his single life may not be so bad as he thought. It was now 7.30 PM and the big Lotto draw was due at 7.45.

The draw was no longer shown live on the TV, so he went to his laptop and opened up the lottery channel on YouTube. He never played a fixed set of numbers as he dreaded the idea of missing a week or making a mistake and realising he should have won the jackpot but lost due to his own error.

Instead, he preferred to buy 'Lucky Dips' or random sets of numbers generated by the lottery computer. This strategy made watching the actual draw pretty pointless. He only knew he had won when he checked on the Lottery app after the draw, which told him how many wins and of what size he had. Nevertheless, he religiously watched the draw being made live, anyway.

Tony watched the draw, which involved a strange-looking machine ejecting coloured balls into a viewing window until the six winning numbers were all on display. Tony watched the draw finish and then started staring at the Lotto app on his phone. It buzzed and a banner message said, "You are a winner."

Tony was not that excited, as he often had a small win by matching three numbers. He clicked on the message and was taken to the details of his win. He suddenly felt very sick and threw up his lamb shank dinner all over his laptop. The results page said, "You have matched six numbers and have won the jackpot."

The shock had caused him to vomit and he now started shaking uncontrollably. He got to his feet and walked around the room, trying to come to terms with the fact that the moment he had been waiting for over 25 years was now here. He started to calm down and the shaking subsided. He got himself a glass of water, although his still shaking hands made it difficult to drink.

He picked back up his phone and read the message again to make sure. He noticed that there was another line to the message that instructed him to call the lottery office to make his claim. He phoned straight away.

"Good evening, Lottery claims department, Martin speaking."

"Hi Martin, I have won the jackpot in tonight's draw."

"Fantastic, let's get on with the validation steps and then we can talk about how we pay you. Did you buy a paper ticket or play online?"

"Online."

"OK then, please give me your username."

"Jackpot Tony one word."

"Very appropriate. I have sent an email to the registered email address. Please open your email and read me the code number in the email."

Tony's phone buzzed to indicate he had received the email and he read back the code.

"Thank you, Tony. I can confirm you have won the jackpot and am pleased to tell you that you are the only winner and as this was a rollover week, the estimated prize is 12 million pounds."

Tony's heart was pounding and he suddenly had difficulty speaking. "Thank you so much," he blurted out.

Martin replied, "The next step is for one of our managers to come and visit you to complete some additional formalities and make arrangements for the money to be paid. Would you be free to meet them on Monday at your home?"

"Yes, of course," replied Tony. He then provided his address and contact details and the meeting was set for 10.00 AM on Monday.

Tony remained in a state of shock for the rest of the weekend. He spent most of the time just sitting in his favourite armchair, staring blankly across the room and thinking what he should do. Before he won, he had imagined being energised at this moment and full of excitement. The reality was the opposite. It was almost that the thought of winning was what he loved and now it has happened he has lost that dream. He now needed to deal with the reality. Slowly, over the course of the weekend, he came to terms with things and had a plan.

Chapter 6

At precisely 10.00 AM, there was a knock on Tony's front door. Tony was surprised to find two men at the door. The first man said, "Hi Tony, I am Raj from the lottery and this is Angus from London Private Bank."

"Do come in?" said Tony and led the men into his lounge, where they all sat down.

"The plan is to first complete the final formalities and then we will arrange to get the money to you. I have bought Angus along with me as we find the best way to proceed is to create a new bank account at a private bank and Angus can set that up now. The new bank account and using London Private is purely optional. We could, of course, transfer the money to your current account, but from past experience, this can cause complications later on."

"What kind of complications?" asked Tony.

"Sometimes there are other account holders who would suddenly have access to your money and the deposit of such a large sum can trigger various money laundering and other security measures at your bank. It is much cleaner to set up the new account in just your name."

"OK, I see," replied Tony.

"The first formality is that I need to confirm your identity. Do you have a current Passport and Drivers Licence that I could see?" asked Raj.

"Sure," said Tony, who got the documents and handed them to Raj. He took photos of the documents using his phone and then completed some paper forms he had in his briefcase. Finally, he gave the forms to Tony and asked that he sign them. Once this had been done, he said, "Congratulations, Tony, the formalities are complete and I can now transfer the jackpot prize of 12,456,725 pounds to you."

"Would you like me to set up a new account for you at London Private to receive the money?" interjected Angus.

"Yes, please, my only other account is also in my estranged wife's name, so I do not want to put it there."

"No Problem," said Angus, who got out his iPad and started typing away. Five minutes later, he announced he had set up the account and asked Tony to download the London Private banking app to his phone. While Tony did this, Raj and Tony arranged for all the money to be transferred into his new account. Once Tony had the app, Angus guided him through getting access to his new account. Once he had access, he could see the 12 million pound plus balance.

"The account comes with a complimentary platinum credit card with a 200,000 pounds credit limit. The card provides a 24-hour concierge service if you ever need help in booking travel or entertainment. There is a virtual card on the app, but a physical card will be sent by courier and arrive in the next 4 hours. I can also provide you with access to one of our life coaches or financial advisers if you want help in shaping your new life or investing some of the money," offered Angus.

"Not just now, thanks," replied Tony. "I want to get my head around my future life plans first."

Raj interrupted, "One other thing, Tony, who have you told so far about your win?"

"Nobody, why?"

"You will find that people's attitudes towards you can change quite drastically once they find out about your win."

"Don't worry about that, Raj. I am not telling anybody. I am to start a new life and leave all those miserable bastards behind."

"Fair enough," said Raj.

The two men then gathered up their things and left Tony to start his new life. As soon as they had gone, Tony phoned the Grand Hotel in Brighton.

"I would like to book the very best room you have available for the next three nights."

"That would be a King Suite at 420 pounds per night."

"That is fine. My name is Tony Rogers and I will be checking in at 2.00 PM."

"We look forward to seeing you, then. I just need a credit card to secure the booking."

Tony provided the details from the virtual card on his new banking app. After making the booking, he went up to his bedroom and packed a small suitcase. He did not pack much as he planned to deck himself out with a whole new wardrobe very soon.

Tony spent the rest of the morning clearing out the house and preparing to leave it empty for some time. When he could be bothered to organise it, he intended to sell the place, as he had no intention of ever living there again. The doorbell rang about 1.30 PM and a courier delivered Tony's new platinum credit card. He was all ready to start his new life, so called a taxi to take him to the Grand.

After checking in, he made his own way to the suite on the hotel's seventh floor. The room was massive, with a lounge area that could easily seat about a dozen people, a dining area, two bathrooms, an office area with a desk, a separate bedroom and even a small private gym. It also faced directly towards the sea and had a private balcony. Tony stepped out and enjoyed the panoramic view along Brighton Beach. In the fresh air, he suddenly felt hungry. He had not had any lunch, so he stepped back inside and ordered a sandwich and a pot of tea to be delivered to his room.

After he had eaten, he felt much better and full of energy to get things done. His first priority was to get himself smartened up, so he looked like the multi-millionaire he now was. He left the hotel and headed towards the trendy Lanes area of Brighton, which was full of excellent designer shops and boutiques.

He passed by a male beautician shop so stopped in for a haircut, facial and manicure; the last two, the first he had ever had. Just opposite the beautician was a Hugo Boss outlet, so he headed there. The young sales assistant could not believe her luck when Tony ordered a whole new wardrobe of causal and formal gear. The bill came to over 12,000 pounds. He had it all delivered to his suite at the Grand.

As part of a detailed pre-planning of the big win he had, buying a new Rolex watch as a priority. He had noticed that the kind of people he intended to mix with always wore very expensive watches. He soon found a jeweller that specialised in watches and purchased a Rolex Daytona Platinum Ice Blue Dial Automatic Chronograph for 103,000 pounds.

Next were shoes. Many people used the quality of shoes to judge the class and prosperity of an individual. He found an upmarket shoe shop nearby and purchased 3000 pounds worth of shoes that he again had delivered to his suite. His final purchase was some designer luggage for his new clothes. He carried that back to the hotel himself.

He arrived back at the hotel to find all his new purchases placed neatly on the enormous bed. He unpacked them all, cut off the labels and hung them in the wardrobe. He had enjoyed the facial and manicure he had earlier, so he decided to call the hotel sap and book himself some more treatments. After discussing the options on the phone with the spa receptionist, he booked an aromatherapy massage for 4.00 PM.

While he waited, he decided to arrange what he would do that evening. He called the hotel concierge and asked him to secure a table for two in the best restaurant available for 7.30 PM that evening. The concierge promised to phone him back once he had reserved a table.

He would need some company for the meal and the rest of the night. He had already researched Brighton escort agencies as part of 'The Planning' and he even knew which girl he wanted from browsing their online directory of profiles. She was a slim 28-year-old French girl called Sadie who promised to be 'a sophisticated, highly educated beautiful companion you will be proud to be seen with in public but an insatiable slut in the privacy of your bedroom'.

Tony phoned the agency's number.

"Platinum Escorts, how can I help you?"

"I am hoping that I will be able to book Sadie to join me this evening."

"You are lucky, sir, she is very popular, but a last-minute cancellation means she is free."

"Fantastic! What is the rate you charge?"

"150 pounds per hour or 1000 pounds for the night plus travelling expenses."

"How long does the night last?"

"From 7.00 PM to 7.00 AM."

"Perfect. I would like to book her for the night."

Tony provided his credit card details and it was agreed that Sophie would meet him in the Lobby Bar of the Grand Hotel at 7.00 PM.

His hotel room phone rang and he picked it up to find it was the concierge with details of his booking.

"I have managed to call in a favour from the manager and get you a table at Le Creuset, which is a Michelin starred French restaurant in The Lanes."

"I have heard it is excellent. Many thanks for that."

"My pleasure, sir."

It was nearly time for his massage, so Tony got changed and went down to the hotel spa on the first floor. He was disappointed to find a man who gave his massage, but he found the experience incredibly invigorating and walked out feeling he was walking on air. He returned to his room and relaxed, watching the TV until it was ready to get ready for his date.

Chapter 7

Tony arrived at the hotel bar just before 7.00 PM and sat down in a large armchair to wait for Sadie. Moments later, he was left slack-jawed as a beautiful woman in a tight black lace dress entered the bar and looked around. He meekly indicated to her and she walked across to where he was sitting.

"Are you Monsieur Tony?" she said in a French accent.

"Yes, and you must be Sadie," he blurted.

"Indeed, a pleasure to meet you."

"Would you like a drink?" enquired Tony, as they both sat down.

"Dirty Gin Martini, S'il vous plait," replied Sadie.

Tony beckoned a waiter over and ordered their drinks.

"What do you do for a living, monsieur Tony?" asked Sadie.

Tony hesitated and then said, "Nothing now, just enjoying spending my money on the pleasures of life."

"Sounds fantastic," said Sadie in her broad French accent, which Tony was finding incredibly sexy.

"Where in France are you from?" enquired Tony.

"The city of Nice, on the Cote d'Azur. Have you been there?"

"Never, but have always wanted to visit."

"If you ever go, then I would be happy to be your guide," replied Sadie.

A plan was hatching in the back of Tony's mind.

The restaurant was fantastic. The food was the most delicious Tony had ever eaten, although that bar was not very high. Sadie dazzled him all night with her beautiful looks and witty flirtatious conversation. This was precisely the life he had been dreaming of for all those years.

After the meal, they went back to Tony's suite at the hotel and Sadie seduced him. He had good sex with his wife in their early years, but this was on a different level. They had sex three times that night before Tony was too exhausted to try again.

The following day, Sadie woke early and took a shower while Tony ordered breakfast to be delivered to the room. After breakfast, Sadie said, "I must leave shortly. I assume the agency explained that the fee only covers me until 7.00 AM."

"Yes, but I want you to stay longer. I am happy to pay more."

"I am booked up for the next two days, but you could make another booking for Thursday."

"Look, Sadie, I want to put a proposition to you. Will you join me for a whole week in Nice from Thursday? We will fly over in a private jet and stay in the very best places."

"You must understand that I am a professional woman and you must pay for my company. For a whole week, you will need to pay ten thousand pounds."

"Yes, I fully understand and am happy to pay."

"OK, I will tell the agency and you will need to contact them to pay and make the detailed arrangements."

"I will phone them this morning."

"Wonderful. I am looking forward to our little trip. It will be so much fun."

After Sadie had left, Tony found a company that chartered private jets from Brighton City Airport and booked a trip for Thursday to Nice. He next phoned the escort agency to pay for Sadie and arrange for her to meet him at the airport at 10.00 AM on Thursday.

All he needed now was to book where they would stay in Nice. He regretted not asking Sadie and was forced to use Google to see what he could find. He decided on the Hotel Negresco, a hotel that used to be a royal place and famous for its lush opulence. It was right on the seafront and at three thousand pounds per night for his sea view suite; he assumed it must be excellent.

Tony put his old dog-eared notebook he called 'The Planning' in his pocket and headed out for some fresh air. He found a coffee shop with outside tables in a small square nearby. He sat in the sun with his Flat White and reviewed his plans.

There were several items that he had already accomplished. He had his new wardrobe, glamourous escort and exotic holiday booked. He decided he did not need to buy the Aston Martin DB11 just yet. What he did need to start arranging was a permanent place or places to live. He would purchase a luxury house in Brighton and a holiday villa somewhere warm and sunny in Europe to start with and then somewhere else further away, way later on, for some winter sun.

After he had finished his coffee, he headed up to the main shopping area of Brighton in search of an estate agent. He had to walk a fair way but eventually found one on the border with Hove. The part of the city of Brighton and Hove that was originally the separate town of Hove, was very different to the hedonistic area of Brighton. Hove was much more low key and quieter. It had some of the city's most desirable houses and was the area that Tony had planned to buy his new luxury pad in.

He told the estate agent that he had recently Inherited some money and was looking to buy a new house for himself in the Tongdean area of Hove. He said he had a budget of up to 2 million pounds. The estate agent showed Tony several available properties.

One, in particular, attracted his attention. It was uncanny how the pictures the agent showed him were almost replicas of the photographs he had in his mind when he had been planning to buy the property over all those years before his win. Tony asked if he could view the property and the agent said he would call the vendor and check when it would be possible. After the call, the agent said, "We are in luck. The vendor and his family are out all day and are happy to let me show you around any time before 6.00 PM."

"Can we go now?" asked Tony.

"I have another appointment in an hour, but it is in the same area, so why not."

Tony followed the agent out of the door to a nearby side street where he had parked this car.

The four-bedroom detached house sat high up on the rolling hills to the north of central Brighton and Hove. The house had stunning views over the city to the sea. There was a large swimming pool and patio with a gazebo and BBQ in the garden. The house itself was modern, with extensive ground to ceiling windows that filled every room with light. The master bedroom had a sea-facing balcony and an enormous en suite bathroom with a spa. It even had a basement media room. His own private cinema was a long-held desire of Tony's.

"What is the price?" asked Tony.

"They are looking for something over 1.75 million," replied the agent.

"I will offer 1.75 million pounds and 1 penny replied Tony."

The agent laughed and said, "OK, I get your point and will phone the vendor and see what they say." The agent went out onto the patio and made the call.

When he came back, he said, "If you can go to 1.8 million pounds, then they will accept."

Tony had already decided he would go up to 2 million, so he was happy to accept.

Tony had no solicitor so was happy to take the agent's suggestion of a local conveyancer they often used. He phoned on the spot to give them instructions and arrange for them to complete the sale of the new house. The agent gave Tony a lift back to the hotel and on the way, Tony instructed the agent to deal with the sale of his old house. He gave the agent a key and said he would have the place cleared by the end of the week.

Back in his room, he contemplated if he should go back to his old house and retrieve any personal objects that he may want to keep for nostalgic reasons. He could not think of anything he felt that strongly about and was keen to have a clean start to his new life. He found a local house clearance company and instructed them to clear the house and dispose of all the contents however they liked.

After the call, Tony felt a bit giddy. Things were all moving very fast. He decided to take it easy for the rest of the day. He ordered some lunch to have in his room and then, after eating, had an afternoon siesta. He felt much better again when he woke.

Chapter 8

The following day, Tony had a leisurely breakfast in the hotel dining room and then a massage in the spa. It was a lovely sunny day, so he decided to go for a walk along the seafront. Tony walked all the way to Brighton Marina. He was getting tired and thirsty, so he went into the tourists' area of the marina in search of a pub. The first place he came across was the Casino. He had always been attracted to the excitement and glamour of casinos but had never actually been inside one.

However, it was on his list of things to do in The Planning. He had nothing better to do, so he went inside. A very helpful woman on the reception took care of his membership formalities and arranged for one of the croupiers to show him around. Her name was Kelly and she had soon convinced him to buy five thousand pounds worth of chips for a bit of a flutter. They started at the Blackjack table or Pontoon as Tony knew it from playing at Christmas with his grandmother. He was not taken with the game. However, it was the roulette wheel that he really wanted to try.

Kelly explained the different ways to bet and the odds they gave. Tony liked the idea of betting on a strip of three numbers known as a Street. It gave odds of 11-1. So he placed 100 pounds on 13.14.15. The croupier spun the wheel and the metal ball raced around the wheel. When the wheel slowed and then stopped, Tony saw the ball was in the slot for number 13.

"Beginners luck," quipped Tony. He placed another 100 pounds on the numbers 22.23.24 next, but it was not a winning streak and he lost. He kept the same numbers for the next spin and this time won with 23.

Kelly kept the complimentary Champagne flowing for Tony and he spent the rest of the day in the Casino. He came out with a small profit of 500 pounds and had a delightful time. He found that time flew by.

He returned to the hotel and had dinner in his suite. He went to bed early, so he was nice and fresh for the start of his trip to Nice the next day.

Chapter 9

Tony arrived at the airport by taxi and was relieved to see what he assumed was his private jet parked on the tarmac outside the terminal. The pilot was waiting for him inside the terminal and was talking to Sadie, who had already arrived. "Monsieur Tony," said Sadie and kissed him on both cheeks. "We were worried whether you were not coming."

"Sorry, traffic was terrible but here now, so shall we go?" replied Tony. He and Sadie followed the pilot out to the plane. The pilot went to the cockpit to finish the pre-flight checks. The steward showed them the aircraft's layout and Tony chose two large leather seats to sit in. They both took up the offer of a glass of Champagne and sat back and relaxed, ready for the flight.

Seven days later, Tony was sitting in the same seat for the return journey, but this time, Sadie was not next to him. She had decided to stay a few extra days in Nice to see her family, so Tony was returning alone. He was alone and depressed. The week in Nice had started wonderfully and Tony enjoyed the very best of what the Cote d'Azur could offer.

The hotel suite was massive and more luxurious than he could ever have imagined. The food in every restaurant was a culinary adventure that was not only delicious but exciting. They drank the best Champagne in the trendiest nightclubs and mixed with the beautiful people. By day, they had their own gazebo in the hotel's private beach club. Sadie was a beautiful and attentive companion. The sex with Sadie was still fantastic.

The problem was he had found out he hated being rich. The main problem was that he could have whatever he wanted. He discovered that the fun for him in wanting something was the expectation and excitement before he got it. He realised that he enjoyed thinking about all the things in 'The Planning' over the years more than when he actually got them. The other problem was the lack of any genuine relationships. He knew that the only reason people were nice to him was that he was paying them, including Sadie.

Once the plane landed in Brighton, he got a taxi straight to his house. As soon as he entered, he realised his mistake. The whole place was completely bare. Everything, including his spare clothes and personal possessions, was gone. All he had was what he was wearing or in his suitcase. His depression suddenly became overwhelming and he sank to his knees and starting sobbing uncontrollably. He was interrupted by a knock at the door, followed quickly by the door opening and the estate agent entering.

"Are you OK, sir?" enquired the estate agent.

"Yes, fine, just a bit overwhelmed to see the house empty," replied Tony.

"That it is a common response, don't worry. I am here to measure up. We are putting it on the market tomorrow."

"You go ahead. I am just leaving," said Tony. He walked out of the house and down the road to the bus stop. He got the bus into the city and booked back into the Grand Hotel.

Tony slept until 7.00 PM then woke and ordered a beer and burger to be delivered to his room. After eating, he went back to bed and did not get up until lunchtime the next day. He got up and had some brunch delivered to his room. He realised he had nobody he could talk to and help him to decide what to do next. He then remembered that Angus from the bank had offered their help if he needed it. He found Angus' business card in his wallet and phoned him.

"Good afternoon, Angus Scott speaking."

"Hi, Angus. This is Tony, the lottery winner."

"Hi Tony, how is it going? See, you have already made a big dent in your winnings."

"Yes, I was not so lucky at the casino in Monte Carlo but don't worry, I have learnt that lesson and will not be playing any more roulette."

"Good. How can I help you?"

"I have been struggling to structure my new life and remember, you said you can help."

"We often find that a sudden windfall can put the recipient's life completely out of kilter and recommend you speak with one of our qualified life coaches who can help you work out the kind of life you really want. Once that is done, we can then create a financial plan so you can invest your money in a way to let you achieve that."

"Sounds perfect. When can I see them? I am keen to start straight away."

"Hang on and I will check when somebody is available."

Angus put Tony on hold and he was forced to listen to some cheesy nineties pop song for a few minutes. When Angus came back, he said, "We have a life coach based in Brighton and she is free at 3.00 PM today, if that is not too soon."

"Not at all. That would be great."

"Are you at the same address as before?"

"No, I am staying at the Grand Hotel, Room 702."

"OK, I will get her to phone you when she arrives at the hotel. Her name is Jenny White."

"Thanks very much."

Having taken positive action to address his problem, Tony felt much better already and decided to go out and get some fresh air. He walked away from the direction of the Casino and towards Hove. Tony sat on a bench in a garden that sat in the middle of one of the beautiful Regency Squares that faced to sea.

He stayed for about 30 minutes, enjoying the sunshine and glorious surroundings before heading away from the seafront in search of a café for lunch. Tony found an Italian bistro just off the top of the square and enjoyed a Pizza and cold beer. After lunch, he headed back to the hotel for his appointment with Jenny.

The hotel reception called his room just before 3.00 PM to say he had a visitor. He asked them to send her up to his room. A few minutes later, there was a knock on his door and he opened it to find a slim woman in her early thirties with a blond bob haircut. "Hi Tony, I am Jenny White."

"Do come in," said Tony and ushered her inside and on to a seat in the lounge.

"Lovely room," said Jenny.

"Yes, it is. Can I get you a tea or coffee?" asked Tony.

"No, I am fine, thanks," replied Jenny. "Shall we get on with it?"

"Suits me."

"I am not here to provide you with financial advice. I am a qualified psychologist and life coach and I am here to help you set some goals that will lead to a happy and fulfilling life for you. Once we have the goals, then my colleagues at the bank can help you structure your finance in a way that best matches them. To start things off, please tell me all about yourself and the recent events that have led you to ask for my help."

Tony told Jenny all about his marriage with Fiona and his long-held obsession with winning the lottery. He then gave her the full details of his recent jackpot win and what he had done since and how it left him depressed.

"Thank you, Tony, that was very useful," said Jenny, without making any judgments. "I need you to explore what kind of life you think would provide you with the happiness you want. I have a whole load of images here on my iPad and I would like you to scroll through them and tap the like sign on those that appeal to you."

"How many can I choose?"

"As many as you like, but between 5 and 9 is a good number."

Jenny passed Tony her iPad. The images were many and varied. Tony picked the six that he liked most. "Which of the ones you picked would you rate the highest?" asked Jenny.

"The older man and woman sitting out having dinner by a tropical beach at sunset."

"What would be the next highest?"

"The couple in the old MG convertible sports car driving along the country road."

"And next?"

"The two guys on the golf course laughing at a shared joke or something."

"And next?"

"The man working at his desk on some complex diagram while the woman next to him looks on in admiration."

"And next?"

"The large family gathering over dinner."

"And finally?."

"The man in a hammock reading a book."

"Many thanks, that is great. Did anything occur to you when reviewing your selections?"

"Not really. I tried not to analyse and just went with my gut instincts."

"No problem, that is a good approach. I noticed that your five most liked images all portrayed activities being shared between two or more people. What does that say to you?"

"I am a bit surprised really, as I am not a very sociable person. I don't really like other people much and have no real friends."

"May I suggest that it is a lack of social interactions that is making you unhappy and you thought that winning the lottery would solve the problem, but you found that the relationships you paid for were not the real ones you craved."

"Wow, that is one hell of a conclusion. Let me have a few minutes to get my head around what you are suggesting."

Tony got up and walked out to the balcony and thought deeply about what Jenny had said. He realised pretty quickly that she had hit the nail on the head.

"You are right. When I fantasised about my life after the lottery win, they were all about being popular and enjoying life with a close circle of friends. For some reason, I connected the money with suddenly being able to make those genuine relationships. I see now that the money makes no difference."

"Fabulous, you have made the first and biggest step towards that happy life."

"What next?"

"I suggest that you try and make some new friends. The best way is to join some clubs for people with shared passions like walking, painting or a sport." "You could also try some online dating and friendship sites on the Internet but be careful and only use the more reputable ones. I would also suggest you try and contact your wife. I got the impression that you have not accepted that that relationship is over, so have one more try at reconciliation."

"OK, I will. Thank you so much for your help. You have been brilliant."

"Thank you, but this is only early days. Let's meet again next week and see how you are doing and in the meantime, if you need to speak, then phone me anytime."

Jenny got up and left to leave Tony to plan his next steps.

Chapter 10

The next day, Tony had decided to try an online dating site and, as recommended, had found a reputable one aimed at companionship rather than one night stands. He was just starting to browse the female membership. He set the filters to women over 35 with no children within a fifty-mile radius. The first page of results did not inspire him much. They all seemed old and worn down by life. He wanted somebody who loved life and would like to share adventures with him.

On the second page, one photo stood out. Mainly because she looked so young, Tony checked her profile and she was 36. Possibly a bit young for him but not a massive gap. Her bio fitted what he was looking for exactly. "I am a single 36-year-old woman with no children. I want to find a man who can be my lifelong companion and share adventures together. I love fine dining, dancing and travel. I am easy-going but fun-loving and curious."

Tony immediately sent a response. "My name is Tony. I am a single 45-year-old man. I have recently separated from my wife and want to start a new, more exciting life with a new partner. I am financially independent, easy going and love fine dining and travel. You might have to polish up my dancing skills, but it will be fun to learn. I hope you will agree to meet me and see if we can become partners in exploring our next adventures."

Next, Tony turned his attention to trying to track down his wife. He was pretty sure he did not want reconciliation with Fiona. He was convinced, however, that he did want to remain friends with her. He also wanted to share some of his new wealth with her. It was only fair that she received a share of the winnings, given the years she had put up with him.

He sent a message to her sister in Australia. "Hi, Susie. I am hoping you can tell Fiona that I need to speak with her. I am sure she has told you that she wants nothing more to do with me. I accept that and am not going to try and persuade her to come back. I respect her decision to leave me and, to be honest. I do not blame her. I have not been a great husband these last few years. I want to remain friends with her and am also keen to repay her financially for putting up with me all those years. I have recently won a tidy sum on the lottery and feel she is entitled to a share."

After the message was sent, Tony went out to grab a burger and a pint at a local pub.

He had just finished his food and was contemplating another pint when his phone buzzed. It was a response from Susie. "Fiona has already met a new man and is happy in her new life here. She does not want your money or your friendship. Leave her alone."

Tony knew that Susie never liked him and had encouraged Fiona to leave him, so he was pretty confident the response was from her. He thought that Susie had probably not even told Fiona he had sent a message, let alone the content. His problem was he had no way to contact Fiona directly.

He knew that Susie and her husband had a second house on the Northern Beaches in Sydney that they used for weekends and holidays on the beach. He and Fiona had stayed there when they had visited her sister several years ago. He was pretty confident that was where Fiona was staying. He decided he needed to fly out and confront Fiona face to face. He decided he better get another pint in the meantime and went to the bar.

When he sat back down, his phone pinged again. This time it was a message from the woman he had sent the message to on the dating site. She said she would love to meet up and sent him her mobile number to make direct contact. He sent a message to her phone. "Cannot wait to meet. I am in the Black Lion pub now if you are in the city centre. Otherwise, how about tomorrow night for dinner."

She sent a message straight back. "I am just leaving work, which is only 5 minutes away, so see you soon. I will have a large glass of Chardonnay if you feel inclined to line one up for me."

He replied with a thumbs-up emoji and went to the bar to get her drink.

Tony waved at her as he saw her enter the pub and she came and joined him at his table. She was much better looking than in her photo. "Thanks for the drink. I need that after the day I have had," said Ursula.

"What do you do?" asked Tony.

"I am in sales for a digital media company in the Lanes. What about you?"

"I used to work for Anglo American but was recently made redundant."

"Sorry to hear that."

"Don't feel sorry for me; with the redundancy money and a win that I have had recently on the lottery, I am in a much better place now. The redundancy has triggered me to improve my life. I can see now what a rut I was in before."

"And you are looking for a new woman to share your new life?"

"Exactly," said Tony. "What about you?"

"I have decided I need to stop dating the hunky good-looking young bad boys and find a real man. One who is not led by his cock and has an emotional age above 15."

"Sounds like you have recently had a rough time."

"Yes, but it was my fault. I now want to change and have a much richer and different type of relationship with a man. One where we are soul mates and share more than a bed."

"I would love to try and see if I could be that person, but I must admit I am worried by one thing and, in the interest of being honest, need to tell you."

"Of course. What is wrong?"

"You are a fair bit younger than me and an extremely good looking woman. I feel that I would be punching above my weight."

"I told you, I have left those superficial things like youth and good looks behind. You are not a bad-looking guy and the age thing does not worry me. In fact, being the younger person will be a nice change. If we develop a real emotional attachment, then those things do not matter."

"That is great to hear. So how about we spend some time together this weekend and get to know each other a little better?"

"That sounds great," said Ursula.

Tony refreshed their drinks and they spent another hour chatting and getting along famously. Ursula was getting tired and hungry, so they decided to call things a day at about 9.00 PM. Ursula agreed to come to the hotel and have breakfast with Tony at 8.30 AM the next day.

Chapter 11

Tony found a table for breakfast and waited for Ursula to arrive. She was about 10 minutes late and full of apologies. "So sorry I am late, but I left my flat without my phone and had to go back."

"No problem. Let's go and get some food from the buffet."

"Sounds good, looks delicious," said Ursula.

After eating, they left the hotel and went for a stroll along the seafront. Tony was pleased that Ursula took his hand as they walked. It was low tide, so they took off their shoes and walked along the shore in the shallow water. The sea was dead calm and the day was getting increasingly hot. "I wish I had bought my swimming costume with me. That water looks so tempting," said Tony.

"Who needs a costume? There is a nudist beach just a bit further along," replied Ursula.

"I am not sure I could do that," replied a horrified Tony.

"Don't be a wimp. This is the start of your new life and you want to get out of your rut. If you are serious about what you told me, then prove it and let's go skinny dipping."

Tony could not see how he could refuse. They reached the nudist beach and Ursula quickly stripped off and raced into the sea; Tony did the same and followed her in. In the ocean, Ursula came and cuddled up to him and kissed him. They frolicked in the water for a short while, but the sea was not warm enough to stay in for very long. Back on the beach, they dried themselves in the sun and they got dressed.

"I need a drink," said Tony.

"Sound like a great idea," replied Ursula and they headed to one of the pubs on the other side of the promenade's main road. They found a seat in a small beer garden where they enjoyed the warming sun some more. "That was fun," said Ursula.

"It was," replied Tony. "Thanks for stopping me from being an old git."

"Next stop, karaoke. How is your singing voice?"

"What!" exclaimed Tony.

"They have a lunchtime karaoke contest in one of the bars on the pier and we are going to enter."

"You are kidding."

"Don't revert to old git mode quite so quickly," teased Ursula.

Again, Tony thought he had no choice, so they headed off towards the Brighton Palace Pier. The karaoke contest was held in a bar towards the end of the pier. They got some drinks and entered the competition and then sat down to listen to their rivals and pick their song. There was one song that stood out and they quickly agreed that was the one for them. They sat back and listened to a drunk Irish woman destroy Purple Rain by Prince.

Next up was an equally awful rendition of Born to Run by Bruce Springsteen. They were just starting to feel that there was not much to beat when a pretty young girl came up and absolutely nailed Sweet Dreams by the Eurythmics. The compere announced their name as next up and they both went up onto the small stage. They found out for the first time as they sang together that they both actually had a decent singing voice.

The performance went brilliantly and they grew from a nervous start to a full-on performance. They left the stage to more applause than the young girl who performed before them and sat back and hoped the rest of the contestants were all lousy. There were just three more singers. The first one gave up halfway through due to nerves; the second was so bad that they were booed off and the last one was just OK.

They won the contest and were each presented with an all rides pass for the funfair at the end of the pier. They both decided they had had too much excitement for one day and decided to come back to the funfair another time.

They made their way to a seafood restaurant in the Lanes and had a late lunch of fresh seafood and a bottle of Chablis. In the restaurant, they were excited to see Kylie Minogue, who was performing that evening in the Brighton Centre conference hall, was also eating with her entourage at a nearby table. They did not disturb her meal, but as she was leaving, Ursula asked politely for a selfie and she was happy to oblige.

Ursula was so thrilled and said, "Cannot wait to post on Instagram, my gay friends will be so jealous."

After they had left the restaurant, Tony said, "Can I be an old git now as I am exhausted? Fancy going back to my suite for a siesta."

"I will go back to my place and have one as well and then get changed and come back to meet you in the hotel before we go out tonight. Rest up, as there will be lots of dancing involved."

"OK, see you about 6.30 PM?"

"Yes, I will message you when I am at the hotel."

Tony went back to his suite and was soon asleep on his bed. His phone alarm woke him at 5.30 PM and he got up and had a shower before getting dressed for his night out. At 6.25, his phone buzzed and he saw the message from Ursula. He went down and met her as instructed in the bar. He was pleased to see Ursula sitting at a table and joined her. "Fancy a cocktail?" said Ursula.

"You read my mind," replied Tony. They ordered their drinks and, while they waited for them to arrive, discussed the plans for the evening.

"We must end up at Dynamo Bongo later, as it is my favourite club."

"Fine with me. How about we try a bit of fine dining first and then go to the club via a bar or pub?"

"Might be tricky getting into a decent restaurant this late on a Saturday."

"I will go and speak to the hotel concierge. He has some good contacts and will sort something out for us."

Tony left and the drinks arrived while he was away. When he returned, he had good news. "The concierge has got us a table for 8.00 PM at a new restaurant that has just opened in St James's Street. It is an Indian/Thai fusion restaurant. The sister restaurant in London has a heap of awards."

After finishing their cocktails, they decided to walk to St James's Street and took the scenic route along the seafront. The full moon was shining down and reflected in the still ocean waters. They paused and enjoyed the view and Ursula said, "I have a good feeling about us. Things seem just right when we are together."

"I agree. I know we have only just met, but I already feel a real bond with you and have enjoyed every second of our time together."

"Did not look like you enjoyed the moment when you found out how cold the sea was this morning."

"Apart from that moment," said Tony, laughing.

They carried on walking and arrived at the restaurant just in time. The food was a set banquet menu and they ordered it with a bottle of wine. The food was very bold with lots of tastes and flavour combinations they had not had before but nearly every one delicious. The following two and a half hours flew by as they experienced the culinary adventure. After the meal, they headed to the club but were disappointed to see a long queue to get in snaking around the block. "Can you be bothered to queue?" asked Tony.

"No and I don't think we will have to. Stay here and I will see what I can do." Ursula left Tony and went to speak with the security guy at the front entrance. Five minutes later, she was back.

"Follow me," she said and led Tony to the front of the queue, where the bouncer opened the rope barrier and let them in.

"How did you manage that?" asked Tony.

"The club is owned by the brother of a previous boyfriend and I told a little white lie about the boyfriend promising me his brother would let me in."

"Well done, fancy some Champagne," said Tony.

"You bet and then we start working on your dancing," said Ursula.

Tony was actually a pretty good dancer and he and Ursula spent most of the night on the dancefloor. By 3.00 AM, they were both flagging and headed back to the hotel in a taxi. Ursula stayed in Tony's bed, but they just had a quick cuddle before both falling asleep.

Chapter 12

The following day Tony woke up to find Ursula had gone. He initially thought she was in the bathroom or lounge but then found a note on the dining table.

I am sorry, Tony, but when I woke up this morning, I was petrified. I am becoming too fond of you too soon. I do not think I am emotionally strong enough to take another disappointment, so I need to cool things down. I still think you are a wonderful man and hope we will have a long and loving relationship, but I need to build things up more slowly. I am away at a conference next week and so we could not see each other, anyway. If you want to, then I would love to cook a meal for you at my place next Sunday lunchtime and we can discuss more then.

Lots of love
Ursula xx.

Tony was devastated. Just when he thought he could start living his life, the opportunity had gone. He was not angry at Ursula but just deflated after being so excited at finding such a wonderful new partner. Hopefully, it was just a temporary problem and they could get things on track again next weekend. His immediate thought was about how he could make next weekend come as soon as possible. Then he had the answer.

He had planned to go and see his wife to resolve their split up, as Jenny had told him to. He would go this week and sort that out and be back by Sunday for lunch with Ursula. He sent a message to Ursula, "I found your note and am naturally disappointed but understand and do not want to rush you. Have a good week and I cannot wait to see you again on Sunday. Lots of love, Tony xxx."

He then got out his laptop and was about to book a flight to Sydney when he recalled the concierge service the Platinum card the bank gave him. He phoned the number on the card and got a very helpful woman who arranged for him to fly first class that evening to Sydney and return by next Saturday morning. The car was to pick him up from his hotel and take him to the airport at 2.00 PM.

Tony wasted no time and had a shower and then went down and had a large breakfast to set him up for the day. He then did some shopping and went back to the hotel and packed. He went down and checked out at 1.40 PM and waited for his driver in the lobby. The driver arrived at exactly 2.00 PM and he climbed into the Mercedes limousine to head to the airport and catch his flight.

Chapter 13

In Sydney, Tony was met by a driver and taken to his hotel. Tony had asked the concierge service to find a hotel as near as possible to where he thought Fiona would be staying on the Northern Beaches. He had been booked into a hotel in Manly called Q station. This hotel was converted from the old quarantine station that protected Sydney from infectious diseases being brought ashore on ships over the 18th, 19th and 20th centuries.

The hotel was situated inside what is now the Sydney Harbour National Park and a short walk or ferry ride to the centre of Manly. Tony was booked into a room in a block that once formed the accommodation for the 1st class passengers on the ship.

He had a veranda outside his room with spectacular views across the harbour towards the city. He had plenty of sleep on the flight over and was ready to hit the ground running. He had a quick shower and got changed before heading to the hotel reception to get help in locating the house he thought Fiona was staying in.

"Good morning, sir, how can I help you?" said the young woman on reception.

"I am looking to find an old friend who used to live at 8 Cliff Street in Manly. Can you tell me how I can get there?"

"It would be about a 30minute walk or I could get you a taxi if you prefer."

"I need to stretch my legs, so I think I will walk. Can you provide a map?"

"Sure, no problem," replied the receptionist.

Armed with his map, Tony set out on his walk, which led him out of the National Park and into the suburbs of Manly. It was mostly downhill and he reached the house in just 20 minutes. He soon recognised the place from when he stayed many years before. It was a semi-detached Federation house from the early part of the 20th century.

As he approached the house, he saw a man in a Brighton and Hove Albion football shirt leave and walk down the road towards the town centre. Intrigued by the coincidence, Tony followed the man to a pub in the main tourist strip of Manly just off the beach. He waited until the man had got himself a beer and then went up to him and chanted 'Seagulls', the nickname of the Brighton team. The man chanted 'Seagulls' back.

"Are you a supporter?" said the man.

"Yes, over here on holiday from Hove. My name is Tony."

"I am Pete. Let me get you a drink."

"Most kind, a pint of bitter, please."

"Only get schooners here and pale ale as is as close as you get to bitter but coming up."

Pete gave Tony his beer and then Tony asked him, "Do you live here then, Pete?"

"Only arrived last week, but that is the plan. I came out with my girlfriend as her sister lives here and she has lent us her holiday house just up the road until we get settled into our own place."

"Is your girlfriend called Fiona?" asked Tony.

Pete looked surprised and worried at the same time. "How do you know that?"

"Because I am her fucking husband."

To Tony's astonishment, Pete got up and ran out of the pub. Tony ambled out to see where he went and saw him running along the beachfront and away from his house. Tony walked in the other direction back to the house and rang the bell. Fiona answered the door and, for a moment, was speechless, then said calmly, "I told you not to contact me."

"I know, but I have good news to share. I am not here to try and get you back but want to share my good fortune and part as friends."

"Don't tell me you have won the lottery?" said Fiona.

"Yes, the jackpot of 11 million pounds and I want you to have some. It is only fair, given what you had to put up with all those years."

"You had better come in," said Fiona.

They went out to a patio area out the back of the house and sat down. Tony explained how he won and then found the money only made him more unhappy and his session with Jenny. He did not mention Ursula. "All I want is to say is how sorry I am for the part of your life I made you waste. I want to share some of the money and hope we can then keep in touch as friends." Tony noticed that Fiona was crying. "What is wrong?" he asked.

"If only you had got this self-awareness while we were still together, we could have made things work, but all you were interested in was winning that bloody lottery."

"Is it too late now?"

"Yes," said Fiona.

"Why?"

"I have a confession. I did not come out here alone."

"I know. I have just had a pint with Pete in the pub down the road."

"How long have you known about him?"

"I had no idea until 30 minutes ago when I followed him from your house."

"Well, anyway, I made him leave his job, wife and two children and come with me to the other side of the world. I can hardly turn round and tell him I have changed my mind and I am going back to my husband."

Tony suddenly realised that it was precisely what he wanted more than anything else. He still loved Fiona and needed her back.

"I am a changed man. I am no longer obsessed with money, although I have plenty of it. I want to use it to share the better experiences in life with somebody I love, not chase materialistic things like flash cars and glamourous friends. I know now that the person I love and the only person I will ever really love is you."

Fiona was now sobbing uncontrollably. "I still love you as well," she blurted out. "Despite hating you for the miserable life we had, I always knew there was a better man inside. What made me most unhappy was that I could not unlock him."

"He is free now and waiting for you to join him."

"What can I do about Pete?"

"Did you love him?"

"Not really. Pete was charming and dashing for a short while and I thought I could love him, but he has reverted to type and spends most of his time in that pub where you met him. My sister hates him even more than you. She said I was an idiot and had swapped one loser for another."

"Let me talk to him and see if I can get him to go back home to his wife. After all, you are still my wife and he has stolen you from me."

"Not exactly how it was, but I would like it if you tried. You will probably find him in the bar of the Manly Pacific Hotel. He is a creature of habit."

Tony set off and walked the 20 minutes to the hotel and, sure enough, there was Pete propping up the bar. Tony put his hand on Pete's shoulder and grabbed his arm so he could not run off again. "Got you," he said. Pete tried to wriggle out of his grip but soon gave up. "Don't worry. I only want to talk. Let me buy you the pint I owe you." He ordered two schooners of pale ale and led Pete to a table. "I will get straight to the point. I have come here to take my wife back. I have spoken with her and she has agreed."

Pete had a big grin on his face. "I am so happy. Leaving Sue and the kids, then coming out here with Fiona, has been the biggest mistake of my life. I don't know what I was thinking."

"Will your wife have you back?" asked Tony.

"No idea. I had not even told her I had come over here. She just thinks I have gone missing."

"You just left your wife and kids without saying a word?" said an incredulous Tony.

"Guess I was too scared."

"Scared of what?"

"Of sharing my feelings. One thing that I have realised is that the issues I had with Sue were all my fault. I kept everything bottled up inside rather than letting her know how I felt."

"Phone her now," said Tony.

"But it is the middle of the night in Brighton."

"I am sure she will be happy to wake up and take this call."

Pete took out his mobile and made the call. It sounded to Tony as it was not going well, but then Tony started crying and opened up and eventually, he was relieved to hear Pete say that he would see her as soon as he could get a flight.

"What happened?" asked Tony.

"She was furious at me for leaving at first. She said she was glad I had left, but then I told her everything was my fault and I was an emotional retard. I said I still loved her and wanted to make things work and have a great family life. She then softened a bit and agreed to let me go back on a trial basis."

They both returned to the house and Pete and Fiona had a private discussion while Tony arranged flights back to the UK. He booked him and Fiona into First Class and Pete in Premium Economy. The car was to pick them up in 3 hours.

Chapter 14

The car dropped Tony and Fiona at the Grand Hotel, where Tony had booked the suite for another week. Fiona was excited when she was shown the luxury suite of rooms. "I have always wanted to stay at the Grand, and it is not a disappointment."

After they unpacked, Tony suggested they invigorate themselves with a session on the spa. He phoned and booked the couples treatment package for an hour later. In the meantime, he ordered some tea and they relaxed in the sun on their balcony overlooking the sea. After the spa, they both felt fantastic and a little hungry, so they left the hotel and found a small café in Brighton Square where they ordered an antipasti platter and a bottle of Prosecco. "I could get used to this life," said Fiona as she sipped her drink.

"I should hope so, as this is our future," replied Tony.

"Where will we live if you have sold our house and all our stuff?" asked Fiona.

"I have phoned the estate agents and he said we can look at the house I found later this afternoon. If you do not like it, then just say and we can look for something else. If you do like it then, we are ready to exchange contracts and could move in 2 weeks."

"It did sound nice from what you said, but let's look later and decide together."

The estate agent picked them up from the hotel and took them to the house at 2.00 PM and they were back in the hotel by 3.00 PM and decided to have a drink in the bar and discuss what they wanted to do. It was not a difficult decision. "I absolutely loved the house. It was exactly what I imagined in my mind when we talked about where we would live after you won."

"That is what I felt when I saw it as well. We must have had the same pictures in our minds."

"Let's complete as soon as we can and start shopping for new furniture and everything else we need. There is so much we will now need to buy."

"I may have been a bit hasty in selling the contents of the old place," said Tony.

"Don't worry. I agree that there is something refreshing on starting again from scratch and having nothing from our horrible old life."

Tony phoned the estate agent and confirmed that they would like to exchange contracts and complete in 2 weeks. The agent told him to contact the conveyancer and arrange to go and sign the contract that afternoon. He did so immediately and agreed that he would visit their offices at 4.00 PM.

After Tony returned from signing the contract, he suggested to Fiona that they should take a holiday somewhere hot and come back when the house was theirs. "I have had enough of travelling for a while after that trip to Sydney. Let's stay here in this lovely room and plan our new life together."

"OK and we can start by forgetting this old rubbish," said Tony and he picked up 'The Planning' notebook and tore it up.

"I fancy an early dinner," said Fiona. "I am sure we will feel tired later, so let's go to a nice restaurant and start thinking about the things we want to do."

"Good idea," said Tony and they both got changed and then left the hotel.

Fiona suggested they start with a drink at one of the pubs in the Lanes. The first pub they came across was the Bath Arms, so they went in there. The barman was wearing a Manly Beach tee shirt. When he pointed this out to Fiona, she said, "It is a small world."

The world seemed a lot smaller still when, 5 minutes later, Ursula came into the pub with another woman. Tony was unsure what to do but then decided honesty was the best policy and said to Fiona, "See that woman with the Pixie haircut who has just come in?"

"Yes, she is very pretty," said Fiona.

"I had one date with her after you left and I am supposed to meet her again for the second date on Sunday. I have not told her that we are now back together and cancelled the date yet. She told me she was away all week at a conference."

"You were punching well above your weight there. Not only is she very pretty, but she can be no more than 24 years old."

"She is 36, but I agree she is a bit out of my league and don't think it would have gone anywhere."

"Did she know you had all won all that money?" asked Fiona.

"Yes."

"I suspect that is the reason you manage to pull her."

"I don't think it was like that at all, but I will go and explain to her what has happened and that I will not be seeing her again."

"I will come with you," said Fiona.

It was irrelevant anyway, as Ursula spotted him and came over to their table.

"Hi Ursula, I thought you were away at a conference."

"Sorry, Tony, but that was a little white lie to give me time to think. I am sorry, but I will not be seeing you again. I enjoyed our date but do not think there is a future for us. Have a great life."

Ursula walked away and left the pub with her friend. "That was easy then," said Fiona.

"You know what. That would have left me devastated if we had not got back together, but now I am so relieved it worked out like that," said Tony.

Tony raised his glass and toasted his wife, "To a fantastic and exciting future together."

"I will drink to that."

The End